Savannah Martin has always been a good girl, doing what was expected and fully expecting life to fall into place in its turn. But when her perfect husband turns out to be a lying, cheating slimeball—and bad in bed to boot—Savannah kicks the jerk to the curb and embarks on life on her own terms. With a new apartment, a new career, and a brand new outlook on life, she's all set to take the world by storm. If only the world would stop throwing her curveballs...

With hotels in downtown filled to capacity months in advance, real estate agent Savannah Martin decides to pick up some extra money renting out her empty East Nashville apartment. She's living with her boyfriend, and the place is just sitting there, begging to be put to use.

But when her latest tenant ends up dead—strangled in Savannah's bed by what might have been a paying customer—the promise of easy money quickly turns sour.

As the hunt for the killer leads to their shared hometown of Sweetwater, Tennessee, Savannah's boyfriend, TBI agent Rafe Collier, is tapped to help with the investigation. But a familiarity with the town and the people in it isn't necessarily a benefit when the main suspect in the murder is the man Savannah decided not to marry. The same man who has never forgiven Rafe for stealing her away...

PRAISE FOR THE CUTTHROAT BUSINESS SERIES

"Move over Stephanie Plum, there is a sassy, sexy sleuth in town! If you enjoy your cozy mysteries with a good shot of romance, and a love triangle with a sexy bad boy and a Southern gentleman in the mix, then you will love this. Very reminiscent of the Stephanie Plum books, but the laughs are louder, the romance is sexier and there is a great murder mystery to top it off."

— Bella McGuire, **Cozy Mystery Book Reviews**

"...a frothy girl drink of houses, hunks and whodunit narrated in a breezy first person."

— Lyda Phillips, **The Nashville Scene**

"VERDICT: The hilarious dialog and the tension between Savannah and Rafe will delight fans of chick-lit mysteries and romantic suspense."

— Jo Ann Vicarel, **Library Journal**

"... equal parts charming and sexy, with a side of suspense. Hero and heroine, Savannah Martin and Rafe Collier, are a pairing of perfection."

— Paige Crutcher, **examiner.com**

"...hooks you in the first page and doesn't let go until the last!"

— Lynda Coker, **Between the Pages**

"With a dose of southern charm and a bad boy you won't want to forget, *A Cutthroat Business* has enough wit and sexual chemistry to rival Janet Evanovich."

— Tasha Alexander, New York Times bestselling author
of **Murder in the Floating City**

"A delicious and dazzling romantic thriller ... equal parts wit and suspense, distilled with a Southern flavor as authentic as a mint julep."

— Kelli Stanley, bestselling author and Bruce Alexander award winner,
Nox Dormienda

Also in this series:

A CUTTHROAT BUSINESS

HOT PROPERTY

CONTRACT PENDING

CLOSE TO HOME

A DONE DEAL

CONTINGENT ON APPROVAL

CHANGE OF HEART

KICKOUT CLAUSE

PAST DUE

DIRTY DEEDS

DIRTY DEEDS

Jenna Bennett

DIRTY DEEDS
SAVANNAH MARTIN MYSTERY #9

This is a work of fiction. Names, characters, places and incidents either are the product of the author's imagination or are used fictitiously, and any resemblance to actual persons, living or dead, business establishments, events or locales is entirely coincidental.

Interior design: April Martinez, GraphicFantastic.com

ISBN: 978-0-9899434-8-2

MAGPIE INK

One

When the phone rings before seven in the morning, it's rarely good news.

Although when the phone beside my bed rang at 6:28 ᴬᴹ on the last Sunday in May, the reason I usually worry was lying next to me, so at least I knew the bad news wouldn't be about him.

Rafe was safe, curled up behind me in bed, with a possessive arm around my waist and a protective hand splayed over my stomach, where his son or daughter was getting ready to serve up my usual helping of morning sickness.

Rafe's presence only helped momentarily, as I have plenty of other hostages to fortune. My brother, my sister, my brother-in-law, three nieces, two nephews, assorted aunts and uncles, and quite a few friends.

Not to mention my mother. We don't always get along, but I'd hate it if anything happened to her, especially before she can come around to my way of thinking and embrace her future son-in-law.

And speaking of her future son-in-law... Rafe has a grandmother and a son of his own, along with a few friends who might also be the reason for this call. The list of potential victims just kept growing as the echoes of the phone rang in my ears.

"You want I should get that?"

Rafe sounded wide awake, although I knew he'd been asleep just a minute ago. That's what ten years of undercover work will do for somebody: make him able to go from dead sleep to wide awake at the sound of a ringtone.

"No." I reached for the phone. "I've got it."

He didn't argue, just settled back down, long fingers making circles across my rounded stomach. Going a little farther south with each sweep.

I knew where those fingers were headed, so I picked up the phone with the intention of getting rid of whoever was calling as quickly as possible. "What?"

There was a beat, and then— "Manners, Savannah," a voice murmured. *Sheesh.* "Mother?"

Rafe's hand stopped making circles. Even he draws the line at trying to get into my panties while I'm talking to my mother. Or perhaps it's simply that the thought of my mother acts like a bucket of ice on his libido.

He removed his hand and flopped over on his back with a sound that was halfway between a laugh and a groan.

"Yes, darling," the phone said.

Yes, of course. I resigned myself to doing without any more of Rafe's attention until I could get her off the line. "What's wrong?"

"Are you alone?" mother inquired.

"No." My voice was laced with a heavy dose of '*duh*,' but of course I couldn't actually say so. Not to my mother. "It's six-thirty in the morning on a weekend. We're still in bed."

"You and...?" Mother hesitated delicately.

I took the phone away from my ear and looked at it before putting it back. Amnesia? Early onset dementia? She's only fifty-eight, but I suppose stranger things have happened.

Probably it was just denial, pure and simple. I proceeded to remind her who I was sleeping with. "My fiancé. The father of my baby. Remember?"

"Rafael," my mother said, with that inflection of sour lemons only she can manage.

"That's right." And she had interrupted something—something I had every hope might go somewhere—so if she'd kindly just get to the point...?

But of course I didn't say that, either. My mother raised a lady. Although I thought it, and trusted that the thought came across in my voice.

Except it didn't seem to, because Mother didn't speak. "What do you need?" I prompted, when I determined the silence had gone on long enough.

She sighed. "I thought perhaps Todd..."

Todd? She called me at six-thirty in the morning because she thought I had Todd Satterfield in my bed?

"I'm sorry," I said. "Rafe's not really into this sharing thing."

And if he had been, Todd would have been the last person he would invite to join us.

Mother's dismay rolled down the telephone line even before her shocked exclamation reached me. "Savannah!"

"Sorry," I muttered, my cheeks hot, while behind me, Rafe made a choking sound. I glanced at him over my shoulder, and saw that he was struggling not to laugh.

I turned away. The sight of him—all hard muscles and golden skin outlined against the white sheets—was distracting, and I couldn't afford to be distracted right now. "Why on earth would you think Todd would be here?"

Behind me, Rafe went still.

"I thought maybe you'd made up," Mother said hopefully.

That we'd... what?

"Rafe and I are engaged, Mother. We're living together. I'm having his baby. We're getting married." Just as soon as we could figure out the details. "There's nothing for Todd and me to make up."

Mother didn't respond, and I tried my question again, using different words this time. "Did Todd say he was coming here?"

"No..." Mother said, making it sound like she wasn't sure.

"Well, what did he say?"

She made a sound. Something like a sigh. "That he was going to Nashville to see a friend."

"And you thought of me? Why?"

We were hardly friends anymore. Todd Satterfield had been my boyfriend for a year in high school, but that was eleven or twelve years ago, and much more recently, I had hurt his feelings and wounded his pride by saying no to his marriage proposal. And then I had added insult to injury by shacking up with Rafe, who—by all accounts, especially Todd's and Mother's—was totally unsuitable for me.

"We didn't think he knew anyone else in Nashville," Mother said.

Why? Todd lived just over an hour away, and had for most of his life. It was very possible—indeed, likely—that he knew people in Nashville.

However, that didn't answer the most important question. "I still don't understand why you're calling me to ask if he's here."

She did a sort of audible squirm, one I could hear through the phone. "He didn't come home last night."

So? "He's thirty years old, Mother. I'm sure it isn't the first time he's been out all night."

"He usually lets Bob know," Mother said.

Bob Satterfield is Todd's father, and my mother's boyfriend. He's also the sheriff of my hometown of Sweetwater, Tennessee, about an hour south of Nashville. And the fact that Mother was communicating with him at six-thirty on a Sunday morning, made me wonder whether Todd might not be the only one who'd been out all night.

"I'm sure he just got caught up in the moment and forgot," I said.

It sounded to me as if perhaps Todd was moving on. I'd turned down his proposal before Christmas, and he had moped around for a few months trying to change my mind, until I got pregnant and it became obvious that I wasn't about to dump Rafe for him. Maybe he'd found himself a replacement. Or at least someone to pass the time with until he met the (new) girl of his dreams.

Mother murmured something that sounded vaguely like acquiescence, or at least not outright dissent.

"I'll let you know if I hear from him," I said. "But he'll probably be home soon." Wearing the same clothes he'd left in yesterday and looking a bit sheepish and worse for wear. "Have you spoken to Dix?"

Mother said she hadn't. "You think he might know what's going on?"

If anyone did, it was likely to be my brother. "They're best friends."

If Todd had someone new in his life, chances were he'd have told my brother about it. Unless my relationship with Rafe had ruined Dix and Todd's friendship, too.

Although if it had, Dix hadn't said anything about it.

Then again, he didn't really talk about Todd, so maybe they didn't spend much time together anymore and I just hadn't realized it.

A ribbon of guilt twisted through me at the thought. I didn't want to be responsible for any bad blood between my brother and his best friend.

But then I banished it. I have the right to fall in love with anyone I want. And just because Dix and Todd are close, doesn't mean I owe it to Todd to marry him.

"Let me know how it goes," I told Mother, and hung up before she could say anything else.

There was a moment of silence.

"What's going on?" Rafe wanted to know.

I turned to face him. "Todd's missing."

He blinked.

"Or not missing, exactly. Apparently, he drove up to Nashville last night to see a friend."

"And your mama thought he was coming to see you?" He arched a brow. Just one. The other didn't even twitch. "Something I should know about, darlin'?"

"No," I said. "I'm not seeing Todd on the sly. Why would I?"

"Can't imagine."

Me, either. "No," I said. "I haven't seen Todd since Easter. And we didn't talk then. Which you already know, since you were there."

He nodded. "He prob'ly just got lucky."

That's what I was thinking, too. "Mother says he usually lets his dad know if he isn't going to be home. But one thing might have led to another, and he forgot."

And now that the phone call was over and we were alone again, maybe one thing could lead to another here, too. I reached out and trailed a fingertip down his arm. The muscles quivered and then flexed under my touch. I smiled appreciatively. Rafe smiled, too, but didn't move.

"You're going to make me do it, aren't you?" I asked.

"Do what?"

"You know." Seduce him, rather than vice versa.

"It ain't gonna hurt you to work for it," Rafe said, "but to tell you the truth, I sorta changed my mind."

I pouted. "It's Todd, isn't it? You don't want him to intrude on our private time."

"If he were at the door," Rafe said, "that might be a consideration. But no, that ain't it."

"You seemed interested before." I hadn't forgotten that hand stroking lazy circles on my belly.

"It's your mama, darlin'. She puts me off my stroke."

Right. And whether that was a literal or metaphorical description, I knew what he meant. I scooted down and curled up next to him, my hand on his chest. "She's gone now."

"She ain't gone. She's down there in Sweetwater thinking about us in bed together."

"She wouldn't be that crude."

He glanced at me, and I elaborated. "A Southern Belle doesn't imagine what someone else is doing in bed. It would be unladylike."

His lips curved. "They teach you that in finishing school?"

"Among other things." I let my fingers go walking again, across his chest this time. "Are you sure I can't make you forget my mother? She's probably getting busy with the sheriff." Doing something very like what we were doing.

Rafe winced. "Putting that picture in my head ain't helping, darlin'."

"Sorry." It wasn't a picture I wanted in my own head, either. My mother doing the naughty with Sheriff Satterfield... talk about a mood-killer. "Try not to think about it," I advised.

"That what you're doing?"

"I'm trying."

"How's that going for you?"

"I could use a little help," I said, skimming my hand down his chest to his stomach, over warm skin, taut and smooth as silk.

He turned toward me. And that was the last thing either one of us said for a while.

After an enthusiastic session between the sheets—as enthusiastic as my morning sickness would allow—and another nap afterwards, we started the day in earnest around nine or so. I had my usual ack emma encounter with the toilet bowl while Rafe jumped in the shower. When he was done, it was my turn to get clean. When we were both dressed, we headed out together, and parted in the driveway: Rafe to ride the Harley north to the TBI headquarters off Gass Boulevard in Inglewood, and me to take the Volvo east to the high-end historic neighborhoods around Five Points.

We were spending most of our time these days at Rafe's grandmother's house on Potsdam Street. A couple of months ago, we'd put it on the market and tried to sell it. We had even come close once or twice, but each time something went wrong, dumping us right back where we started, with no purchase agreement and no buyers. So by the beginning of May, the house was just sitting there, newly renovated and empty. After the last time my apartment was broken into, I'd become a bit leery of staying there. And then there was the baby. I still had six months of pregnancy to go—assuming I made it that far—but once the baby was born, it would have to live somewhere, and my rental was a meager one-bedroom with no space for a nursery. Mrs. Jenkins's house had three stories, more bedrooms than we could ever hope to fill, and a nice, big yard. Plus, it was free. The only drawback was the neighborhood: on the edge—or to be fair, beyond the edge—of the gentrified parts of town. It was still a bit like the wild west out here, with drug deals going down on the corners out of souped-up cars driven by angry young men whose pants were belted below their butts.

Nobody had given us a hard time, however, and the fact that Rafe looked like he belonged, and like he could take care of himself—and me—probably contributed to that fact.

And things were looking better all the time. There was another big Victorian being renovated up the street, and on the next block, a real estate investor had picked up a couple of empty lots and was building infill homes. Slowly but surely, gentrification was creeping into the Potsdam area, too. By the time our son or daughter was ready to go to school, we might be living in the middle of a hip and happening neighborhood.

Meanwhile, I had another month to go on the lease for my apartment. I couldn't sublet it, not for that short of a time, so what I'd done instead, was sign it up for one of those short term bed and breakfast websites. With the new Nashville convention center recently completed, the hotels in downtown are booked solid for the next several years, and by-owner rentals have become big business in the urban core. My apartment is a quick jog across the river from downtown—just a hop, skip, and a jump, really: less than a mile—and I'd stayed pretty busy with renters for the past several weeks. Someone was in there now, too. A woman named Ursula had arrived on Thursday and was leaving again this morning. She was in town for a job interview, she'd told me in her email, with some PR firm or other on Music Row.

As I drove up Main Street past the building on Fifth and Main where the apartment is located, I glanced up at the second story balcony. The French doors fronting Main Street were closed, with no sign of life beyond. She might have left already, to catch an early flight back to New York or Los Angeles or wherever it was she was from. But checkout wasn't for another forty-five minutes, so I'd come back later to strip the bed and clean the bathroom.

Then I was past, and continued on toward Brew-ha-ha, the coffee shop on the corner of Tenth and Main. Over the last month, I had developed a craving for sesame bagels with chive cream cheese, and if I didn't get one, I'd spend all day thinking about it. We'd end up having bagels for dinner, and that wouldn't make Rafe happy. The time between dinner and now wouldn't make my small inhabitant happy, either. For being as tiny as the baby was—just a couple inches long— it had a voracious appetite, and a very definite opinion as to what it wanted to eat. This month, it seemed to want bagels. And chives. My body was probably lacking something important.

Then again, I didn't have cravings for potting soil or sidewalk chalk, so I could live with the need for bagels.

Brew-ha-ha was doing a brisk business when I walked in. It took time to get to the counter to place my order, and more time while someone put it together on a tray. Meanwhile, I scored a seat at a tiny round table over in the corner, wedged myself in, and pulled out my phone.

My mother's early-morning phone call was bothering me.

Not because I was worried about Todd. As I'd told my mother, he was thirty years old. He was the Assistant District Attorney for Maury County. He'd been married and divorced, so this wasn't his first rodeo. The man wasn't a novice when it came to life, love, or for that matter crime.

Not that bad stuff can't happen to anyone, of course, but I didn't really think anything had happened to Todd. He simply isn't the kind of person whom bad things happen to. He's much too conservative and careful to involve himself in situations where something bad could happen.

No, he was probably home by now, or at least on his way there. He had woken up in someone else's bed this morning, and had had to do the walk of shame in the same clothes he'd worn to dinner last night. Embarrassing, but hardly fatal.

What bothered me was that she'd called at all. She knew that Todd and I barely spoke anymore. She knew that I was living with Rafe and was carrying his baby. And she had to know that we wouldn't be into threesomes.

Yes, I'm sure she was counting the days until I called her to say I'd kicked Rafe out of my life and was moving on—she had a long wait, if so—but it seemed very strange that she'd even consider the possibility that I might be having dinner, let alone anything else, with Todd Satterfield.

The phone rang on the other end. Finally, my brother picked up, just as the plate with the bagel and cream cheese descended in front of me.

"Thank you," I told the server, a tattooed and pierced guy in his early twenties.

"You're welcome," my brother told me, as the server nodded and walked away. "What did I do?"

"Nothing. I wasn't talking to you." I tucked the phone between my ear and my shoulder, and got busy spreading cream cheese over half the bagel.

"Your boyfriend?"

"No. I was talking to the bagel guy."

"Problem?" my brother asked.

"With the bagel? Of course not."

"With your boyfriend?"

"No." Bagel being schmeared, I took the phone in one hand and lifted the bagel with the other. The first bite was like ambrosia, better than the best cheesecake I've ever had. I suppressed a moan and asked, "Why?"

"Why, what?"

"Why would you think there's a problem with Rafe?"

"Mother called," Dix said.

"About Todd?" I took another bite of bagel. *Mmmm.*

"Did she call you, too?"

I swallowed. "At six-thirty this morning. To say he didn't come home last night." I lifted the bagel again, but spoke before I bit into it. "I don't understand why she'd call *me*. She knows I'm living with Rafe."

"Selective memory," said my brother. And added, "Or wishful thinking."

"She doesn't want me to be, so she's pretending I'm not?"

"Something like that."

Great. "So about Todd..."

"He's home," Dix said. "I called him."

"Didn't Mother and the sheriff call him?"

"He must have had his phone turned off. Or been asleep, or something."

Or just avoiding the grownups' calls. "So nothing's wrong?"

"Not that he said," Dix said. "He told me he'd spent the night somewhere. When I tried to find out who he'd been with, he said he doesn't ask me questions about my love life."

"You have a love life?"

The question just fell out of my mouth, I swear. It wasn't intended to be flippant. I was just so surprised. It was six months since my sister-in-law Sheila died. And while I knew that Dix and my friend, MNPD homicide detective Tamara Grimaldi, had become friendly, if they were making love, it was news to me.

"None of your business," Dix told me.

No, it wasn't. If he and Tamara Grimaldi were doing the horizontal mambo, I'd just as soon not know. That was their affair—no pun intended.

"So Todd's back home and safe," I said instead.

"So it seems," Dix answered.

"Good." I hadn't really been worried, but found I was relieved anyway. "So what are you doing today?"

"Hanging out with the girls," Dix said, referring to my nieces Abigail and Hannah. "Church this morning, and then Hannah has a birthday party this afternoon."

"Have fun." In four to six years, that could be me. "Say hi to Catherine if you see her." Catherine is my other sibling, two years older than Dix.

Dix said he would, and then asked how I was spending the day. "Bagel," I said. "In twenty minutes I'm going over to the apartment to change the linens and clean the bathroom. The latest tenant is supposed to have moved on by then."

He sounded interested. "How's that working out for you? The short term B&B thing?"

So far, so good. "I've had five tenants over the past month. One girl stayed for a week—she was in town to record a song, she said—and the rest stayed a few days each. One couple, a single guy, and the rest women." Between them, they'd covered my rent and utilities for the month.

"What's Collier doing?" Dix wanted to know.

"He went to the TBI building to use the gym. Something about practicing hand-to-hand combat with somebody."

"I should work out with your boyfriend sometime," my brother said.

"Why do you want to learn hand-to-hand combat?" He was a lawyer. It wasn't like he had much occasion to get into fistfights. And the kind of law he practices—family law, wills and estates—doesn't even leave much opportunity for legal rumbles.

"I don't," Dix said. "I just want to get in better shape."

"Maybe you should ask Grimaldi to help you." The detective was in excellent physical condition.

"That's why—" Dix began, and changed his mind. I could hear the snap when he closed his teeth on the rest of the statement.

I arched my brows, but didn't comment. If Dix wanted to beef up for Tamara Grimaldi, who was I to give him a hard time? I liked Tamara, and I wanted Dix to be happy. And besides, him taking up with her in any kind of serious way, had the potential to disturb my mother almost as much as my taking up with Rafe had done, so it might take some of the pressure off.

"I'll mention it to him," I said. "Maybe you can drop the kids off with Catherine next Friday, and come up for the night. Now that we're living in Mrs. Jenkins's house, we have plenty of room." Unless he'd prefer to spend the night with Grimaldi, of course. "You and Rafe can work out in the morning."

"Maybe," Dix said. He sounded intrigued. "I'll think about it."

"You do that." The second half of my bagel was calling my name, so I cut things short. "I'll talk to you later, OK?"

"OK," Dix said and hung up. I picked up my plastic knife to give all my attention to slathering cream cheese over the second half of heaven.

Two

By the time I had finished my bagel and made sure it wouldn't make a repeat appearance—which happened sometimes—checkout time at Casa Martin had come and gone. My tenant had left, per our agreement, and I could get in and prepare the place for the next short-term renter, who was coming in Wednesday and leaving next Friday.

Rafe was still in the middle of his workout, so I didn't bother calling, just sent him a text saying I was headed over to the apartment and if he wanted to, he could meet me there if he finished what he was doing in the next forty-five minutes or so. His presence would keep me from doing some of the heavy lifting, so I figured he'd probably come running just as soon as he got the message. I had less than a week to go until I was through my first trimester, and after two previous miscarriages—one with Rafe last fall, one with my ex-husband a few years before—we were both counting the days. True, bad things can happen later in a pregnancy, too, but the majority of miscarriages take place in the first trimester—both of mine had—so we would both breathe a little easier once that milestone was passed.

At any rate, Rafe was wont to take things out of my hands these days, so I wouldn't injure myself or the baby by carrying anything too heavy. Like a load of laundry or a scrub brush. If I hadn't been brought up to expect to have things taken out of my hands, I might have found it stifling, but as it was, I appreciated it. Nobody wanted this baby more than I did. Not even Rafe.

I parked on the street and hustled across the courtyard and into the building. It was hot and humid, the time of year during which we all move as quickly as we can from air-conditioned home to air-conditioned car to air-conditioned office. The fabric of my shirt stuck to my back, and I wished I'd thought to pull my hair up into a tail or bun before going out, since the back of my neck was sticky.

The mailbox should be empty, since I'd had my mail forwarded to Mrs. Jenkins's house. But I checked it anyway, and found a note from the HOA strongly suggesting I attend Monday night's meeting. As a renter, I'd never considered myself eligible for the home owners' association—the actual owner of the complex had that privilege and responsibility, I figured—but I stuck the note in my bag anyway. It seemed a bit pointed, as it had my name scrawled on it. To my knowledge, in the almost three years I'd lived in the apartment, I had never been invited to an HOA meeting, and especially not so firmly.

Upstairs, I stood in front of my door for a moment, listening, before I knocked. From almost a year of doing real estate, I know that sometimes places that are supposed to be empty, aren't empty, and you run the risk of walking in on a copulating couple, or a man waggling his you-know-what in your direction. Just because Ursula Whatever-Her-Name was supposed to be gone, didn't mean she had actually left. Much safer to make sure the place was empty before I walked in on something I'd wish I could unsee later.

There was no sound from inside, and no answer when I knocked, so I inserted the key in the lock and pushed the door open. "Hello?"

There was no answer to that, either. Ursula must indeed be gone.

I hung my bag on one of the hooks in the hallway, just as I'd done every day for two and a half years before I moved out, and rolled up my metaphorical sleeves.

First things first. There's a laundry closet in the hallway opposite from the kitchen, just a few steps from where I was standing. I turned the washer on and dumped detergent into the water, taking a moment to make sure it foamed up nicely before I went in search of dirty towels and sheets.

The dishtowel in the kitchen still hung where I had left it, on the handle of the oven, and it still smelled fresh. But I snagged it anyway, just in case, and dropped it into the washer. The kitchen trashcan was empty, so Ursula must have taken the bag with her when she left. Nice of her. Not everyone who had stayed here had been so considerate.

The living room looked good, too. The pillows were fluffed and the coffee table free of junk. Ursula was either really good at picking up after herself, or she hadn't spent much time here.

The door to the bedroom was closed—I rarely do that; the place feels small enough without closing all the doors—and I skirted the dining room table and headed in that direction. Behind me, the washer stuttered to a stop as the water reached capacity. I twisted the knob and pushed the door open, hustling to get the bed stripped and the sheets and towels gathered before the water got cold.

Momentum carried me a few steps into the room before my feet caught up with my brain and I stumbled to a stop.

God.

Ursula hadn't left. She was still in bed. But not with anyone. And nobody was waggling anything at me. Her eyes were fixed, staring at the ceiling, her skin a bluish-gray.

"Oh, God!"

I made it to the toilet, but just barely. The bagel made a comeback, along with everything else in my stomach.

You'd think I'd be used to throwing up by now. I did it most every morning as I attempted to brush my teeth. But morning sickness is a different kind of throwing up. You gag, and feel normal afterwards.

This wasn't like that. This was a sick rush that left me weak and trembling, hanging on to the toilet bowl so I wouldn't slide to the floor.

God, what had happened?

Stupid question, when it was all too apparent what had happened—she'd killed herself, or someone else had killed her—but my mind wasn't working properly. I knew I needed to drag myself to my feet. Splash some water on my face and call 911. But I couldn't get my body to cooperate. I just sat there on the cold tile floor, fighting back waves of nausea while my head spun.

And then I heard it.

The sound of the front door opening and closing.

Someone's coming.

Steps in the hallway.

If he finds you here, he'll kill you, too.

Steps on the carpet in the living room.

Hide!

I glanced around. But a hiding place didn't magically appear. I was in a small bathroom. The only place to hide was behind the shower curtain, and whoever was out there would hear the rustle of fabric and the sound of the rings sliding along the rod if I tried to get behind it at this point.

Steps halted in the doorway of the bedroom, and I froze.

The sound that followed was inarticulate. I want to say it was a curse, but I think it was more elemental than that. A grunt, as if from an emotional jab to the solar plexus. A quick intake of breath.

Nonetheless, I recognized it.

"Rafe," I managed.

A beat, then a rush of feet across the carpet before he appeared in the doorway. "Savannah!"

He was pale, as pale as I'd ever seen him. "Christ! You OK?"

He dropped to his knees next to me and reached out.

"I threw up," I said, leaning against him. The heat of his body felt good. I was cold all the way through.

He didn't say anything, just wrapped his arms around me and held on.

"She's dead," I told him, the words muffled against his chest. "I didn't touch her. But she's blue. So she's dead, right?"

"Yeah." His voice rumbled through his chest.

"We have to call the police."

"In a minute. She ain't going nowhere."

No. And whoever had killed her—unless she'd simply died on her own—was long gone. Another minute wouldn't hurt.

"Why does this keep happening to me?" I wailed, without really expecting an answer.

Rafe's arms tightened. "It didn't happen to you. For a second—"

He didn't finish the sentence, but he didn't have to. I hadn't noticed it, consciously, but now that I thought about it, the woman on the bed did look a little like me. Same general body-type—height and weight, minus the pregnancy—and same wavy, dark blond hair fanning out over the pillow.

I tilted my head back to look at him. "You don't think...?"

He quirked a brow. "You piss anyone off lately? Enough to wanna kill you?"

"Not that I know of." Most of the people I had upset to that degree were in jail. There was Shelby Ferguson, I suppose—my ex-husband Bradley's current wife—who might be harboring a slight grudge, but she had her hands full with an infant and with making conjugal visits to Riverbend Penitentiary, so I doubted she'd take the time out to come here to kill me.

"It's probably something simple," I said, trying to keep my voice steady and keeping my mental fingers crossed that I was right. "Maybe she went out somewhere, to kick up her heels on her last night in Nashville, and picked up the wrong guy."

Rafe made a noise in his throat. It was a non-committal noise. And he was right. Too soon to guess.

"You OK?" He looked down at me, one hand sliding down to rest against my lower back.

I shook my head. "No. But I'll survive. I don't feel like I'm going to throw up anymore. And we have to call 911."

"I'll take care of it. I want you to wait outside."

He got to his feet, then helped me up. That hand against my back began steering me toward the living room.

"Outside the bedroom?" I asked.

"Outside the apartment," Rafe answered, and kept walking.

Perforce, I did, too. "What do you want me to do? Sit on the stairs?"

I couldn't go home. Back to Mrs. Jenkins's house, I mean. The police would want to talk to me when they got here. And it was much too hot to be comfortable standing around outside.

"That'll work," Rafe said. "I just need you to stay outta the crime scene."

So it was a crime scene. I had surmised as much—women in their twenties or early thirties don't usually drop dead with no warning—but it was still a fazer to hear the words.

"Are you sure it mightn't be an accident?" I asked hopefully. "An overdose or something?"

He hesitated and shot me a glance. Maybe he could hear how much I wanted not to get tangled up in another murder investigation. "It might could."

"Do you know how...?"

"She died cause she couldn't breathe," Rafe said. "Could be drugs. Could be something got stuck in her throat."

Or it could be that someone wrapped his hands around her throat and squeezed. I glanced over my shoulder, to see if there were bruises on her neck, but since the bedroom was around the corner by now, it wasn't like I could see anything.

"I was going to wash the sheets," I said weakly as we passed the laundry closet. "The washer is full of water."

Rafe glanced at it, and then at me. "You're gonna have to wait until the crime scene crew's come and gone."

Was he kidding? I shuddered. "I won't be washing those sheets. If the police don't want them, they're going straight in the dumpster."

We passed through the door into the hallway, and I immediately found myself breathing a little easier. Guess Rafe had known what he was doing after all, when he told me I had to wait outside the apartment.

He closed the door behind us, then pulled out his phone. "Hold up this wall for a second, darlin'." He put my back against it. I closed my eyes and listened to the phone call.

It didn't take long. Instead of calling 911, he cut through all the red tape by dialing Tamara Grimaldi directly. And once she answered, the conversation was short. "It's me. I need you to come to Savannah's apartment. Bring a crime scene crew."

Grimaldi said something, and Rafe answered with, "See you then," and hung up.

I blinked at him. "Didn't she ask what happened?"

"She knows what happened," Rafe said, dropping the phone into his pocket.

"How?"

"She works homicide," Rafe said. "She knows I ain't gonna call her unless somebody's dead."

"How did she know it wasn't me who was dead?" It was my apartment, after all. It seemed like a reasonable question.

"If you'd been dead," Rafe said, "she woulda been able to tell."

"How?"

"I woulda been hysterical."

I blinked at him. He smiled sweetly. I blinked again. "Hysterical?"

He shrugged. "I've kinda gotten used to you, darlin'. Somebody kills you, I ain't gonna be calm."

"That's so sweet," I said, touched. He squinted at me, and I added, "You're always calm. You were calm when you walked into Perry Fortunato's bedroom and found me tied to the bed. You were calm when a hundred cops were pointing guns at us outside *La Havana*. You were even calm when you walked into Julio Melendez's warehouse to save me from Hector Gonzales."

"No, I wasn't."

"You looked calm."

"That don't mean I was calm," Rafe said. "And anyway, you weren't dead."

No. And he was right: he hadn't been calm when he burst into Perry's bedroom or Julio's warehouse. He'd looked upset for all of a second and a half in each instance, until he'd seen me and ascertained that I was still breathing.

"My hero," I said.

His lips curved. "I bet you say that to all the boys."

"No." I hadn't had occasion to meet many heroes, so I'd never said it to anyone else before now. But this wasn't the time for it. "So now what?"

"We wait," Rafe said.

"You're not going back inside?"

He shook his head. "It ain't my case. Tammy won't be happy if I stomp all over her crime scene."

I guess not. Although he was fellow law enforcement, so it seemed to me like he should be able to.

Then again, jurisdictions, I guess.

Rafe nodded when I said so. "A murder in Nashville falls under the MNPD. If they need help, they'll ask us for it."

Which they hadn't. At least not yet. "And if they don't ask, you can't butt in."

He shook his head.

"I guess we'll just sit here, then."

"Guess so." He slid down to the floor beside the door. After a moment, I joined him, with an unladylike groan.

He reached out and took my hand. "You OK, darlin'?"

"I'm getting there," I said. The nausea was gone, or as much as it is ever gone these days. As long as I didn't dwell too much on what had happened, and where, I was all right.

"Baby OK?"

I put a hand on my stomach. "As far as I can tell. I can't really feel him move yet."

He quirked a brow. "Him?"

"Or her. It."

We sat in silence for a moment.

"What do you think happened?" I asked.

"To her?" He didn't wait for me to nod. "Mighta been what you said. She went out and picked up the wrong guy. It happens. Or whoever she came to town to meet killed her. Or it mighta been something like an overdose. Alcohol poisoning. All I know right now is that she suffocated. Can't tell you why yet. Didn't look at the body close enough."

I nodded. "I'll just sit here and keep my fingers crossed that it was an accident."

"You do that." But he didn't sound too encouraging. And frankly, it probably was too much to hope for.

The police, meaning Detective Tamara Grimaldi, came up the stairs less than five minutes later. MNPD headquarters, where Grimaldi works, is just a mile away, a straight shot across the bridge into downtown, so I wasn't surprised she had made it here so quickly.

I first met Grimaldi last August, after Rafe and I stumbled over my colleague Brenda Puckett's butchered body in Rafe's grandmother's house. She—Grimaldi—took one look at me and wrote me off as useless. I took one look at her and quailed.

I don't anymore. I've learned that she's human, and she has decided that I'm not the pathetic waste of oxygen she originally thought. Or at least that I'm not *just* a pathetic waste of oxygen. My girlish ways still annoy her, just as her brusqueness and businesslike demeanor still intimidates me, but we've become friends.

She looked grim as she crested the stairs and came down the hallway toward us, dressed in her usual masculine pantsuit and low-heeled shoes. I knew there was red polish on the nails inside the shoes—I'd seen her wearing sandals and Capri pants at my brother's house less than a month ago—but from looking at her right now, you'd swear she didn't have a feminine weakness in her arsenal.

She squatted in front of me, dark eyes steady on my face. "You OK?"

I nodded.

"Baby OK?"

She wasn't supposed to know about the baby—we were keeping the news about the pregnancy quiet until I was through the first trimester, for obvious reasons—but I guess maybe Dix had told her.

"Yes, thank you."

She moved her attention to Rafe. And she didn't ask him whether he was all right, just looked at him for a second. What she saw must have reassured her, because she got to her feet. "I'll be right back. Just let me see what we've got, and then I'll be back to talk to you."

I nodded.

She glanced at Rafe. "You coming?"

He hesitated. "You mind?" he asked me.

I shook my head. It was obvious the detective wanted him to accompany her, so whether I minded or not didn't really matter, anyway.

They disappeared into the apartment. I leaned my head back against the wall and closed my eyes. And opened them again at the sound of a door closing down the hall.

My neighbor, Mr. Sullivan, came toward me. "Something wrong?"

I hesitated. But really, there was no point in trying to keep it a secret. He'd figure out the truth once the crime scene crew arrived and strung their yellow tape across the door. Anyone who watches TV these days know what that looks like. "Dead woman."

Mr. Sullivan blinked. "The blonde?"

"Yes. Did you see her?"

He nodded. "When I came home from work yesterday she was letting herself in. I thought it was you at first, so I said hello. When she turned, I saw it wasn't. Same hair, different face."

"She spent a couple days here," I explained. "For a job interview." And since I suspected, after that summons from the HOA, that subletting my apartment for short-term rentals was against the rules, I thought I'd better not say anything about the fact that she was a paying guest. "I spend most of my time at Rafe's grandmother's house these days. I just came in to get the sheets this morning, and found her."

Mr. Sullivan clicked his tongue. "That's a shame. Pretty woman."

"Did you talk to her at all?"

He shook his head. "Not after I realized she wasn't you."

Bummer. "Thanks," I told him.

He nodded. "Did your friend find you?"

"Friend?"

Mr. Sullivan opened his mouth, but before he could answer, the door to my apartment opened, and Rafe popped his head out. "Darlin'..."

He looked grim, his mouth set in a straight line, and my heart started thudding faster. "Yes?"

He nodded to Mr. Sullivan, but addressed me. "Gonna need you to come back inside for a minute. Sorry."

"It's OK," I said, scrambling to my feet.

"We'll get you outta here after that. They should be coming to take her away soon."

And none too soon for me.

I turned to Mr. Sullivan. "I've been invited to attend the HOA meeting on Monday night. Maybe I'll see you there."

"Always make sure I go," Mr. Sullivan said cheerfully. "Good eats." He winked at me. "You have a good day now."

He wandered off down the hall toward his own apartment. I followed Rafe back into my own.

Three

Grimaldi was still in the bedroom, and the corpse was still on the bed. I knew it would be, so I steeled myself before going through the door, and tried not to look in that direction. But it was hard: sort of like attempting not to stare at an accident on the highway.

Grimaldi was standing at the dresser with a wallet in her hands.

It wasn't mine. This one was bright teal, and had Kate Spade written all over it. Mine doesn't, and besides, it's a demure cream.

Grimaldi turned to look at me. "Jocelyn Rivera," she said.

"That's her name?"

She nodded.

"That isn't what she told me."

Grimaldi's gaze sharpened. "What did she tell you?"

"Ursula Something. York. Or Wells. Or maybe London. Something short and sort of British." Classy. Elegant.

"You have the information at home?"

I nodded.

"Look it up and let me know. Did she tell you what she was doing in Nashville?"

"Job interview," I said. "With a PR firm on Music Row."

"Do you remember the name of that?"

I shook my head. "But I can look that up when I get home, too."

"Please do."

"Twenty bucks says they've never even heard of her," Rafe said.

Grimaldi looked at him. "Gambling is illegal."

"I won't tell."

She shook her head. I looked from one to the other of them. "What's going on? Why would she give me a fake name? It's not like I'd know who she was either way." I'd never heard of Ursula until she contacted me, and if I'd ever heard the name Jocelyn Rivera before, I didn't know when or under what circumstances. To the best of my knowledge, I'd never before seen or heard of the woman in my bed.

"Your girl," Rafe said, "ain't what she told you she was."

"What is she?"

"Best guess," Grimaldi said, "a call girl."

I gulped as the room took a slow spin. "I rented my apartment to a prostitute?"

"Afraid so." Rafe put an arm around me and drew me close, to where my back was against his front.

"Am I in trouble?" Surely renting space to a prostitute was illegal. It was facilitating or something, wasn't it?

"Did you know?" Grimaldi asked.

"Of course not!" For that matter, I had only her word for it now. "What makes you think that's what she was?"

"Little black book." Grimaldi lifted it between two plastic-gloved fingers.

"She didn't just... I don't know... have a lot of boyfriends?"

"Sure she did," Rafe said. "Boyfriends who paid."

Ewww.

"Was she…" I glanced at the corpse, "entertaining in my bed?"

"I assume so," Grimaldi said.

My face twisted. In that case, it wasn't just the sheets that were going; the whole bed would be hitting the dumpster after the police released the crime scene.

"Good thing we ain't living here no more," Rafe said cheerfully.

"If we'd been living here, this wouldn't be a problem." I turned back to Grimaldi. "She wasn't in town for a job interview?"

"I won't know until I check with the company she supposedly had the interview with, and I can't do that until you get me the name, but I don't imagine so. No."

"I'm an idiot." I turned and thunked my head against Rafe's chest a couple of times, since there was no wall handy.

"Was no way you coulda known," he told me, rubbing his hands up and down my bare arms.

"Of course I could have. If I'd thought about it. *You* would have thought about it."

I still had my forehead against his chest, so I couldn't see his face, but I could hear that arched eyebrow in his voice. "Not sure I like what you're implying, darlin'."

"Not that you spend your time thinking about prostitutes." *Sheesh.* "Just that you're a bit more knowledgeable than I am when it comes to this stuff."

"Stuff?"

"Criminal stuff." And again, *sheesh.*

"I'm going to need to see a list of all your clients," Grimaldi said, and I lifted my head to look at her. "The people you've rented your apartment to. Everyone who's stayed here since you moved out. There's been more than just she, right?"

Yes. There had. "You think this has happened before?"

"Not the murder," Grimaldi said, with a glance at the victim.

Of course not. But— "You think I've rented my apartment to other escorts?"

She shrugged. "There have been reports of prostitutes utilizing short term rentals rather than hotels or motels. Less chances they'll draw attention to themselves that way."

"Oh, my God." I thunked my head against Rafe's chest again.

"Go home, darlin'," he told me. "Get the information together for Tammy. We'll finish up here, and then I'll be home, too."

"Right." I took a breath and straightened. "I can do this."

"We're counting on it, darlin'. Just make a list of everyone you've rented the place to. Names, contact info, payment info. Anything you can remember. And anything you know about Ursula."

I nodded.

"I'll walk you out." He did, and stopped in the hallway to give me a kiss. "Drive carefully. Take care of my baby."

I said I would, and then I headed down the stairs while he went back inside my apartment, to where a dead prostitute was sprawled across my bed.

By the time he came home—back to Mrs. Jenkins's house—it was afternoon, and I had finished compiling my list for Tamara Grimaldi. In the past month, I had rented out the apartment five times. Once to a couple, once to a single man, and three times to single women.

Grant Howard was the guy. He'd spent a full work-week—Monday to Friday—on what he'd said was a consulting job for a law firm. I had no reason to disbelieve it, but at the moment I was questioning everything.

The couple was the Ericksons, Maude and Harold, a retired couple from Wisconsin, who had been vacationing. They'd asked me for information about the Grand Ole Opry and sightseeing tours of the country stars' homes, so I tended to think they'd been who they said they were. Besides, I had actually met them, and I don't think I had ever seen a woman who looked less like a prostitute than Maude Erickson.

One of the single women had been named Victoria Wallace, with a Canadian email address, and she'd been in Nashville for a whole week, as well, ostensibly to record a demo.

Another had told me her name was Shauna Bangs, and in retrospect, that name should have set my radars to buzzing. She'd stayed two nights, Friday and Saturday last week. I'd barely had time to change Grant's sheets before she'd arrived.

The last woman—or last before Ursula, or Jocelyn—had been Wendy Morgan, who had stayed from Monday to Thursday this week. I'd had to scramble to get the sheets changed between her and Ursula, too. She'd told me she was in town just looking around, since her husband was up for a position at Vanderbilt University in the fall, and she wanted to see whether she could live here. It sounded reasonable, but by now I was second-guessing everything.

When Rafe came through the door just before one o'clock, I was sitting at the kitchen table tearing my hair out. Not literally, although I had fisted my hands in it a few times, so my mother would have told me to go brush.

He pulled out the chair across from me, turned it around, and straddled it. "You OK, darlin'?"

"Fine," I said, blowing out a breath. "I wasn't the one who was strangled in my bed."

He didn't say anything to that, just kept watching me. I took another breath and blew it out, more slowly.

"I'm a bit freaked out," I admitted. "Shauna Bangs sounds like she'd be a hooker, doesn't she?"

His lips twitched. "I'd say so."

"What about Victoria Wallace? Wendy Morgan? Grant Howard?"

He shrugged. Muscles moved smoothly under the tight T-shirt. "Could go either way."

"Right." I blew out another breath. "I can't believe I've been renting my apartment to prostitutes. My mother will have a fit."

"Not if you don't tell her."

"What are the chances she won't find out?"

"I ain't telling her," Rafe said. "You ain't telling her. How's she gonna know?"

"Grimaldi will tell Dix and he'll tell Mother?"

He shrugged. "It coulda happened to anyone."

Maybe. Anyone gullible enough not to put two and two together when Shauna Bangs asked to rent the place, anyway.

I sat back and smoothed my hair. "Did you discover anything else I should know about?"

"As a matter of fact."

Uh-oh. "What?"

"Before you started doing this..."

"Renting out the place?"

He nodded. "Did you install extra security?"

I blinked. "No. There was already a lock and a chain on the door. And there's a locked door downstairs, too. I figured that was enough." Besides, he'd be the one I would ask to install said security, so if I had, he'd be the first to know.

"So if there's a camera setup in the bedroom, you didn't put it there?"

"No." And then what he'd asked registered. "There's a camera setup in the bedroom?"

And on the heels of that realization, something else occurred to me. "How long has it been there?"

"Hopefully only since we moved out," Rafe said.

Hopefully. "That's disgusting. Who wants to watch themselves making love?"

Rafe shrugged. "I don't mind looking at you naked."

I didn't mind looking at him naked, either. But I preferred him naked in the flesh, not on screen. And anyway, it wasn't watching him on tape that worried me. It was watching myself, with all my flaws and imperfections.

"Perry Fortunato had a camera in his bedroom." And Perry was about as creepy as they came. Among other things, he'd taped his wife cheating and himself committing rape.

"The tape's been destroyed," Rafe said.

"Perry's tape?"

He nodded. "I made sure of it."

For the record, this wasn't the tape of Connie Fortunato and Beau Riggins—both dead now—getting it on in Perry and Connie's bed, nor was it the tape of Perry raping and strangling Lila Vaughn.

No, the tape we were talking about was of me, stripped to my lingerie and heels, tied to Perry's bed. The tape that culminated with Perry bleeding to death on the floor while Rafe cut me loose.

"Did you watch it first?" I asked.

He shook his head. "I was there. I know what you looked like."

"Did the cops watch it?"

"Tammy told me they didn't." He shook his head. "That's old news. Can we get back to today?"

"Sure," I said. "I assume you didn't put a camera in our bedroom?"

"Not without telling you first, darlin'. If I wanna film us in bed, I'll talk you into it. But I ain't gonna do it without your permission. Not only would you kick me out, but I'd go back to jail."

"It's illegal?"

"One-party consent state," Rafe said. "Except for areas where someone might reasonably expect privacy. That includes bedrooms, bathrooms, and locker rooms."

"So if you wanted to film us making love, I would have to consent, too?"

He nodded.

Good to know. "So if you and I didn't, who put the camera there?"

"My guess is Jocelyn," Rafe said.

"Why?"

He shrugged. "Blackmail?"

"I guess it would depend on who she was having sex with."

In my bed. Ewww. I made a face and continued, "Was there film in the camera? Or however that works these days?" Digital cartridges or CD-ROMs or whatnot.

Rafe shook his head. "There ain't no camera. Just the setup for one."

"So what's her name—Ursula or Jocelyn or whatever—could have had a camera running, and whoever killed her realized it, and took it with him when he left?"

Rafe nodded. "The crime scene crew's going over everything. If it's in the apartment, they'll find it. But my guess is it left with the killer."

"They're there now?" Probably throwing fingerprint powder all over my apartment again. Nasty stuff. Hard to get rid of.

Rafe's lips twitched. "Sorry, darlin'. We'll get somebody in to clean the place after they're done."

"I can clean it," I said. "It's just annoying." Especially the fourth or fifth time it happens.

"No kidding." He glanced at the paper in front of me. "That the list?"

I nodded and pushed it toward him. "One man, three women, one couple."

He turned it around and skimmed it. It wasn't very extensive. Just the names, the email addresses or phone numbers they'd used to contact me, their payment information, and whatever they'd given as their reason—or excuse—for coming to Nashville and needing a place to stay.

"You see any of these people in person?" Rafe asked.

"The couple. They insisted on paying by check. Wouldn't use a credit card, and I'm not sure they knew what PayPal is. So I arranged to be there to let them in and take their money." And if they'd been using my apartment for illicit threesomes or foursomes, I'd eat the piece of paper their names had been written on. "Nice people. Late sixties, maybe. She was wearing a T-shirt with a sparkly kitten on it. He looked like Santa Claus."

Rafe's lips twitched. "That don't mean nothing."

"Sure it does. I've never seen any man who looked less like a pimp. Besides, he totally adored her. I could tell. They were holding hands. I hope we'll be that cute in forty years."

Rafe didn't seem to have an answer to that, and I added, "I also saw Victoria Wallace. She was the first, so I was a little worried. And curious."

That single eyebrow arched. "What d'you do? Spy on her?"

I shrugged, blushing. "I parked on the street and watched for a while. I'm not entirely sure it was her, but a woman came out who wasn't one of the usual people. Unless someone else had a visitor or has rented their place, I'm thinking she was it."

"Uh-huh." I could tell he was trying not to grin. "Could you tell anything from the way she looked?"

"She didn't look like a porn star, if that's what you mean. Average height, on the skinny side, long, brown hair, dressed in jeans and cowboy boots."

"She looked like a country singer."

I nodded. "And that's what she was supposed to be."

"You'd recognize her if you saw a picture of her?"

"I imagine so." I hadn't seen her up close, but my eyesight is aided by contacts, so I see reasonably well even at a distance.

He returned his attention to the list. "Anyone else?"

"No. After her came the Ericksons—whom I met when they arrived—and by then I had calmed down about having strangers in my apartment, so I didn't feel the need to look at the rest. Some of the neighbors probably saw them, though. Mr. Sullivan saw Ursula. Or Jocelyn. If Grimaldi went door to door, she might rustle up a few witnesses."

"Spicer and Truman are doing that," Rafe said, eyes on the list. His lashes—long and sooty—cast shadows on his cheeks.

I watched for a moment, then pulled my thoughts together. "Am I going to be in trouble over this?"

He glanced up. "Why? You didn't strangle nobody."

"Of course not. I meant because I've been renting the place out." And to hookers. Or at least one hooker, if Shauna Bangs happened to be someone who simply had an unfortunate last name. "I have an invitation from the homeowner's association to attend their meeting tomorrow night."

"So?"

"They've never asked me to attend before. I'm not a homeowner."

"Ah," Rafe said and pushed the list away. "Yeah, they might have something to say about it."

No kidding.

"Can you come with me?"

He looked at me, and I batted my lashes. He grinned. "Sure. If I don't have to work."

"You don't usually work nights." Our standing joke was that once he retired from undercover work, I would meet him at the door with a pipe and slippers at five o'clock every day. It was usually more like five thirty or six when he arrived, and he doesn't smoke a pipe nor wear slippers as a rule, but if I were home, I met him at the door, occasionally in my skivvies, and sometimes in nothing at all. Once in a while he'd take his rookies out on a S&C field trip at night, to practice surveillance and counter-surveillance, but those were scheduled ahead of time, so if he had one tomorrow night, he'd already know about it, and would already have told me.

"You never know what might come up," Rafe said, which I suppose was true. "But if I don't have to work, I'll go along." And then he leaned back on the chair and stretched, and that tight T-shirt pulled tighter across his chest and shoulders.

"Speaking of something coming up..." I said.

He grinned. "Pregnancy's really doing a number on you, ain't it?"

I shrugged. "I want you when I'm not pregnant, too." Although sitting at the kitchen table didn't hurt. Best as I could figure out, the baby currently growing in my belly had been conceived on this table.

"I guess I can spare five minutes," Rafe said.

"That's all it's going to take?"

He didn't answer, just got to his feet and held out his hand. "Care to join me in the shower?"

"Don't mind if I do," I said, and let him pull me to my feet.

Two hours later we walked into Grimaldi's office in the police headquarters building downtown.

I suppose I could have emailed her my list of tenants—that's probably what she'd expected me to do—but I was curious. Someone had died in my apartment, and although I knew I wasn't responsible, it was personal.

I'd been to Grimaldi's office a few times before. It isn't very big, although it blows the former coat closet that I work out of at Lamont, Briggs and Associates out of the water. It was probably about eight feet square, and what room wasn't taken up by the desk and two visitors' chairs, was covered by paperwork. Tamara Grimaldi is one of the best homicide detectives in the Nashville police. She handles a lot of cases, and as far as I know, manages to close most of them. She solved my sister-in-law Sheila's murder back in November, as well as my friend Lila Vaughn's murder last September, and my colleague Brenda Puckett's murder before that. If someone had to drop dead in my apartment, I couldn't ask for anyone better to handle the investigation and get me off the hook.

She was sitting behind the desk scowling at her computer screen when we walked in, and didn't waste any time transferring the scowl to us. "Took you long enough."

I resisted the temptation to apologize. "We got sidetracked." I stepped forward and put the list on her desk.

"Uh-huh." Her voice was dry. I got the feeling she knew exactly what had distracted us.

I stole a glance at Rafe. He was grinning, of course. "Anything new?" I asked.

Grimaldi shook her head. "The medical examiner won't be in the office until tomorrow. Not that I expect any surprises in the autopsy. The crime scene team is still working. Spicer and Truman are still conducting interviews."

She put her finger at the top of my list, where I'd written down everything I could remember about Ursula Kent aka Jocelyn Rivera. "This the firm she said she was interviewing with?"

I nodded. "They're a legitimate company. I tried calling, but of course they're closed today."

"Of course." She shook her head. "Why don't you leave the investigating to the professionals, Ms.... Savannah?"

I scowled at her. And immediately stopped when I remembered my mother's admonition about wrinkles. "It's not as if they'd have answered if *you* called. If they're closed on Sundays, they're closed no matter who's on the phone."

"Maybe, maybe not," Grimaldi said. "Most people answer when the police call." She smiled smugly.

I rolled my eyes but didn't argue, since she did, after all, have a point. "I feel responsible," I said instead. "She was killed in my apartment. If I hadn't agreed to rent the place to her..."

"If you hadn't rented her your place, she'd have died in someone else's bed," Rafe said.

And then it wouldn't be my problem. Although she'd still be dead, which I guess was his point.

"I feel stupid," I said. "I believed that she was here for a job interview."

"There was no way you could have known any different," Grimaldi said. "Did you even speak to her?"

I shook my head. "It was all by email. She contacted me online."

"So you never even heard her voice. You had no way of knowing whether she was telling the truth or feeding you a line."

I suppose not. But I still felt like I should have guessed something was up. I don't know how, but somehow.

"So what happens now?"

"For you," Grimaldi said, "nothing. Unless something comes to light that implicates you further, you're off the hook."

"What do you mean, 'further'?" Nothing was going to come to light to implicate me at all. *Sheesh.* It wasn't like I would have killed this woman even if I had known who she was and that she was entertaining men—for money—in my bed.

"Go home," Grimaldi said. "Enjoy the rest of your weekend."

"What about him?" I gestured to Rafe.

"Take him with you. He's all yours."

"The TBI isn't involved?"

The guy who was all mine shook his head. "The detective don't need no help with this case, darlin'. She'll figure it out on her own."

All righty, then. I got to my feet. "It was nice to see you. Even under the circumstances."

"The circumstances could be better," Grimaldi agreed.

"Will you let me know what happens?"

She hesitated, and I pushed. "She was killed in my apartment. She even looks like me. The least you can do is tell me when you arrest her murderer. Not that I think I'm really in danger, or anything..."

Rafe's hand tightened momentarily around my arm.

"No," the detective agreed.

"But it's personal. I'd like to know."

Grimaldi nodded. "I'll let you know what I found out."

"Thank you." I headed for the door with Rafe right behind me.

"You let me know if you need any help," he told Grimaldi over his shoulder.

"You'll be the first to know."

Although from the tone of her voice, it would be snowing in hell when she called.

"Professional rivalry?" I asked Rafe when we were outside the door and on our way down the hall toward the elevator.

He shrugged. "Something like that. Tammy can be territorial."

"Don't call me that!" floated down the hallway after us.

I grinned, and so did Rafe. "So now what?"

"You hungry? It's almost dinner-time."

It wasn't. It was not even four o'clock. But we'd used up a bit of energy earlier, in the interlude between the murder and the trip to police headquarters. And we'd both skipped lunch. Not to mention that Rafe had worked out this morning, and had probably burned a lot of calories that way, too.

"I could eat," I said. I could always eat these days.

"Burger and fries?"

"Why not?" I was eating for two, after all. And most of what I ate seemed to go toward creating the baby, anyway. My stomach was getting a little bigger, but I wasn't noticing a lot of extra padding anywhere else. With luck, I'd be able to get rid of it all once the baby was born.

"My kinda girl," Rafe said and put his arm around my shoulders.

"And don't you forget it." I leaned my head on his shoulder as the elevator doors closed and we began our descent.

Four

Every Monday morning, LB&A—Lamont, Briggs and Associates, the real estate firm I work for—has a weekly sales meeting. We all sit around the big table in the conference room and talk about our new listings, new clients, and anything else that's going on.

I had thought I might skip the meeting this week. I had no new listings, nor any new clients, and I didn't really want to talk about the fact that I'd found a dead body in my bed this weekend. And besides, I was pregnant. I needed my sleep.

But Rafe got up and went to work in the morning as usual, and woke me up before he left, and since I was awake anyway, I decided I might as well go.

To be honest, I was having second thoughts about the whole real estate career. I'd had my license for about a year, and in that time, I hadn't generated much business at all. If it hadn't been for Rafe paying most of the bills, I'd be scraping the bottom of the savings account right now. I'd earned enough in commissions to afford to renew my license and maintain my association membership for another year, but that was pretty much all I'd managed to do, and I wasn't sure that was reason enough to carry on.

Don't get me wrong: I enjoy houses. I like looking at them, and I like selling them—when I have the chance to. It was just that other things kept coming along to distract me. Like dead bodies.

Maybe I should talk to Rafe about going to work for the TBI. Or maybe I should talk him into quitting his job and getting a private investigator's license, and I could be his office assistant. Like Effie Perine with Sam Spade.

Except this Effie and Sam would be sharing a bed.

Anyway, the story about the murder had been on the news last night, along with an interview with the head of the Fifth and Main home owners association, Prisca Miller. She and the cameraman had been standing in front of my apartment building. The building is close to the LB&A office, and some of my colleagues drive by to get to work. I was sure some of them knew that I used to live there. And while the police hadn't released Jocelyn's name, someone had discovered that she was a prostitute plying her craft in a short term rental apartment. Prisca clearly wasn't happy about that. In fact, I got the impression that the fact that Jocelyn had been a prostitute was a worse crime than Jocelyn being murdered.

I didn't know Prisca well. She was fairly new; I didn't think I'd seen her at all during the first couple of years I'd lived here. It was only in the last year, year and a half maybe, that I'd noticed her coming and going. And she didn't live in my building of studios and one bedroom apartments, but instead owned one of the townhouses on the other side of the courtyard. I had no idea what she did for a living, but it had to be something that paid well, since she was always very elegantly dressed. Besides, those townhouses didn't come cheap, nor did the brand-new Mercedes she was driving.

She was a couple years older than me—early thirties, maybe— with nostrils that flared angrily as she told the camera how upset she was about what had happened. And she was absolutely gorgeous, with coloring similar to Rafe's: coffee-with-lots-of-cream complexion, dark eyes, and hair that was just a shade or two lighter than black. It was pulled back so severely that her eyebrows were slightly elevated, and her voice was crisp with annoyance as she addressed the camera.

"This is an untenable situation, and the city needs to do something to crack down on the short term rentals that are cropping up everywhere. It's a well known fact that these so-called B and B vacation rentals are a haven for prostitution and worse. The city needs to institute legislation to keep this from happening to our homes!"

Her eyes were lit with semi-religious fervor, and I could imagine the viewers at home nodding along with her.

"We'll take care of this situation internally at our next HOA meeting," Prisca promised; rather ominously, I thought, "but the city needs to do its part in dealing with the larger problem. We need legislation prohibiting short term rentals in our condo complexes. This has to stop!"

In homes all across Nashville, people stood up and cheered.

"Maybe I'll just skip the HOA meeting Monday night," I'd told Rafe.

He gave my shoulders a squeeze. "I'll go with you. Moral support."

Sure.

But first, there was the LB&A sales meeting to get through. I took a seat in the conference room and crossed my fingers under the table in hopes that no one had watched the news and would connect the dead body with my building.

I should have known better. Our acting broker Timothy Briggs opened the meeting with the usual rundown of new listings, new clients, upcoming closings and the scheduling of open houses for the next weekend. I volunteered to host someone else's, since I didn't have any listings of my own. I'd done a lot of that over the past year, usually for Tim, who had more business than he knew what to do with, especially now that he had to ride herd on the rest of us.

"We'll talk about it later," he told me, and carried on.

The meeting concluded without any mention of my apartment building or the murder that had taken place there, and I got to my feet feeling relieved. It really wasn't like Tim, to be honest. Usually he's the first to give me a hard time. He's mellowed some since I saved him from a murder rap back in February—and saved his life while I was at it; or at least Rafe did—but he has a crush on my fiancé, and doesn't always manage to restrain himself from needling me.

"A word, Savannah?" he said, just as I was congratulating myself on having had such a narrow escape.

I turned to look at him.

"In my office."

Uh-oh.

I wanted to ask what it was about—although I could guess—but several of the others were still in the conference room, gathering their paperwork and preparing to go, and I didn't want to start something in front of them. Tim was actually being considerate, offering to do whatever it was he planned to do in private, and since he's very much a performer at heart, one who loves being in front of an audience, I figured I'd better not look this particular gift horse in the mouth.

"After you." He gestured me through the door in front of him. I passed into the hallway with my heart knocking against my ribs.

When I first went to work for LB&A, the company was called Walker Lamont Realty, and the broker and owner was Walker Lamont. He was the one who hired me, and we had a good relationship, all the way up until the moment he decided to kill me. I put him in prison over that, and our relationship is no longer quite as good. In fact, Walker escaped a couple of months ago, and came after me, and it took the combined efforts of myself, Rafe, and Grimaldi to lock him back up.

But I digress. When Walker went to prison the first time, he made Tim interim broker, and Tim promptly renamed the company Lamont, Briggs and Associates, to remove some of the stigma of being associated with Walker's name. Lamont, Briggs and Associates became LB&A in pretty short order, and I figure it's only a matter of time before Walker's name is gone altogether.

Walker's office used to be the big corner office in the back of the building, from whence Tim now rules the roost. He closed the door to the hallway and waved me to a seat before making himself comfortable in the padded leather chair behind the desk.

I folded one leg over the other and tried not to feel like a teenager being called to the principal's office.

Not that I ever had. I was a very proper girl. My mother wouldn't have had it any other way.

Tim didn't react to the leg-crossing. He bats for the other team, and if it had been Rafe sitting here instead of me, it would have been a totally different story. Tim damn near salivates whenever Rafe's name comes up. As it was, he didn't waste any time in asking me, "How's Rafael?"

He is one of only two people in the world who call my boyfriend by his full name. The other one is my mother, on those occasions when she can't avoid referring to him.

However, Mother's inflection is very different from Tim's. She always sounds like she smells something bad when she utters the name. Tim curls his tongue around each syllable as if he imagines curling that same tongue around Rafe's ear. It's disconcerting.

I shook off the mixture of annoyance and amusement. "Fine."

"He certainly is," Tim said, smacking his lips.

I made a face. It wasn't the first time I'd walked straight into that particular bad pun. "He's at work. At least that's what he said when he left this morning."

Tim nodded. "We need to talk."

Uh-oh. I smiled hopefully. "About Rafe?"

Tim didn't, just leaned back and picked up a pen to twirl between his manicured fingers. "I saw the news last night."

"I swear," I said, "I had nothing to do with it."

"The dead prostitute?"

I nodded. "I had no idea what she was doing. She told me she was coming to town for a job interview. If I had known she was a hooker, I wouldn't have rented my place to her."

And then something occurred to me. "How do you know about that? They didn't give out my name on the news."

"I recognized the building," Tim said. "I drive by it every day."

Right. But... "There are a lot of apartments at Fifth and Main. How did you know it had anything to do with me?"

"I didn't," Tim said. And added, "Until now."

I grimaced. Not the first time I'd walked right into that one, either.

"And I knew you'd been using your place as a short term rental. I took a guess."

Right.

"It won't be happening again," I assured him. "I've learned my lesson." From now on, I didn't plan to do any more renting. And anyway, the homeowners' association would probably slap my wrist and make me cease and desist at the meeting tonight. Or Prisca Miller would, personally.

"I don't care what you do on your own time," Tim said, in blatant disregard of the fact that he takes a lively interest in Rafe, and Rafe is who I usually do. Not to be crude about it. But Tim has had a crush on Rafe since the first time they met, and the fact that Rafe is now shacked up with me—or I with him—has done nothing to curb Tim's fascination. "But you being plastered all over the news isn't going to do LB&A any favors."

The unfairness of that statement took my breath away. "What do you mean?" I wheezed indignantly. "I'm not plastered all over the news. Nobody mentioned my name, let alone the company."

"They will," Tim said.

"No, they won't. I had nothing to do with the murder."

He rolled his baby-blues. "I'm not worried about the murder. I'm worried about one of our agents running a brothel."

"A brothel?!" My voice squeaked, and I took a breath and tried to calm down before I continued. Shrieking like a trailer park wife is unladylike. "I rented my apartment to a woman who was coming to town for a job interview. I had no idea she was a prostitute. It isn't something you ask!"

"Nonetheless—" Tim said.

"Haven't you forgotten that it's just a few months since *you* were implicated in a murder? Your name and face were all over the news. All of Nashville saw you, because you dumped a dead body in the park instead of going to the police and telling the truth!"

"They wouldn't have believed me," Tim said. "And anyway—"

I wasn't finished. "Walker murdered several people. Everyone knows it. And Brenda broke so many real estate rules and regulations it's a miracle the firm is still standing. After what the three of you did, how could this possibly make anything worse?"

"That was then," Tim said. "This is now."

Now? "It's four months since you dragged a dead body out of your bed and into the trunk of your car. It's three months since Walker broke out of prison and tried to kill me. Again. That was plastered all over the news, too. It hasn't been so long that anyone's forgotten."

"Be that as it may," Tim said, "your situation isn't helping."

"Detective Grimaldi will figure out what happened. And then everyone will know I had nothing to do with it."

"I'm not talking about the murder," Tim said. "I'm talking about you renting your place to prostitutes."

"I rented my apartment to a woman who was coming to town for a job interview." Or so she had led me to believe. "Do you really think I would have rented it to someone I knew was going to be entertaining paying clients in my bed? How stupid do you think I am?"

Tim opened his mouth, and I held my breath. It really isn't like him to let an easy opening like that slip by. But he didn't take the bait, which was even more worrisome. "I'm sorry, Savannah," he said. "But

LB&A doesn't need another scandal. I'm not sure we can survive one. You're going to have to find somewhere else to work."

"But I don't want to work anywhere else. I like it here." It was convenient, and besides, it was the only place I'd ever worked. Walker hired me straight out of real estate school.

"We can't afford any more bad press," Tim told me.

"But you can't just fire me! I have to be associated with a brokerage. If I wanted to leave here, I'd have to sign on with another broker first. It's illegal to be a real estate agent without a broker!"

I was telling him things he already knew, of course. I just didn't know what else to do. He was firing me? After I helped him beat a murder rap just a few months ago? After Rafe and I saved his life when someone was gunning for him?

"You're a lousy real estate agent," Tim said, and although I knew he was right, it still hurt. Not to mention that it was insulting. I was gathering breath to say something cutting when he continued, "You haven't even sold a house a month since you started working here."

No, but... "It isn't like I'm costing you money! I pay my monthly fees."

"You're playing at being a real estate agent," Tim said. "You're not taking it seriously. And you're making us look bad. All these dead bodies..."

Rich, coming from the guy who had dumped the body of one of his clients in the park.

Although he had a point. I had made more money from renting out my apartment these past few weeks, than I had made in any one of my real estate transactions. And my mother might actually be right. She had warned me right from the start that real estate is a cutthroat business, not suitable for a gently-bred Southern Belle. Maybe my elbows just aren't sharp enough to make any headway in a business inhabited by sharks.

"I'll spend the week looking into another brokerage," I told Tim. "But you can't fire me until I do. That would mean I'd have to retire my license, and I don't want to."

Tim looked reluctant, but conceded my point. "We'll keep you on the roster until the end of the month. But I'd appreciate it if you didn't come in again this week. And if you cleaned out your desk."

It was just one blow after another, wasn't it? My desk—which took up most of the space inside a converted coat closet off the reception area—made me feel like a real agent even when I hadn't had a closing in months. And now he wanted me to empty it.

"What happens if I... if the case is solved by the end of the week? Will you reconsider?"

Tim hesitated. "If you bring in a couple of clients. Maybe."

Silence fell.

"I suppose the open house is out for next weekend."

Tim nodded. "I'm sorry, Savannah. Liz'll do it. She's brand new; she's looking for opportunities to meet clients."

Like I had been a year ago. He hadn't had any problems letting me sit open houses for him then.

"And I have to do something to help the company perform better. Things have been in the crapper ever since Brenda died. She was a horrible witch, but she sold a lot of houses. And when Walker went to jail, I took over as broker, so my productivity is down. Several of the other agents left, because they didn't want to be associated with us. And you're not bringing in much business. And then there are all the scandals..."

At least one scandal of which he was the focus. But I didn't point it out again. He seemed sincerely distraught—not so much about firing me, but about the fate of the company, as well as, I'm sure, the lack of money going into Tim's pockets—and I couldn't deny that he had a point. There had been a lot of scandal surrounding LB&A, and in Tim's eyes, this last one must be the proverbial straw that had the potential to break the company's back.

I got to my feet. "I'll get my things out of the office."

"Thank you," Tim said.

"I'll give you a call in a week, and tell you where to send my license. Meanwhile, you have my number if you need to talk to me."

He nodded.

"I'll see you around."

I walked out of his office with my head held high. And I walked down the hallway the same way. Most people had left after the meeting, for which I was grateful. I didn't know whether any of them knew about Tim's plan to get rid of me, but I didn't feel up for facing anyone at the moment.

Fired. How mortifying.

Up front, Brittany, the receptionist, was seated behind the big desk flipping through the pages of the most recent *Cosmo*. She looked up when she heard me coming down the hall. And then she looked down again when she saw I wasn't anyone interesting.

I didn't read anything into that. It wasn't unusual, after all.

"Anything for me?" I asked on my way past the desk.

She shook her head without looking up. I passed by and into my office.

It didn't take long to pack the few belongings I had there. Few, both because the room is small and because much of what I previously kept at the office got broken a couple months ago, and I hadn't bothered to replace it. It took five minutes to throw all my pens and pencils into the bottom of a bag, add papers, notepads, and the like, unpin my map of Nashville by zip code and school zone from the wall and roll it up, and take down the pictures and little reminders pinned to the bulletin board above the desk. My street index—mostly useless now that everyone has GPS and smart-phone map features—went into the bag next, along with a Barbara Botticelli bodice ripper I had tucked out of sight in the bottom drawer after I learned who Barbara was, and more accurately who she'd been imagining every time Mac the Black MacTavish leveled his pistol and said, "Stand and deliver."

Rafe, in case you wondered. It's a long story. And anyway, Barbara and her AKA are dead now. Wherever she is, I think she has more important things to worry about than what Rafe looks like naked.

As I shoved the book down into the bag, it occurred to me that maybe I should write my own bodice ripper. Barbara wasn't around to do it anymore, so the reading public was probably suffering from withdrawal. I'd read plenty of them, so I'd probably be able to write one. And I had the perfect inspiration in-house. Barbara had had to rely on imagination and a single night with Rafe thirteen years ago, while I had him every night.

If nothing else, it would give me something to do other than worry about the dead prostitute in my bed, and the fact that I was losing my job.

Rafe wouldn't mind. He'd get a kick out of it. Especially the research for the love scenes.

Maybe we could roleplay.

I felt my temperature kick up a degree.

Safer to think about my mother's reaction instead. I had no problem imagining the flared nostrils and look of shock that would greet the announcement that I had decided to try my hand at penning steamy historical bodice rippers.

It would almost be worth it, just for that.

A throat cleared over by the door, two feet away, and I looked up, grinning.

The young woman standing there cleared her throat diffidently. "Hi. I'm Liz."

The new girl.

Or not exactly a girl; she must be about my age, if not a year or two older. But the new LB&A hire, the one who would be sitting Tim's open houses from now on.

I wiped the amusement off my face. It took no effort at all. "Of course. What can I do for you?"

"I just wanted to introduce myself," Liz said. "I'm new here."

"Welcome. I'm on my way out the door." Literally as well as figuratively. The last thing I had to do was unplug the laptop and take it with me. Since Rafe moved in and brought his own computer, I've taken to leaving mine at the office most of the time.

"That's OK," Liz said. "I just wanted to meet you. Did your sister find you?"

I had started to bend to crawl under the desk where the plug was, but now I straightened. "Sister?"

"She stopped by on Saturday morning," Liz said. "Looking for you."

I blinked at her, and she added, "I was doing floor duty."

I used to do floor duty too, last year. It's a good way to pick up clients when you're a new agent. I hadn't picked up any clients that way, but I'd picked up Rafe, so I considered it time well spent.

"My sister was here?" I have one sister. Catherine. She's four years older than me, and she lives in Sweetwater with a husband and three kids. If she'd been in Nashville this weekend, she hadn't mentioned it to me.

Liz nodded. "I told her you weren't here, and she said she'd leave you a note."

"A note?" Why didn't she just call me? She has my number.

"She was in here a couple of minutes," Liz said, looking around at my postage stamp of an office.

"In here?" I looked around, too. There'd been no note, not that I had seen. Maybe it had fluttered to the floor?

I bent to look under the desk. There was no note, but since I was there anyway, I unplugged the laptop.

"Maybe she typed a message on your computer," Liz suggested.

Maybe. But since the computer was now unplugged, looking for it would have to wait. I began winding up the cord. "I'll give her a call and see what she wanted. Thanks for letting me know."

"No problem," Liz said and wandered off. "Nice to have met you," she informed me over her shoulder.

"Likewise." I tucked the laptop under my arm, took the bag in my other hand, and flipped off the light before leaving the office and the building. The last thing I saw before I walked out, was Brittany turning a page of Cosmo. She didn't look up when I walked out.

Five

The first thing I did, after getting in the car and turning on the air conditioning, was dial Rafe, to tell him what had happened. After firing me, Tim could forget about Rafe flirting with him the next time they met. I wondered whether he'd thought of that before he let me go, and whether it would do any good to remind him.

There was no answer, though—Rafe must have been busy putting rookies through their paces—so I left a message telling him to call me when he was free, and dialed my sister's number instead.

Like Dix, and like our father and grandfather before him, my sister is a lawyer. It's the family business. I'm the only Martin-child of our generation who didn't make it through law school. I started, but left before graduation to marry Bradley Ferguson.

While it didn't take me long at all to regret anything and everything to do with Bradley, I've never regretted dropping out of law school. Sure, it would have been easier to make a living as a lawyer. If I were a lawyer, I wouldn't be in this situation now. But I also wouldn't have met Rafe again, and for that I would be willing to put up with anything.

Besides, there is just no part of me that wants to be a lawyer, and I'm glad I'm not.

But I digress. Catherine met Jonathan McCall in law school, and they got married and moved back to Sweetwater, where we changed the name of the family business from Martin and Sons, Esq. to Martin and McCall. Catherine practiced law until she got pregnant, and then stayed home with Robert, Annie, and Cole, while Dix and Jonathan held down the fort. Once Cole's out of diapers and in school, I'm sure Catherine will go back to work, but for now, she's happy being a mom and taking on the occasional client. She represented me in my divorce from Bradley, and if it had been up to Catherine, she would have taken him for half of everything he owned and nailed his hide to my wall.

She was home with Cole, and picked up on the second ring. "Savannah? Something wrong?"

"I'm not sure," I said. "You didn't tell me you were going to be in Nashville on Saturday."

"That's because I wasn't," Catherine said.

"Did it have anything to do with Todd?"

There was a beat. I imagined her taking the phone away from her ear to look at it before putting it back. "Did what have to do with Todd?"

I told her what had happened yesterday morning: that Mother had woken me up at six-thirty to ask whether Todd was with me.

Catherine hooted. "She must have been drinking."

"At six in the morning?"

"Maybe not. But she had to have lost her mind to think you'd have Todd there."

No question. "But it wasn't you, right? You didn't come up to Nashville to meet Todd?"

There was another pause. I imagined another incredulous look at the phone. "Have you lost your mind?" Catherine asked. "First of all, I'm very happily married. Secondly, Todd's not my type. And third... don't you think my husband and kids would notice if I weren't there?"

Well, yes. "So what were you doing in Nashville on Saturday? And why didn't you call me?"

"I wasn't in Nashville on Saturday," Catherine said. She sounded snippy.

"Are you sure? Because the girl at the office said a woman came by who said she was my sister."

"I'm positive." Catherine sniffed. "I'm not even sure I know where you work, Savannah. And why would I look for you at the office on a Saturday? I'd assume you'd be spending the day with Rafe. At home. In bed."

Which was pretty much what I had done. Not in bed—not all of it—but with Rafe.

"And," Catherine added, "I know where you live—in that big old house of Rafe's grandmother—so I would go there to look for you, not to your office."

"So you weren't here."

"No," Catherine said, with rather strained patience. "That's what I'm telling you."

"So who was? I don't have any other sisters." And my only sister-in-law was dead.

"No idea," Catherine said, "but I suggest you start by asking the girl at the office for a description."

She hung up in my ear.

She had a point, though. I dialed the office, and when Brittany answered the phone, asked to be connected to Liz. When Liz came on, I asked her to describe my 'sister.'

"She looked like your sister," Liz said, and from the tone of her voice, I got the distinct impression she thought I was either pulling her leg, or a little bit nuts.

"You mean she looked like me?"

"Uh-huh," Liz said.

"Dark blond?"

"Yes." And shouldn't I know that about my own sister?

"Younger or older?"

She hesitated. "Maybe a little older. And... um... a little thinner?"

"I'm pregnant," I said.

"Oh." She sounded relieved. "I don't think she was."

No. And she wasn't my sister, either. Dix and I take after Mother's family, the blond and blue-eyed Georgia Calverts. Catherine looks like our dad: shorter, more compact, with dark hair and brown eyes. I'd always attributed her slightly Mediterranean coloring to the Martins' French heritage. Until this past Christmas Eve, when my Aunt Regina, my dad's sister, told me that it's a leftover from the War Against Northern Aggression, when our great-great-a-few-more-greats-grandmother Caroline had an affair with one of the grooms while her husband was off fighting the Damn Yankees. The result was my great-great-great-grandfather William, who inherited some of his father's coloring.

But I digress, again. Whoever had been in the office looking for me wasn't Catherine.

"I don't suppose she told you her name?"

"No," Liz said. "Um... don't you know your sister's name?"

"It wasn't my sister. I'm trying to figure out who it was."

"Oh." She didn't say anything else, but I could hear the gears in her head grinding. And no wonder. It isn't the kind of thing that happens every day.

"If I brought you a picture, would you recognize her?"

"Probably," Liz said. "I mean... I didn't see her long. But I think I would."

"I'll get back to you on that. Thanks for your help."

My next call was to Tamara Grimaldi. "Something happened," I told her.

"Another dead body?"

"No." Although that reminded me... "Is there any news about the first one?"

"The autopsy is done," Grimaldi said. "She was strangled. We already knew that, but it's nice to have it confirmed."

'Nice' wasn't exactly the word I would have chosen in connection with strangulation, but OK.

"Manually? Are there fingerprints?"

"No prints," Grimaldi said. "With a chord or wire. Or some sort of fabric. Tie or belt."

"The wire from the phantom camera?" Was that why someone had taken it away?

"Could be," Grimaldi said. "What happened?"

"What do you mean...? Oh." Right. "Tim fired me."

I stopped and blinked. Where had *that* come from? I mean, it happened, but it wasn't like I'd been fretting over it. Was it?

"That's interesting," Grimaldi said. "Why?"

"He said I made the company look bad."

"Rich," Grimaldi said.

I thought so, too. "That wasn't what I was going to tell you, though. While I was cleaning out my office, one of the new girls stopped by to ask whether my sister found me."

"Have you been missing?"

"Of course not. She said my sister came into the office on Saturday morning, looking for me."

"I see," Grimaldi said.

"I spoke to Catherine."

"Let me guess. She wasn't in Nashville on Saturday."

I shook my head. "No. So I asked Liz for a description. She said my sister looked like me."

"Your sister doesn't look anything like you," Grimaldi said.

"No. The dead girl does, though."

There was a moment of silence while we both thought about it.

"She said she might be able to identify a picture," I added.

"I'll send Spicer and Truman over there with one. Her name is Liz?"

I said it was.

"Anything else?"

Was there?

I shook my head. "Not at the moment."

The detective hesitated for a moment. "You OK?"

"Not really," I said. "Tim made it clear that he didn't want to see me again. I have the rest of the week to prove to him that I can be an asset to the company, but basically, he wants me to go away and not come back."

Grimaldi's silence was questioning, and I added, "In addition to making LB&A look bad, I'm not bringing in enough business."

"So if you bring in more business, he'd be willing to disregard the fact that you make him look bad?"

"Something like that."

There was another pause. "I can be available in an hour or so," Grimaldi said. "Would you like to grab some lunch? I have a couple more questions anyway."

That would be nice, actually. Especially as I suspected the couple of questions were just an excuse to make me feel better. She liked me. She really liked me. "Twelve o'clock at the FinBar?"

"See you there," Grimaldi said, and hung up.

THE FINBAR IS ONE OF several eateries located within a block or two of the LB&A office. Some are restaurants, more are bars. The area has a well-earned reputation for nightlife.

The FinBar is a sports bar of the urban and hip variety, with exposed brick walls, lots of green plants, and brass everywhere. Old world tavern meets big city restaurant. The concession to the sports bar name are the flat screen TVs mounted everywhere, and tuned to whatever sport is going on at the moment. When I walked in, I could see international golf, Mexican soccer, and good, old, all-American baseball on three different screens.

Grimaldi was already there, in a booth under the American League. She was manipulating buttons on her cell phone, and didn't notice me until I slid into the booth across from her. Then she looked up for a moment, registered that I had arrived and was who she was waiting for, before finishing her conversation or note-taking or whatever it was she was doing. That complete, she handed me the phone. "Have you ever seen her?"

On the small screen was a picture of a woman with streaky dishwater-blond hair and a lot of makeup. It looked like a professional portrait; maybe something an actress or a singer might use to find work. Or a call girl.

"Alive, you mean?" I handed it back to her. "Not to my knowledge. She doesn't look familiar. I assume she's the dead woman from my apartment?" Because to be honest, it was a little difficult to reconcile this beautiful, smiling face with the mottled monstrosity I'd seen in my bed yesterday morning.

Grimaldi pocketed the phone. "And also your sister."

"Liz identified her?"

She nodded. "She said the victim spent a couple of minutes in your office, ostensibly writing a note."

"That's what she told me." The waitress approached, and I ordered sweet tea and Grimaldi a Coke before picking up the conversation again.

"Did you find a note?"

I said I hadn't. "But Liz suggested that she—Ursula, or Jocelyn— might have written something on my computer."

"Did you check?"

I shook my head. "By then, I had already turned it off and unplugged it. It's in the car, if you want to take a look."

Grimaldi looked torn. "Are you parked in the lot?"

I nodded.

"Would you mind getting it? There's supposed to be wi-fi here."

"Not at all." I slid out of the booth. "When the waitress comes back, would you order me a Cobb salad? And a side of fries?"

Grimaldi arched her brows, and I shrugged. "Cravings."

"Of course," Grimaldi said politely, although I'm sure she knew the cravings were just an excuse, and I really just wanted the fries because they taste good and I could get away with indulging.

By the time I walked to the car and got back inside with the laptop tucked under my arm, the drinks had arrived, the food orders had been given, and Grimaldi had unearthed an electrical outlet hidden beneath the table. I handed her the computer cord, and she ducked down to attach it while I plugged the other end into the side of the laptop and booted up. And hesitated.

"I imagine I don't have to worry about fingerprints?"

Grimaldi shook her head, black curls disheveled from her trip below the table. "We know who she is."

OK, then. I applied my fingers to the keyboard and tapped in my password. A few seconds later, my desktop came up.

"Nothing unusual here," I told Grimaldi. There were no documents open, and when she had me look through my folders, there was nothing there that I didn't recognize, either. Everything I saw was mine.

"Let me see." She twitched her fingers.

Sure. I turned the laptop around and pushed it toward her, and watched as she tapped in a few commands.

"What are you doing?"

She shot me a glance across the table. "Checking to see whether anyone has created any new documents this weekend."

"And?"

She shook her head.

"Can you tell the last time—before now—that someone did create something?"

"I'm not a tech whiz." But she tapped on the keyboard again. "Let's try the obvious first. If that doesn't work, I'll take this with me and hand it off to someone in the IT division."

Sure. I watched as she tapped some more.

"Nothing new in your inbox," she told me.

Good to know. Then again, it just went to prove what Tim had said. I wasn't bringing in any business. If I'd had real estate clients, they'd be communicating with me. My webmail wouldn't yield a big, fat zero.

"Bingo," Grimaldi said.

"What?" I leaned forward, but of course all I could see was the back of the computer.

She glanced up at me. "Email sent at 10:14 Saturday morning."

What? "I wasn't in the office at 10:14 on Saturday." Or anywhere else near my email box. At 10:14 on Saturday, I was pretty sure Rafe and I had been indulging in some after-breakfast nookie.

Grimaldi shook her head. "No. But someone else was."

I got out of my side of the booth and squeezed in on hers. "Let me see." I nudged her toward the wall with my hip.

"You don't have to push." But she yielded some room to me. I peered at the screen.

Yes, indeed. An email had gone out from my email account on Saturday at 10:14 AM. It had my signature line on it, but I certainly hadn't written it.

> *Todd,*
> *If you're not busy, could you please come and see me tonight? 7 o'clock? My apartment at Fifth and Main.*
> *Savannah*

I stared at the screen with my eyes bugging out of my skull and my mouth hanging open. "She emailed Todd?"

"Looks that way," Grimaldi said, fingers once again moving across the keys. "Let's see if he responded."

Yes, let's.

"My mother called me yesterday morning," I said while I watched Grimaldi type. "Before six-thirty. To ask whether I'd seen Todd. Apparently he didn't make it home Saturday night."

"No kidding?"

I shook my head. "I talked to Dix. He said Todd got home eventually, but apparently he spent Saturday night somewhere else."

"He tell you where?"

"I didn't talk to Todd. Things are still awkward." What with Todd proposing and me choosing Rafe and all. "My mother told me. That's why she called. Apparently they all thought he might be with me."

"Why?"

"That was my question, too. Mother said she thought we might have," I made air quotes with my fingers, "made up."

Grimaldi arched both brows. "I don't imagine Collier thought much of that."

"He didn't seem to mind. That kind of thing doesn't usually bother him." He couldn't doubt how totally crazy about him I was, after all. He knew Todd was no threat.

Grimaldi looked like she might have disagreed, but if she did, she thought better of expressing it. "Looks like I might have to have a talk with Mr. Satterfield," she said instead.

I leaned back. "That should be interesting."

She gave me an inquiring look, and I elaborated. "He's the ADA for Maury County. His father is the sheriff. And you're a Nashville homicide detective trying to finger him for murder."

She leaned back, too. "You think he's capable of that?"

It was a good question. And because I wanted a little extra time to think about my answer, and because it was a little uncomfortable sitting so close, especially now that her attention was off the computer and on me, I removed myself from the detective's side of the table and returned to my own. On the way there, I thought about what to say.

It was a tough question. There were people I knew, who without a doubt were capable of violence. Rafe, because I'd seen him do it. Grimaldi, because it was her job. Sheriff Satterfield, who may never have been at a point where he actually had to kill someone, but who had to be willing to make that choice if the occasion arose.

Dix would kill anyone who threatened his children. So would Catherine and Jonathan.

Mother... I wasn't sure whether she'd be capable of killing anyone. She might not consider it ladylike.

And for myself...

Well, I had once taken Rafe's gun out of his hand and put myself between him and what I perceived as danger. As it turned out, it had just been Grimaldi, but if it had been someone worse, I think I would have been able to pull the trigger. At least in that moment, and if I didn't have too much time to think about it.

Whether I would have hit what I was aiming for was a totally different matter, of course.

But Todd... I honestly wasn't sure. He'd been raised a Southern gentleman, and along with that came knowing his way around a gun. He could probably shoot—and hit what he was shooting at. If someone broke into his house, I could see him defending himself, or his father. Or if it came to that, my mother. And if things had been different, me.

But self-defense is a far cry from murder. And shooting someone is very different from wrapping your hands—or a tie or even an electrical chord—around their neck and pulling until they become blue in the face and their eyes turn bloodshot.

"If you're asking whether he could have strangled that woman," I said eventually, "I find it hard to believe. Self-defense, yes. But cold-blooded murder? I'm not so sure. Have you met Todd?"

"Briefly," Grimaldi said.

"Did he strike you as someone who'd strangle a prostitute?"

"He didn't strike me as someone who'd have anything to do with a prostitute. But this was a prostitute who looked like you, and who was found in your apartment."

Well, yes. And a prostitute who—it seemed—had contacted Todd the same day she died and invited him to come see her that night. From *my* email account.

"It isn't going to be easy for you to investigate this," I pointed out. "Especially if he doesn't want to talk to you. Between him and his father, they can throw plenty of roadblocks down. You have no jurisdiction in Maury County."

"I don't. But I know someone who does." She smiled. Or maybe smirked was a more accurate description.

"Good for—" I said, and then stopped, suspiciously. Grimaldi smirked harder. "Oh, no. You don't mean...?"

"That's what we do," Grimaldi said, "when we run across something that involves several jurisdictions. We ask for help."

From the Tennessee Bureau of Investigations.

Where my boyfriend worked.

The same boyfriend who was from Sweetwater and who knew the town and the people in it, and knew how things worked down there.

I tried to imagine Rafe heading to Sweetwater to interrogate Todd.

My mind boggled.

Six

The food arrived before I had time to pull myself together, and we got busy eating. With the pregnancy, I was pretty much always hungry these days, and the various upsets of this morning hadn't affected my appetite. I spent the first few minutes after Grimaldi dropped her bomb forking lettuce into my mouth. What I really wanted, was to dive into the steaming pile of French fries I'd ordered with my salad, but that would be foolish and also fattening. While I had the excuse of being pregnant right now, I still had to lose the baby-weight after the baby was born, so I didn't want to pack on too much poundage, either. So vegetables first, and then I could indulge in fries.

Grimaldi had ordered a burger, and I tried not to look too envious as she bit into the hefty beef-patty slathered with melted cheese and dripping juices. But I don't think I succeeded, because she swallowed and told me, "You could have ordered a cheeseburger, you know. I wouldn't have said anything."

"Fattening," I answered.

Grimaldi—who couldn't possibly weigh more than a hundred and thirty pounds, most of it lean muscle—shrugged. "You're pregnant. You need the protein. And besides, I happen to know that your man doesn't like you starving yourself."

No, he didn't. Whenever we went somewhere together, Rafe usually delighted in ordering me hamburgers and milkshakes and slices of cheesecake.

"He does like to feed me," I admitted. "He wouldn't like it if I got fat, though."

"He wouldn't care," Grimaldi answered and lifted her burger. "He isn't with you because you're blonde and pretty."

I wasn't too sure about that. Or rather, while I knew that that wasn't the only reason he was with me, I suspected it had a little something to do with it. And probably more than a little.

I'm the metaphorical princess from the castle on the hill: Margaret Anne Martin's perfect younger daughter, the Southern Belle to end all Southern Belles. Rafe, meanwhile, grew up in the trailer park on the other side of town, the son of LaDonna Collier, who got herself in the family way at fourteen by a colored boy. As kids, we went to different schools: I'd gone to the 'nice' schools on the 'nice' side of town, and he'd gone to the less nice schools on the less desirable side of town. We'd ended up together at Columbia High, but by then those racial and societal lines had been firmly drawn. We both knew where we stood. While Rafe had noticed me back then, he knew he'd better stay away from me unless he wanted Dix and Todd to gang up on him, and while I certainly knew who he was, too, I was so uptight that if he spoke to me, I pretended I couldn't hear him.

After graduation, I went to finishing school and Vanderbilt University, and then I married Bradley. Rafe went to prison, and by the time I was Bradley's wife, he had served half his time and been released, and was working undercover for the TBI. Different worlds. I can't imagine he ever thought he'd end up with someone like me. I know I never imagined I'd end up with someone like him.

And yes, I admit it: the fact that he's different is part of his appeal. Which is why I think the fact that I'm different, is part of my appeal for him, too.

While I cogitated, I'd continued to fork lettuce into my mouth, to enough of a degree that I thought I could justify having a French fry. The salt and general potato goodness exploded in my mouth. I managed not to moan, but my eyes may have crossed involuntarily, because Grimaldi smothered a laugh. Or maybe it was a snort. "It's no wonder he likes to feed you, if that's what you look like when you eat something you like."

I swallowed. "Sorry. My mother brought me up to eat like a bird. It's a hard habit to break."

"You're gonna have to try," Grimaldi said, "because you don't want your little girl growing up like you did."

No, I didn't. And I didn't want my little boy growing up to think it only mattered what someone looked like on the outside, either.

"I'm not sure whether I'm having a boy or a girl yet." And I tried not to think too hard about it, since, given my history, there was a fifty/fifty chance I'd lose this baby, too.

Grimaldi put down her burger. "Let me see your hands."

Really? I dropped my fry, wiped my fingers on my napkin, and held out my hands. "Do you read palms?"

She shook her head. "My Nonna used to say that palms up means a girl, palms down means a boy."

My palms were up, so if Grimaldi's Nonna was right, I was having a girl.

I took my hands back, since she made no move to take them. "Nonna?"

"Grandmother," Grimaldi said. "My father's mother. Good Italian peasant stock."

She took another bite of burger, which I thought signaled the end of the subject. She doesn't like to talk about herself. I guess maybe we're not on those terms yet.

Maybe I should ask Dix if she'd been more forthcoming with him. All I knew about her was that she lived on the west side of town, near Charlotte Park, and that she became a homicide cop because her mother was murdered when Grimaldi was fourteen, and the killer was never caught.

Which is a pretty big and personal thing, if you think about it, yet I didn't know any of the normal day-to-day details.

"Do you have siblings?"

Grimaldi swallowed. "A brother and a sister."

"Like me." I smiled.

"Both younger than me."

While I was the spoiled baby of my family. *Check.*

"Where do they live?"

"Tony's in Columbus," Grimaldi said. "Francesca in Chicago."

"Is that where you're from?"

"Columbus or Chicago?" She didn't wait for me to clarify. "I grew up in Cleveland."

"I've never been to Cleveland."

"You haven't missed much." Again she didn't wait for my answer. "It's just like any other big city. It's nicer here. People are friendlier."

"That's just on the surface," I told her. "People talk about Southern hospitality and graciousness, but it's really just skin deep. We don't mean it. It's just how we were brought up."

Her lips twitched. "So when your mother looks at me and says 'Nice to meet you,' she doesn't actually mean it?"

"Probably not." And then it registered. "When did you meet my mother?"

"At the hospital," Grimaldi said. "After you were shot. Remember?"

Oh. Sure. "At that point she might actually have been sincere. You weren't dating my brother then."

"I'm not dating your brother now."

"Only because you don't ever leave the house when you're together," I said. But since there was no sense in trying to talk about it if she wouldn't even admit there was something to talk about, I changed the subject. "Can I be there when you tell Rafe he has to go to Sweetwater and accuse Todd Satterfield of murder?"

"I don't want him to accuse anyone of murder," Grimaldi said. "And I thought I'd tell him over the phone."

"That's probably a good idea." Rafe isn't terribly fond of our hometown. There are very few good memories for him there. And it was less than a month since I had dragged him down there for my high school reunion. He wouldn't be happy about having to go back so soon. "You could send someone else, you know. Rafe doesn't like to go to Sweetwater."

"I wasn't going to ask him to," Grimaldi said calmly. "I was just going to tell him that someone has to, and see whether he chooses to go himself, or whether they send someone else. I think he might have an advantage, knowing these people, but I'm not going to force him."

Good to know. "I'm not sure Rafe's relationship with Todd and the sheriff is a plus. The sheriff used to arrest him, and Todd wanted to marry me."

"It isn't easy to interview an assistant District Attorney in connection with murder," Grimaldi said. "Most people would be intimidated. I don't have to worry about that if I send your boyfriend."

No. Or if he was intimidated, Rafe wouldn't show it.

He and Sheriff Satterfield had actually mended a few fences the last time we were in Sweetwater. About time, too, after so many years. I couldn't imagine Bob Satterfield being thrilled to have Rafe showing up asking questions about his son, however. Blood being thicker than water, and all that.

"Don't wear yourself out worrying about it," Grimaldi advised. "Not until we know there's something to worry about."

Good advice. Except I was pretty sure already there was something to worry about. "A woman's dead. Strangled in my bed. My former boyfriend is implicated. And my current boyfriend has to go interrogate him. As far as I'm concerned, that's enough reason to worry."

Grimaldi didn't answer. Which was answer enough, really.

I went back to Mrs. Jenkins's house after that, and pushed my box of stuff into a closet. Grimaldi had kept the laptop; apparently it was evidence and I wouldn't get it back for a while. Good thing I didn't have any work to do.

I still couldn't believe that Tim had fired me. Or semi-fired me.

Could I drum up enough business in what was left of the week to convince him to let me stay?

Was it even worth trying?

Or was it time to admit defeat and move on? I'd been thinking something similar just this morning myself, before he ever said anything to me. I hadn't expected to have my mental questions answered quite so promptly and decisively, though.

Fired. *Gah.*

Frustrated, I sat down at the kitchen table with a notepad, the same one I had used to make my list for Grimaldi yesterday. I hadn't even remembered to ask her whether any of my other guests had been prostitutes, too.

A reminder to do that went at the top of the page. Then I gnawed on the top of the pen for a minute before I started making a list of my options.

A) Convince Tim to let me stay at LB&A.

That would mean I'd have to dig up at least two clients in what was left of the week. If I hadn't managed to do that in the time I'd had my real estate license—almost a year—my chances of succeeding in the next four days were pretty slim.

B) Get another job to help Rafe pay the bills.

There were two strikes against that one. I had no education, and I was pregnant. Most people are leery of hiring pregnant women. Of course, I could cease to be pregnant, but I couldn't make myself wish for that. I'd rather be unemployed and pregnant than the opposite.

So for now, at least, that option had to go on the back burner. I could revisit it in a year, after the baby was born. Assuming I wanted to go to work then.

C) Go back to law school to finish my education so I could get a job later.

The pregnancy kiboshed that one, too, for the moment. When I left to marry Bradley, I'd had a year to go before I could take the bar exam. Now I had six months before the baby came. And going back to school if I couldn't finish didn't make any sense.

Aside from the fact that I still didn't really want to become a lawyer.

D) Let Rafe continue to pay the bills, which he was quite capable of doing, and switch my license to another real estate brokerage.

No guarantees anyone else would want me, with my notoriety. (Which I personally thought Tim was exaggerating, but what did I know? Maybe everyone else would agree with him and think I was too prone to attract trouble.) And besides, Tim was right. I really wasn't very good at practicing real estate. There was no incentive for anyone else to take me on.

E) Let Rafe continue to pay the bills, while I prepared to become a full time mother and part time romance writer. If Elspeth had done it, how hard could it be?

I turned over a new sheet of paper and chewed on the pen some more. Maybe if I actually tried to write something...

The peal of the phone saved me from having to put anything down on paper.

"Afternoon, darlin'," Rafe told me.

"Hi." As usual, the sound of his voice made me a little breathless and weak in the knees, even while I was sitting down. And at the moment he wasn't even trying. We just hadn't been together long enough yet that I had stopped counting my good fortune every minute of every day.

"I gotta make a road trip."

"Let me guess," I said. "Grimaldi called you."

"Yeah." He sounded resigned.

"You don't have to go yourself, you know. She said you could send someone else if you wanted."

"That may be what she told you," Rafe said, "but when she called and requested the TBI's help, she asked for me, cause I know the players."

"You can still say no. It isn't really your job." His task was to train the undercover rookies. He wasn't a field agent.

"Not sure I'll still have a job if I say no. The boss asks you to do something, you say yes."

I suppose. "Would you like me to go with you?"

"Not sure that'd be a good idea, darlin'."

"Not for the interview." That would be unprofessional. "Just for the ride."

He hesitated, and I pressed my advantage. "There's something I want to talk to you about. If you go to Sweetwater, there's no telling when you'll be back."

Under the circumstances, the sheriff might not be above slapping him in jail overnight. He'd need someone to post his bail.

"Everything all right?"

"I got fired," I said.

There was a pause. I thought he'd ask me what happened, but he didn't. "I'll be there in thirty minutes. Be ready to go."

He didn't wait for my answer, just hung up. I got up from the table and went to get ready.

When Rafe showed up, he was driving a white SUV with the official TBI seal on the door.

Mother would have told me that whistling is unladylike, but she wasn't here to hear me, so I did it anyway. "Nice ride."

Rafe's lips quirked. "I figured it ain't gonna hurt to look like I'm official."

"You *are* official."

"Not sure Satterfield and his daddy'll see it that way, darlin'."

I climbed in on the passenger side and fastened my seatbelt while Rafe put the car in gear and we rolled around the circular gravel driveway toward the street. "I was so happy that you and the sheriff worked things out last time we were in Sweetwater. This is going to ruin everything again, isn't it?"

He turned right on Potsdam and shot me a look out of the corner of his eye. "Not much I can do about it."

No. "Will you be calling the sheriff? To tell him you're there?"

"No," Rafe said. "Satterfield's a big boy. I don't need to tell his daddy I wanna talk to him."

True. Todd was definitely of age. A year younger than Rafe; two years older than me. He didn't need his parent present while being interviewed, and Rafe was under no obligation to tell the sheriff he wanted to talk to his son.

"I'm gonna try to catch him at work," Rafe added, as we turned the corner of Dresden and headed for the interstate. On our left was the Milton House, the old folks home where Mrs. Jenkins had been living when I first met her. Horrible place. The home she was in now was much nicer, and she seemed to like it there. "I don't wanna have to do this at home."

Where the sheriff would be. And where it would be less professional.

I glanced at the dashboard clock. "We'll get there in time, don't you think?" It was barely two o'clock, and I assumed the Maury County District Attorney's Office had regular business hours.

"Should." The entrance to the interstate was coming up, and he slowed down to turn onto the ramp before speeding up again. "If there ain't too much traffic."

"Too early for rush hour," I said. "And the weather's good. Unless there's an accident, we should be fine."

He nodded, and spent a minute or two focused on merging with traffic, first on I-24, and then the I-40 to I-65 interchange, all of which came up within a mile of one another. Once we were on Interstate 65 headed south, he spoke again. "What was that you said about getting fired?"

I told him what Tim had said.

"Bastard," Rafe growled.

"He has a point. I'm not very good at my job. I should have a thriving career by now, with referrals and people calling me and closings every month. Instead I'm hunting down one lead at a time, and sitting other people's open houses for them."

He didn't argue with that, probably because he couldn't. "That don't change the fact that most of this so-called notoriety's come from him and his boss. He's the one who dumped a body this winter!"

"I reminded him of that," I said.

"What'd he say?"

"Basically, that that was ancient history, and this is now, and me renting my apartment to a prostitute is the straw that broke LB&A's back."

"Bastard."

"Yes, but he has a point."

Rafe shrugged. Outside the car window, the Wedgewood Avenue exit flashed by, with its access to the Tennessee Fairgrounds and the Fort Negley Civil War site. Four months ago, someone had taken a potshot at Tim up on Fort Negley, and Rafe and I had kept him alive until the ambulance could get there. It was really quite annoying that that didn't seem to matter at all now.

Granted, it hadn't been a very deadly shot. It hit him in the shoulder, not near any vital organs, so chances were he would have survived without our help. But still, he'd been shot and it was thanks to me and Rafe that he hadn't had to drag himself down the hill and over to the emergency room. A little gratitude might have been nice.

"What are you going to ask Todd when we get there?" I changed the subject, since I didn't want Rafe to ask me what I was planning to do for work now. I hadn't decided yet, so it would be a difficult question to answer.

He glanced at me, half incredulous, half suspicious.

I clarified. "You don't really think he had anything to do with strangling that woman, do you?"

"Dunno," Rafe said and turned his attention back to the road.

"What do you mean, you don't know? You can't really think that! You know Todd. He isn't capable of cold-blooded murder."

He shot me a look. "You sure you wanna come with me, darlin'? We ain't gone very far yet. I can turn around and take you back home."

"Yes, I'm sure," I said. "And don't threaten me. You know Todd. How can you possibly think he's capable of strangling someone?"

He sighed. "Not sure I do. But what I think can't be part of this, Savannah. I gotta treat this like any other interview. The victim contacted him and invited him to spend time with her on the night she was killed. He's a suspect."

"He probably thought the email was from me."

Rafe glanced at me again. "Then he woulda figured it out when he got there, wouldn't he?"

Yes. Todd knows me well enough to be able to recognize me. Although it made the fact that she looked like me a little bit extra sinister. And perhaps not entirely coincidental. "That's not reason enough to kill someone, though."

He didn't answer, and I added, "Is it?"

He shrugged. "Depends on the situation, I guess."

It was my turn to glance at him. "You know something, don't you? Something you're not telling me?"

He shook his head. "I don't know nothing. But I have a couple ideas. I wanna see what he says first, though, before I start talking about any of 'em."

That made sense, much as I wished to understand what was going on. I sat back in my seat and watched the scenery flash by as we passed Brentwood and headed south toward Franklin and, beyond, Maury County and Columbia.

Seven

The Columbia town square is dominated by the courthouse: big and white with pillars and a clock tower reaching toward the sky. It was built in 1903, and is a pretty massive structure, but by now, not quite big enough to house all the entities that make up the city and county government. As a result, the District Attorney's office is actually located within the County Clerk's office, on the corner of East 7th Street and Town Square, across the street from the courthouse. Two stories, red brick, turn-of-the-(last)-century, with a green and red striped awning. Rafe pulled into an empty parking space in front of the building next door and cut the engine.

We sat in silence for a moment. If I hadn't known better, I would have guessed he was nervous, and bracing himself for what he had to do.

I reached out and put my hand on his arm. He was still wearing the T-shirt and jeans he had left in this morning, and his skin was simultaneously cool and warm under my fingers. Cool from the air conditioning that had been blasting out of the vents while the car was in motion; warm from the blood pumping underneath.

"Why didn't you change your clothes before we left?"

He looked at me, and then down at himself. "Didn't wanna take the time."

"Are you going to feel comfortable walking into the District Attorney's office in a T-shirt and jeans?"

My mother always impressed upon me that clothes make the man—or in my case, the woman. I do my best to dress appropriately for every occasion. And it isn't as if Rafe doesn't own a suit. He does. A very nice one, that fits him exceedingly well.

His lips quirked. "You afraid he's gonna intimidate me, darlin'?"

"Something like that," I admitted.

He chuckled. "Satterfield don't worry me. I'm here to do a job. He'll have to deal with the way I look."

"Of course." Rafe in a suit is an impressive sight, all the more so because I see it so rarely. But Rafe in snug jeans and a T-shirt that hugs his chest and stretches tight across his shoulders isn't exactly hard on the eyes, either. And effective in quite a different way. That gun strapped to his hip didn't hurt at all, either. "You'll be careful, right?"

"What's he gonna do," Rafe asked, opening the car door and swinging his legs out, "have me kicked outta his office?" He slammed the door shut and came around to my side of the car and opened my door so he could keep talking to me. "He knows better. If he don't talk to me, he'll look even more guilty."

"He may refuse to talk to you because you're you. He may insist on talking to someone else."

"There ain't no one else," Rafe said. "Sit tight. I'll be right out."

He made to slam the door again. I put out a hand to stop him, and unhooked my seatbelt with the other. "I'll walk around while I wait."

Rafe looked suspicious, and I added, "I won't follow you inside and try to eavesdrop. That would be totally unprofessional." Even though it killed me to know I wouldn't be able to hear their conversation.

His lips twitched, and I looked around. "I'll just go look at the brochures." There was a rack of them in the doorway of the building in front of us. "It's too hot to sit in the car with the air conditioning off, and there's no telling how long you'll be."

"Suit yourself," Rafe said with a shrug. Muscles moved under the tight T-shirt, and a woman who was restocking the brochures faltered for a second. I rolled my eyes. Rafe grinned and turned back to me. "If you get too hot, get back in the car and turn on the air."

"Or maybe I'll just come looking for you," I said.

"Maybe you won't." He grabbed me by the shoulders and dropped a kiss on my mouth, quick and hard. "Behave yourself, darlin'."

He walked away before I could respond, because frankly, it always takes a few seconds to unscramble my thoughts after one of Rafe's kisses. Being near him reduces me to a metaphorical puddle of love and lust. By the time I had recovered my faculties, he had passed under the green-and-red striped awning on the outside of the County Clerk's office, and had pulled open the glass-fronted door beneath. Before he ducked inside, he shot me a wicked grin over his shoulder, as if he knew exactly what I was struggling with.

I lifted a hand to fan myself.

"Hot," the woman restocking the brochures remarked. She was fanning herself, too. With a brochure about Bella Terra, the other Antebellum mansion in Sweetwater. I recognized the picture.

"Definitely." It was hard to know whether she was making an observation about Rafe or the weather, but either way I couldn't argue.

THE BUILDING NEXT DOOR TO the County Clerk's office turned out to be the Maury County CVB—the Convention and Visitor's Bureau—and the lady's name was Becky. We spend a pleasant few minutes talking; about Rafe, about the fact that he and I were both from Sweetwater, twenty minutes away, and about the fact that I was expecting. She had no idea who Rafe was, beyond the good-looking guy who had just sauntered into the building next door, leaving a trail of pheromones in his wake. It was a nice change. I'd gotten so used to coming home to this part of the state and having everyone looking at me askance because I've taken up with the black sheep of my hometown, that it was nice to have someone not even recognize either of us.

I'd assumed Rafe would be inside the County Clerk's office talking to Todd for a good, long time, so you can imagine my surprise when not even five minutes had passed when he came back outside.

"Excuse me," I told Becky.

She nodded, eyes on him. "That was fast."

I smiled weakly. "Maybe the line was short." No sense in giving her any details about what was actually going on.

As I moved closer to Rafe, I studied his face for any indications as to what had happened, but he was, as usual, hard to read. The only times I know what Rafe is thinking, is when he wants me to.

So I asked. "What happened?"

He shrugged. "Nothing."

"Wasn't he there?"

"He was."

"Didn't he want to talk to you?"

"No," Rafe said, opening the car door for me, "but he knows he's gotta."

I scooted into the seat. "So...?"

He closed the door behind me and walked around the car. When he was in the driver's seat, with the door closed, he answered. "He won't talk without representation."

"He can't represent himself?" Rafe put the key in the ignition and cranked the engine over. "He *is* a lawyer."

"He wants someone else to represent him. Can't blame him for that." He backed out of the parking spot.

Maybe not. Under the circumstances, having representation might be a good idea. But that didn't mean I understood why we were leaving. "He works in the District Attorney's office. There has to be a lawyer there who can represent him."

"He didn't want one of them," Rafe said. "I'm guessing he wants to keep this quiet from his colleagues as long as possible. Bad for business."

He got the car pointed north, and we set off at a sedate 15 mph. I waved to Becky on our way past.

We made a complete circuit of Public Square—all one way traffic—and ended up back where we started, on the corner of East 7th. Todd was on his way out of the building, tall and slender in a navy suit, with a briefcase in his hand. I heard the *beep-beep* as he unlocked his car door.

"Where are we going?" I asked Rafe as we headed east out of Columbia. I could guess, but I didn't want to assume.

He shot me a look. "He don't wanna represent himself. And he don't want one of his colleagues to represent him. Who do you think he trusts enough to have his back?"

I grimaced. His best friend. "My brother."

"Got it in one," Rafe said, and stepped on the gas.

Twenty minutes later, we had changed locale from the Columbia town square to the one in Sweetwater. A little smaller, with a statue in the middle instead of the big, white City Hall, but with the same Victorian brick buildings lining the square. Rafe pulled into a parking spot and turned to me. "I don't imagine you're gonna be willing to wait outside."

I shook my head.

"Didn't think so." He opened his door and came around the car to open mine.

"That's my brother in there," I pointed out. "And my brother-in-law. I have to at least go in and say hi. After that, I can go to Audrey's and look at the clothes, or have a cup of tea at the Café on the Square, or something."

Or I could position myself somewhere inside Martin & McCall where I might be able to pick up some of the conversation through a wall.

"We'll figure it out." Rafe put his hand at the small of my back as we headed to the door. I opened it and let him hold it while I passed through, into the coolness of the interior. It wasn't even June yet, and already the temperatures were approaching ninety-five. Summers in the south can be killer, where just the few feet between the air-conditioned car and the air-conditioned building are enough to make the hair stick to your temples and the shirt to your back.

The reception was blessedly cool, and Darcy, the receptionist, looked up with a professional smile that turned warmer when she saw me. "Savannah."

I smiled back. "Good to see you."

She pushed back from the desk. "Do you need to see your brother? Or Jonathan?"

"Both. Either." I gestured. "Rafe's here to see Dix. He and Todd Satterfield have an appointment. Todd will be arriving in a minute, too. I'm just stopping in to say hi before they get started."

Darcy looked at Rafe. Like most people in Sweetwater, especially those of a certain age, she doesn't approve of me taking up with him, but my brother also pays her salary, so she knows better than to let her disapproval show too visibly. "I'll let him know you're here."

"Not necessary," Dix said, opening the door to his office. "Sis."

I tilted my face up, and he dropped a kiss on my cheek before putting out a hand. "Collier."

"Martin." They shook.

"Men are weird," I said. "You're practically family. Why do you call each other by last name?"

Rafe grinned down at me. "It's a guy thing. And besides, you do it with Tammy."

Dix didn't say anything, but I thought I saw his posture stiffen infinitesimally.

"Not to her face," I said. "When I talk to her, I call her 'Detective.' It's just when I talk about her that I call her Grimaldi."

My brother looked from one to the other of us and shook his head. I thought he might have muttered something, too, but before I could ask—or not—he raised his voice. "Come on into my office. Todd called. He's on his way."

"Darlin'..." Rafe said.

"Yeah, yeah," I answered. "I'll leave when he gets here."

"Might be better if you left now," Rafe said.

Dix nodded. "I'm not sure seeing you will help, sis."

Fine. "I'll go visit with Audrey. Just let me use the bathroom first."

"Use Audrey's bathroom," Dix said, blocking the way. "I want you out of sight by the time Todd gets anywhere close to the town square."

I opened my mouth to tell him that Todd wouldn't see me if I were locked in the restroom, but he got in first. "That way, you won't be able to listen through the vent, either."

I closed my mouth again, grimacing, as Rafe grinned. "Busted," he told me.

I shrugged. "You can't blame me for trying. That poor woman died in my bed. She lied to me. And she used my computer and my email address to get Todd there." If he'd been there. And I thought he had. A little belatedly, I had remembered Mr. Sullivan's question about whether 'my friend' had found me. Rafe had interrupted our conversation before I'd had the chance to ask Mr. Sullivan which of my friends he'd been talking about, but if he'd seen Todd with me before—and he probably had, since Todd had come and gone for a bit before I got involved with Rafe—Mr. Sullivan was likely to have seen him.

"Nobody's blaming you, darlin'." Rafe put an arm around my shoulders and dropped a kiss on the top of my head. "But this'll be easier if Satterfield don't come face to face with you the minute he walks in the door."

Dix nodded. "He's already upset. Seeing you will only make it worse."

"Fine. I'm going." I slipped out of Rafe's arm and turned toward the door. "Come find me when you're finished. I'll either still be at Audrey's, or I'll have moved on to the café."

The last thing I heard before the door closed, was Dix telling Rafe, "Come with me, and I'll tell you how this is going to go down."

AUDREY'S ON THE SQUARE IS the closest Sweetwater comes to high fashion: a very elegant boutique where my mother and her friends shop. I've been known to buy a thing or two there, as well, including the purple dress I wore to my high school reunion last month, as well as the red dress I bought last fall to make Todd propose.

(He did. But while I'd been trying it on, I'd been imagining Rafe taking it off me, which should have clued me in on what my answer was likely to be. Unfortunately, it took actually being faced with the proposal to realize that I didn't want to marry Todd.)

Audrey has been Mother's best friend for thirty-five years, since my mother came to Sweetwater as a young newlywed, straight out of college. They've gone through three births, three weddings, five grandchildren, and the loss of a husband and a daughter-in-law together—all of them my mother's. Audrey never married, that I know of, and she has no family now that her parents are gone.

Like my mother, she's in her late fifties. Unlike my mother, who looks soft and ladylike with champagne-colored hair and elegantly understated clothes—a Summer, if you happen to be familiar with the color analysis thing—Audrey is a Winter: tall and angular, with jet black hair cut in a sharp wedge and bright red lipstick, usually dressed in dramatic black and white or strong primary colors. There's nothing soft about her. I love her, and have never doubted that she loves me, but she's not at all the cuddly type of pseudo-aunt.

When I walked through the door, she was ringing up sales for a customer, a woman her own age, and she looked up and smiled when she saw me. "Savannah! This is a surprise!"

She came out from behind the counter and walked toward me, leggy on cobalt blue patent leather heels that matched the cobalt, white, and black color block dress she had on.

"I didn't know I was going to be here," I explained, returning the air kisses she deposited an inch from each of my cheeks, French style. "But Rafe had to talk to Todd about something, so now they're both across the square with Dix running interference."

Audrey's face clouded. "Everything's all right, I hope?"

I hoped so, too. The idea of my fiancé having to arrest my wannabe husband—and the Assistant DA—for murder was disconcerting. "I'm sure it'll be fine. Go back to what you were doing. Sorry to interrupt."

Audrey nodded, but she didn't look convinced. Nonetheless, she returned behind the counter and accepted the customer's credit card. They went back to their murmured conversation while I wandered off to the right, looking at dresses.

A couple of minutes later, the bell above the door dinged when the customer left, and Audrey came over to me. "Find anything you like?"

"I'm finding lots of things I like." Everything in Audrey's store is beautiful. She has excellent taste. "But I'm really just passing time until they're finished and we can drive back home. I can't afford a new dress. I'd just grow out of it in a few months, anyway."

"Margaret Ann told me you're expecting," Audrey nodded. "Savannah, darling... are you sure you have thought this through?"

I dropped the slippery silk I'd been fingering, and watched it slither down to hang from the hanger before I raised my eyes to Audrey's. "Thought what through? Having Rafe's baby?"

She nodded.

"Yes, I've thought it through. I love him. I want his child."

"Life can be difficult for a mixed race child in the South, Savannah. As I'm sure your boyfriend can testify."

The man who had gone through most of his early life being known as 'LaDonna Collier's good-for-nothing colored boy'? Unquestionably.

"Times have changed," I said steadily. "People don't care so much about color anymore. Not even here in Sweetwater. And we live in Nashville, anyway. People are less traditional there. Nobody looks at us twice when we go out together. Nobody's going to blink if I have a brown baby."

Something—a thought, a shadow—crossed Audrey's face, but she didn't respond, other than to return her attention from the town square outside the window to me. "Your mother's worried."

"My mother just wants to control my life."

"Your mother wants you to be happy," Audrey corrected. "As does every mother."

"I'm happy. Rafe makes me happy. Being his wife and having his baby will make me even happier."

Audrey didn't sigh, but she looked like she was thinking about it.

"It'll be OK," I said. "I love him. He loves me. And we'll both love the baby. If a baby grows up being loved, it'll turn out fine, whatever color it is."

She didn't look convinced, but she nodded. And changed the subject. "What's going on over at Dix's place?"

"They're talking," I said. "Dix, Todd, and Rafe."

"About?"

"Not me. And I'm not sure I should tell you."

Audrey arched her perfect, black brows.

I sighed. "Did you see the television footage yesterday, about the dead prostitute?"

Audrey nodded.

"Rafe's investigating it. At the request of the Nashville police."

"Why?" Audrey asked. "Was she from here?"

"Not as far as I know. But I think there's a connection to something local." Although I'd better not tell her exactly what, since it was probably confidential, and since Audrey would run directly to Mother and share everything I told her. And while it would be nice to have my mother be a little less insistent that I should have married Todd instead of taking up with Rafe, I didn't want her to know that he might be involved, however peripherally, in the strangulation of an escort. Especially one who looked like me and who had been killed in my bed. After contacting him and asking him to stop by for a visit.

And besides, if word got around and he wasn't involved—and he probably wasn't, right?—he could sue for slander. He's a lawyer. So it was best not to take any chances.

I smiled prettily. "It's just lawyer talk, I bet. Between the TBI and the District Attorney's office." And Dix. "I just came down to keep Rafe company on the drive. I imagine we'll be on our way back again within the hour."

Audrey nodded.

"So what have you and my mother been up to lately?"

We spent a few minutes talking about my mother and Audrey lunching together and attending the Home and Garden show and making plans for an outdoor wedding that someone was planning to hold on the grounds of the Martin Mansion next month, and then I excused myself and headed back across the square to the café, where I found a table by the window and ordered another iced tea to have something to sip on while I waited. Because it had been three hours or so since lunch, and since I was hungry again, I ordered a bagel with cream cheese as well, and settled in to wait.

Eight

It was almost an hour later that Rafe came out of the Martin and McCall office. He stopped just outside the door to look around, and to put on a pair of sunglasses before he set out across the square toward Audrey's. I had already paid for my tea and bagel, so I went to intercept him. There was no sense in having him face Audrey, especially as I had no idea whether she'd actually be nice to him. She seemed more inclined to be understanding than my mother, but that didn't mean she wouldn't be rude to Rafe.

He changed direction when I hailed him, and came to meet me, right in front of the monument to the fallen of the Civil War. "Ready to go?"

"If you are."

He nodded. "Let's get outta here."

"That bad?"

He just shook his head, but his expression said plenty.

"I'm sorry." I reached out and stroked his arm, partly to offer comfort and partly because I just enjoy touching him. The skin was still soft, but the muscles underneath were tense. "Maybe it really would have been better if someone else had gone."

He shrugged.

"Did... um... my name come up?"

The look he shot me was incredulous. "It was me and Satterfield, with your brother running interference. The dead woman looked like you and was killed in your bed. Hell, yeah, your name came up."

"You know what I mean," I said.

"Did we talk about the fact that he proposed and you said no and then crawled into my bed and got yourself knocked up?"

"It wasn't like that." Although the fact that he seemed to be going out of his way to be vicious told me something about how uncomfortable the conversation must have been for him.

"I was there," Rafe said. "It was exactly like that."

"The way I remember it, I didn't crawl into your bed. You dumped me there, and then proceeded to strip. And it was lucky we even made it that far."

First, because we almost ended up making love on the kitchen table, and then because someone shot at us through the front windows once we made it into the hall.

He sighed, and probably would have closed his eyes for a moment if he hadn't been driving. "I'm being an ass."

"You're upset," I corrected.

He shot me a look. "You think?"

"I'm sorry."

This time he blew out a breath. "It ain't your fault, darlin'. Just one of the most uncomfortable interviews I've ever sat through. And that includes the ones where I was the one in the hot seat."

I winced. "Did you at least learn something useful?"

Rafe hesitated. When he opened his mouth again, I thought he'd answer, but instead he said, "Your house is coming up on the left. You want I should stop so you can say hi to your mama?"

"No." God, no. I don't visit my mother unless I have to. Not because I don't love her—I do, in spite of everything—but because she's a major pain in my behind.

"You sure?" He slowed the car.

"Positive. Go past."

We went past. "And don't try to distract me," I added, as the Mansion faded into the background. "I want to know what happened."

Rafe stepped on the gas again, and the SUV picked up speed. "He came, we talked, I left."

Shades of Julius Caesar.

"I know that," I said. "Give me a break, Rafe. She died in my bed. I want to know what Todd said."

He hesitated again, and then he slipped the phone off his belt and handed it to me. "I recorded the interview. And you don't get to listen to all of it. But you can listen to a little."

"Really?" I fumbled my way through finding the recording and turning it on. There was a slight hum of dead air in the background, with some sort of little click, and then Rafe's voice. "I'm gonna record the interview, if you don't have a problem with that."

There was a pause, during which I assumed Todd looked at Dix and got the OK. "Fine."

"Introduce yourselves, if you don't mind, for the record."

"Assistant District Attorney Todd Satterfield," Todd said, his voice clipped. I could tell from his delivery, hardly muted by being second-hand, that he was feeling annoyed. Or perhaps he was feeling something else instead. Worry, maybe. Whatever it was, it was giving his voice an edge. It was also making him go on the offensive. "Is that gun loaded, Agent Collier?"

I imagined Rafe glancing down at it. "That a problem?"

"It's a federal offense for a convicted felon to carry, own, or possess a firearm," Todd said smugly.

I could imagine my brother rolling his eyes. I could also imagine

Rafe's expression, eyebrow raised. "If my being armed worries you, I can leave the weapon in the car until we're done here."

I expected Todd to say something, but he didn't. All I heard was silence. They were probably having some sort of staring contest, to see who would break eye contact first.

I paused the recording and turned to Rafe. "Is that true?"

"What?"

"That a convicted felon can't carry a gun."

He nodded.

"How come you can?"

He was a convicted felon. Two years in medium security prison for assault and battery before the TBI arranged for his early release and had him absorbed into their undercover program.

"The bureau had my record expunged when I went to work for them," Rafe said.

"Ten years ago?"

He shook his head. "Six months ago."

I blinked. "Didn't you carry a gun during the time you were undercover?" Surely they hadn't sent him out to infiltrate the biggest South American Theft Gang in the Southeast without some means of defending himself?

"I never got caught carrying," Rafe said, which wasn't the same as to say he hadn't carried.

"So for ten years, you carried illegally?"

He glanced at me, lips quirking. "I did a lot of things illegally, darlin'. Carrying a weapon was the least of it."

"But didn't Wendell know you had a gun?"

Wendell Craig was Rafe's handler, his contact at the TBI. Now that Rafe was legitimate, so to speak, Wendell was his boss.

"Course he did. He gave it to me. But they couldn't expunge my record then. If Hector found out, I'd be sleeping with the alligators."

Hector Gonzales had been the head of the biggest SATG in the

Southeast, and Rafe's target for ten years. Now he was safely behind bars in Atlanta, thanks in large part to my boyfriend. And yes, if it had somehow gotten back to Hector that Rafe's criminal record had been expunged, he would definitely have smelled a rat.

"Alligators?" I said. Usually the expression is 'sleeping with the fishes,' isn't it?

"Rumor has it he'd dump inconvenient evidence in the Everglades. Alligator Alley. By the time the gators were done with the bodies, there wasn't much left for anyone to pin on him."

Yikes. The less said about that, the better. I turned back to the real issue. "So the gun's legal."

He nodded.

"Why did Todd ask you about it?"

"Cause it ain't supposed to be possible to expunge a criminal record where the crime was assault or DUI. Satterfield would know that, being in the business."

I nodded. "I don't imagine he asked because he was concerned about you possibly breaking the law."

"I don't imagine so," Rafe agreed, "no."

"So if it isn't supposed to be possible to do, how come you have a license to carry?"

"Wendell pulled some strings and got it done anyway," Rafe said. "In exchange for services rendered, or somesuch."

"I see." Mitigating circumstances. Special conditions. Whatever.

I turned the recording on again, as Rafe made tracks in the direction of the interstate.

"Now that that's outta the way," his voice on the phone said, "let's see if we can get this done. I don't wanna spend all night here if I can help it."

"Don't you enjoy spending time in your hometown, Agent Collier?" Todd asked nastily.

There was another pause. I imagined Rafe considering, and discarding, the option of pushing Todd's teeth down his throat.

"We go back a couple decades at least," he said eventually, evenly. "I don't mind if you do away with the title."

"I prefer to keep this professional," Todd said.

Sure. That's why he kept taking little digs at Rafe. Who told him, "I'd prefer not to be here at all. But seeing as someone had to go down here and take your statement, since you chose to leave a crime scene without notifying the cops..."

Oops.

I waited for Todd to deny it. He didn't. All I heard was dead air, humming quietly, and then Rafe spoke again. "You can choose to cooperate or not. If you don't, I'll go back to Nashville and tell Detective Grimaldi that you declined to make a statement. I imagine the next thing that'll happen, is she'll call your daddy to execute an arrest warrant."

"Don't threaten me," Todd snarled.

"I ain't threatening you, Satterfield. That's the God's honest truth. The detective sent me down here to take your statement. If you won't give it to me, someone else'll have to take it."

Dead air silence hummed from the phone again. "Does Savannah know you're here?" Todd asked.

"She's next door."

"Here?" I imagined Todd twisting on his chair.

"Across the square," Dix said. "At Audrey's."

"How much does she know about all of this?"

There was another beat, this time while Rafe thought about what to say. "Pretty much all of it. She found the body."

"Christ," Todd said, the first time ever I had heard him take the Lord's name in vain.

"How about you just tell me what happened? Get it over with."

Todd hesitated, and I imagined a flurry of looks across the table: silent communication between Dix and Todd, and maybe between both of them and Rafe.

"We know she sent you an email," Rafe prompted. "I guess you thought it was from Savannah?"

There was another pause, and then Todd's voice. "I hoped it was."

I turned the recording off. "I don't think I want to listen to any more of this. No offense."

"None taken." Rafe reached out and took his phone back. "Maybe I'll just tell you what he said."

"Maybe that would be best." I sat back and folded my hands in my lap. It was a tiny bit smaller these days, what with the extra roundness of my stomach. "I assumed he was still upset about what happened this winter, but actually hearing him say it is different."

He nodded. "I didn't much enjoy it, either."

"I hope you didn't apologize."

"I'm not that sorry," Rafe said. "Besides, he told me he hoped I'd fucked something up badly enough that you finally saw the light and dumped my sorry ass. I think he's waiting for me to cheat or something."

"You're not going to, are you?"

He didn't answer, just looked at me, eyebrow arched.

"Right," I said. "So did you talk about it? About me? After what I just heard?"

He shook his head. "We stuck to the case. I figured that was safer. Less chance he'd shoot his mouth off, and less chance I'd push his face in and get myself arrested."

Good move. "So he admitted to getting the email."

He nodded.

"And did he admit to going to see me? Her?"

"He said he didn't. That he had other plans. And that he spent the night somewhere else. When I asked him for a contact number to confirm his alibi, he refused. Said I'd have to get a warrant before he'd give me that information."

We'd reached the interstate now, and Rafe fed us onto the ramp going north.

"Do you believe him?" I asked.

He glanced at me. "Would you?"

Not really. Or at least I found it almost unimaginable, if he thought the message was from me, that he wouldn't come running.

Then again, if he had gone to my place, and had found Ursula-Jocelyn there instead of me—whether alive or dead—why not just admit it? If she'd been alive, all he'd have to do is say that he got there, a woman he didn't know was there instead of me, and he left again. The fact that she got killed after he left, had nothing to do with him. He didn't even know her, so what reason would he have to kill her?

And if he got there and she was already dead, why hadn't he called the police right then and there? All he'd done had been to respond to an invitation from an old friend. A bit embarrassing, perhaps, given the circumstances, but not criminal. As far as I could see, there was no reason at all why he'd lie about any of it.

I said as much.

"There's every reason for him to lie," Rafe answered.

"What do you mean? What reason?"

Rafe waited until he had merged with traffic on the interstate to answer. "She died between six and eight. If he got there at seven, he coulda killed her."

"Sure. But why would he kill her? He didn't know her."

Rafe didn't answer, and I turned to look at him. "He didn't know her. Did he?"

"Turns out he did."

"He did?"

"I played a hunch," Rafe said. "Pulled the picture of her up on my phone and asked if he could identify her."

"And?"

"He didn't wanna look. I think he thought I was gonna show him a picture of the corpse."

I wasn't sure I could blame Todd for not wanting to see that. Although Rafe seemed to think Todd's reaction was somehow suspicious.

"So your brother took a look," Rafe said.

"Dix knew her, too? How? She wasn't even from around here."

"People move," Rafe said.

"Sure. But Grimaldi said nothing about her being local. She was born in Ohio and lived in Atlanta."

I stopped, as what I'd said registered.

Atlanta. Where Rafe had spent time making sure Hector Gonzales was behind bars.

And more to the point, where Todd had also spent time. Specifically, the time I'd been married to Bradley. My mother swore that my divorce had prompted Todd's divorce, just as she swore that he'd married his ex-wife because he couldn't have me.

Hell—heck—he'd said so himself once. *She looked like you, so I thought she'd be like you, too. But she wasn't. She was common and didn't dress right and didn't really care about anything but herself.*

Or maybe some of those words were my mother's. I distinctly remembered her calling Jolynn common.

Jolynn...

"What was the dead girl's name, again? Her real name?"

"Jocelyn Rivera," Rafe said.

"Not Jolynn?"

He shook his head.

"So she wasn't Todd's ex-wife."

He didn't answer.

"She *was* Todd's ex-wife?"

He nodded.

"Shit," I said. "I mean..."

"Shit works. Shit works very well."

Yes, it did.

"So the dead woman in my bed was Todd's ex-wife Jolynn."

It was several minutes later. That's how long it had taken me to actually process the information that had just been dumped in my lap. It was pretty overwhelming, you have to agree. Not only had the girl told me her name was Ursula Kent and that she was in town for a job interview when she was really Todd's ex-wife and a prostitute, but now she was dead and Todd was, presumably, a suspect.

How could he not be, after all? If the girl had been any random hooker, it might have been different, but his ex-wife...? That turned every assumption I'd made on its head. If he'd gotten to my place and she'd been dead, he had every reason in the world not to call the cops. He'd incriminate himself. And if he got there and she was still alive...

"This can't be a coincidence."

"No," Rafe agreed. We were still on our way home, headed north on I-65 at a good clip, trying to beat the rush hour traffic. "I don't imagine it is."

"Did you know this when we drove down here?"

"No," Rafe said, and didn't sound happy about it.

"How can that be? I mean, Grimaldi looked into her. That's how we know her name wasn't really Ursula."

He nodded. "I guess she went back to her maiden name after the divorce. Satterfield confirmed her given name was Jocelyn, but that she liked to go by Jolynn. Maybe Grimaldi hasn't gotten around to digging up the rest of it yet."

Hard to believe. The detective is nothing if not thorough.

"Or maybe there's another reason she didn't tell me," Rafe added. "Wanted to see if he copped to it on his own. Or didn't want me going down here thinking he's guilty."

"Do you think he's guilty?"

"It's his ex-wife who's dead. His ex-wife who turned to prostitution after he divorced her. Either of those facts won't look good when it comes time for reelection. And she tricked him into coming to

Nashville by pretending she was you. That prob'ly didn't make him happy. If nothing else, he's a suspect."

It was hard to argue with that.

"You didn't arrest him, though. Does that mean you aren't sure?"

"I need an arrest warrant to arrest him," Rafe said. "Unless I catch him in the middle of committing a crime, and I didn't. It was just an interview."

"But he lied, didn't he?"

"That ain't reason enough to arrest him," Rafe said. "Lots of people lie when you ask them questions."

Right. "What if he runs away?"

He squinted at me. "You think he will?"

It was weird, thinking about Todd this way. Like he was just another criminal, another suspect in another crime, and not a man I'd grown up with. A man I'd known my whole life. A man I had once considered marrying.

Then I shook it off and concentrated on answering the question. "There isn't anything keeping him here. His dad, sure. But Bob's an adult. He'll survive. And his job, but that might be in jeopardy anyway. He doesn't have a family of his own. No wife or kids. No home other than the one he's sharing with his father. If he's dating anyone, I haven't heard about it."

And if he was, chances were he wouldn't have jumped at the chance to come see me. Or who he thought was me.

"You think I oughta tell Tammy he's a flight risk?"

I hesitated. "That might mean she'd go ahead and arrest him, wouldn't it?"

He shrugged. "It might could."

I tried to imagine my mother's reaction if Todd got arrested for strangling a prostitute—one who happened to be his ex-wife—in my bed.

Arrested by her son's girlfriend, whom he had taken up with improperly soon after his wife's murder.

Or better yet, arrested by her daughter's fiancé, who had beat out Todd for that same daughter's affections.

The mind boggled. My voice came out half-choked. "This is a big mess."

"Welcome to my world," Rafe said.

Nine

We got back to Nashville just as rush hour started, and had to creep slowly through the I-65 North to I-40 East to I-24 West interchange. Once, about six months ago, I'd almost killed myself traversing that part of the interstate, thanks to a little help from a multiple murderer in the lane next to mine who gave me a nudge at the wrong moment, straight into an eighteen-wheeler.

Nothing like that happened this time. Rafe navigated expertly across the various lanes and got us off at the exit on Spring Street, just before traffic started getting really snarled up toward Trinity Lane.

"Do we have to take the car back to the TBI today?" I asked as we wound our way onto Ellington Parkway.

He shook his head. "I'll take it to work in the morning and ride the bike back tomorrow night."

"We have to go to the HOA meeting at Fifth and Main tonight. Remember? Unless you think we shouldn't?" I would be very happy to hear that he thought we shouldn't, since I had a bad feeling about it. I'd love an excuse not to show up.

Unfortunately, Rafe thought we should go. "Somebody mighta seen something. And if they're all gonna be there, we might get lucky."

Maybe. I was pretty sure I wouldn't get lucky, though. Prisca Miller's voice on TV, when she'd said she'd take care of things at the next meeting, had been pretty ominous.

"Tammy'll be there," Rafe added, as we exited the parkway at Douglas Avenue and went west. "Between the two of us, we'll keep you safe."

Safe?

"What makes you think I won't be safe? Prisca Miller looked ready to evict me," which wouldn't be a big deal, since I'd already moved out, "but I don't think I'm in any actual danger."

"A woman was strangled in your bed," Rafe said. "A woman who looked like you. On the off-chance that your ex-boyfriend didn't just lose his mind and decide to bed his ex-wife pretending she was you, and then ended up strangling her when the reality didn't match the fantasy in his head, we can't be a hundred percent sure whoever did it knew who he was strangling. He mighta thought it was you."

And if that wasn't a thought designed to drop the bottom out of my world, I don't know what would.

"From now on," Rafe added, "and until this guy's caught, I don't want you going around by yourself."

I took a deep breath. "Not a problem. Tim fired me, remember?"

"Bastard."

"Maybe I'll just stay home and write my own bodice ripper. *Stand and Deliver*. Or maybe *Outlaw Inlaw*."

"What?" Rafe said.

The HOA meeting was scheduled for seven o'clock. We were there five minutes early, and had to sit in the back, because the room was already full.

The HOA meetings took place in the condo association's meeting room, on the first floor facing the courtyard. When we walked in, it looked more like a party than a business meeting. The room was abuzz with voices, and everyone was sipping drinks from plastic cups or carrying paper plates with snacks. There was a table set up at the side of the room, the plastic tablecloth weighed down with carrot sticks and pretzels and stuffed mushroom caps on trays. Obviously some of my neighbors had more time to prepare hors d'oeuvres than others.

I recognized several people I sort of knew, including Mr. Sullivan, who was deep in conversation with a trim, older lady from the building next to ours. I also recognized Tamara Grimaldi. She was standing near the front, talking to Prisca Miller and a short blonde whose name I didn't know, but whom I knew as another officer of the HOA. A secretary or treasurer or something of that ilk. She looked like a squat book wedged between two bookends, or a marshmallow squeezed between pieces of chocolate and graham cracker.

Not that she was fat. A tiny bit plump, perhaps, or what Barbara Botticelli might have called voluptuous, but even that might have been due to standing between two much taller individuals.

Grimaldi and Prisca were around the same height and with similar coloring, but where Grimaldi was lean and businesslike in her dark pantsuit and low heeled shoes, Prisca Miller looked like a teenage boy's wet dream. She was zipped into a suit jacket two sizes too small, with a matching skirt that stopped several inches above her knees. I couldn't see a top under the jacket, so I had to believe she had closed it over just a bra. My mother would have considered her shoes unladylike in the extreme—not because they were short-heeled and frumpy, but because they looked like something a dominatrix might wear: shiny black patent leather with a four inch heel and a one inch platform. My feet hurt looking at them, and I've been brought up to believe you're not fully dressed without at least a two-and-a-half-inch heel. Her hair tumbled down her back in glossy, espresso-colored waves, while

Grimaldi's black curls were cropped short and clustered close to her head. And while the detective's face was scrubbed clean of makeup, Prisca had the smoky eye thing going, along with a pair of lips so glossy red they looked lacquered.

Next to me, Rafe gave a low whistle, and I turned to him, eyes narrowed. "You didn't just do that."

He grinned down at me. "She ain't my type, darlin'."

"Then don't whistle."

"I didn't whistle at her," Rafe said. "This place is hopping. I had no idea this was going on."

Me, neither. This was the first time I had ventured into one of the HOA meetings. Being a renter, I had assumed they weren't for me. But now I sort of wished I had stopped by before. In real estate, the more people you know, the better off you are. Someone usually always knows someone who's looking for a house to buy, and here were at least fifty people I could have mined for their connections.

"You hungry?" Rafe asked, gesturing to the laden table.

"I could eat." I can always eat. At least lately. And we'd... let's say we'd gotten sidetracked between the time we arrived home and the time we had to leave to come here. Sidetracked in a way that had involved exercise but no food, and which had provided fodder for the bestselling bodice ripper I might one day write.

I'm serious, if Barbara Botticelli had had Rafe in her bed every day, there was no limit to the success she might have found.

Anyway, I was starving.

"I'll take you out for a proper meal when we're done here," my hero told me, "but for now, let me get you a plate. What d'you wanna eat?"

What I should eat, were celery sticks and baby carrots. What I wanted was everything else.

"Um... maybe a deviled egg and a couple of meatballs and some stuffed mushroom caps and a couple of crackers with cheese?"

Rafe arched a brow.

Fine. "And a carrot stick."

He grinned. "Coming right up. Why don't you have a seat, darlin'. You look ready to chew the upholstery."

I did? How mortifying. A Southern Belle isn't supposed to look hungry, and when food is put in front of her, she's supposed to nibble daintily. In fact, if I were to behave like my mother's daughter, I'd make the plate Rafe was bringing suffice, and would tell him that he needn't take me out for dinner afterwards. Not that I had any plans of doing that. I was already looking forward to a proper meal after this one. So what if I had to move into the pregnancy wardrobe a little early?

Before I could sit down, though, Grimaldi beckoned for me to come closer. And when the police beckon, it isn't like you can say no. I made my way through the throng to the front of the room, nodding and smiling to strangers and people I'd seen before along the way.

"Evening, Detective."

"Ms. Martin." She nodded.

We've gone back and forth a few times lately about the fact that we've sort of become friends and she's sort of dating my brother, so it would be nice if we progressed to first names. Grimaldi seems reluctant, and it's hard for me to address her as Tamara, too. We both do our best in social settings, but the fact that I'd become Ms. Martin again, indicated that this was business.

"Are you alone?"

I shook my head. "Rafe's getting food."

Prisca's eyes slid to my midsection, and I could read the thoughts like a bubble above her head. *Like you need it.*

"I'm always eating these days," I added—directed at Grimaldi but loud enough that I was sure Prisca could hear every word, even above the hum of everyone's voices. "Hopefully most of it will turn into baby, and there won't be that much left to lose after he or she is born."

There: the two proverbial birds with one stone. I wasn't fat, I was pregnant, and Rafe was off limits, because he'd impregnated me.

Grimaldi nodded. "This is Prisca Miller, president of the home owners' association. And Shannon Duncan, treasurer. Ms. Miller, Ms. Duncan, Ms. Martin."

"Nice to meet you both," I said.

Shannon murmured something in return, and watched me. Prisca's attention immediately slipped over my shoulder, and moved up and down and up again. She didn't quite lick her lips, but the inclination was there in her eyes.

So much for my pregnancy keeping her from ogling my baby daddy.

I rolled my eyes, and saw Grimaldi's lips twitch. Rafe's did too, when he came to a stop beside me. "Here you go, darlin'." He was carrying a plate with everything I had asked for, including the single carrot stick.

I took it. "Thank you."

He grinned. "My pleasure." He watched me bite into the carrot before turning the grin on Grimaldi. "Tammy."

She nodded back. Not a big smiler, the detective, especially when faced with the dreaded diminutive. I wouldn't have blamed her for taking his head off.

She didn't. Just answered, cordially enough, "Mr. Collier. This is Ms. Miller, head of the home owners' association, and Ms. Duncan, treasurer."

Rafe nodded. "A pleasure."

Shannon murmured again. Prisca preened, fluttering her eyelashes and cocking her hips, sticking her chest out. She had a nice chest, and nice, white, straight teeth behind the blood-red lipstick. And hair she flipped over her shoulder, flirtatiously. "Likewise. I've noticed you coming and going."

I munched my carrot stick while I watched, as unobtrusively as I could, to see whether Rafe would take the (rather obvious) bait. Despite evidence to the contrary, I can't quite shake the feeling that women like Prisca are his type, while I'm not.

In this case he spent about ten seconds on her, just long enough to be neighborly and flattering, but not long enough to indicate any real interest, before he turned back to Tamara Grimaldi. "We need to talk."

"Later." She was much too seasoned to indicate, with so much as a sideways glance, that she didn't want to have the conversation in front of Prisca and Shannon, but then Rafe was much too seasoned to do that in the first place.

"I'm taking Savannah for something to eat when we're done here," he told her. "You should join us."

It wasn't a suggestion.

"Of course," Grimaldi said.

He nodded. "I'll catch you up then." And then he turned to me. "Ready to go sit down?"

I nodded, my mouth full. He put his free hand on the small of my back. "Nice to meet you both," he told Prisca and Shannon.

Shannon nodded, with a look at me. Prisca simpered. "You, too."

"No better than she ought to be," I informed Rafe under my breath as we walked away.

He chuckled. "Don't hold back, darlin'."

"She looked at you like she wanted to take a bite."

He shrugged. "Ain't nobody taking bites outta me these days but you."

"Damn straight," I said, and made him smile.

The meeting got underway a few minutes later. I kept nibbling on my food and listening with half an ear to the proceedings.

Frankly, it was boring, even more so than the—similar—meeting I'd attended at LB&A this morning. The reading of minutes from the last meeting gave way to reports from the treasurer and secretary, and old business gave way—finally—to new business. By then, I was half asleep. Being pregnant didn't just make me constantly hungry, it made me constantly sleepy, too.

New business turned out to be the murder, not surprisingly, and Prisca introduced Grimaldi, who got up to give an update on the investigation, and an appeal for anyone who had seen anything to please come forward. As she made her way toward the podium, everyone straightened and rubbed sleep from their eyes. Guess I wasn't the only one who'd been bored.

I wish I could tell you she shared some fabulous clue I didn't already know, but alas: it was just the same basic information. A woman had been found dead in one of the apartments, and the police were investigating. Anyone who knew anything they thought might have bearing on the problem, should please contact Detective Grimaldi.

Prisca raised her hand. "Is it true that the victim was a prostitute?"

Since she'd gone out publicly—on TV, no less—with that bit of news last night, it was perhaps a little late to ask, not to mention a bit disingenuous.

I waited for Grimaldi to tell her so—she certainly would have told me—but given that the cat was out of the bag, so to speak, and the information already disseminated, I guess maybe Grimaldi felt there was no point in holding back. "We're working on that assumption."

"What was she doing here?"

Prisca glanced over her shoulder as she asked, toward where Rafe and I were sitting. I thought about sticking my tongue out, but decided it would be unladylike.

Grimaldi explained that the dead woman had rented one of the apartments for a few days while she was in town for a job interview. Or so she had said.

Prisca wrinkled her nose. I couldn't see her, her back was to me, but I could hear it in her voice. "Job interview?"

"Obviously an excuse," Grimaldi said. She isn't stupid, and I'm sure she knew what Prisca was doing, or trying to do.

"Is there any danger to the rest of us?" Mr. Sullivan wanted to know, before Grimaldi could flatten Prisca, assuming she was planning to. Maybe I was the only one who wanted to see Prisca writhing in humiliation on the floor.

"At the moment," Grimaldi told him, "we believe this was a one-time thing, not connected in any way with the building or the residents."

I wondered if that meant I was off the hook, too—contrary to what Rafe had implied in the car earlier—or whether she just meant that nobody else was in danger. Technically speaking, I guess I wasn't a resident anymore.

A few other people had questions, too—nothing earth-shaking, nothing I hadn't already thought of and talked to Rafe about—and then Grimaldi reiterated that anyone with information, no matter how insignificant it might seem, should feel free to contact her, or speak to her after the meeting. She went and sat back down amidst sporadic applause.

Prisca got up and click-clacked up to the front on her heels. "Any other new business?"

Nobody spoke.

"Any other old business?"

Seemingly not.

"Move to adjourn."

"Second," Mr. Sullivan said, loudly.

"The meeting is adjourned." In lieu of a gavel to bang, she clapped her hands, like she were dealing with a class of recalcitrant five-year-olds.

Rafe turned to me. "Ready to go?"

I glanced around. The invitation to the meeting had been, in my opinion, pretty strongly worded, and so far I'd gotten off easy. No one had cornered me and laid into me for renting my place to a hooker, even unwittingly. No one had laid into me for being stupid, even. Nobody had yelled at me for unleashing a murder on them.

But that could change. Maybe we should get out of here before it did.

However, there was one thing I needed to do first.

"What's that?" Rafe asked.

I hesitated. I didn't really want to involve him, especially with what I expected to learn, but with the way he was sticking close to me tonight, my chances of getting away, even for a short conversation, were probably pretty slim. "Yesterday morning, Mr. Sullivan asked me whether my friend found me. You came out before I could ask who he was talking about."

His brow arched.

"It was probably just the dead woman," I added, although I didn't really believe it myself.

"Or not." He got to his feet and helped me up. "Let's go find out."

I sighed. "Let's."

MR. SULLIVAN WAS PLUNDERING THE stuffed mushroom caps when we approached the table. "I hope you weren't looking for anything in the way of spinach dip," he said cheerfully, "because it's mostly gone."

"We were actually looking for you." I gave him my friendliest smile.

"Yeah?" He looked from me to Rafe and back. "Why?"

"Well, yesterday morning, when we were sitting in the hallway outside my door..."

He nodded.

"You asked me whether my friend found me. I assume you weren't talking about the dead woman, right?"

Mr. Sullivan shook his head. But since his mouth was full of sausage-stuffed mushroom, it took a minute before he could answer. I looked around, and caught Shannon Duncan looking at us. Prisca Miller was deep in conversation with Detective Grimaldi again.

"Your gentleman friend," Mr. Sullivan said. "He used to come around last year. Good-looking blond fella." He slapped Rafe on the shoulder. "No offense, young man."

"None taken," Rafe said. "When did you see him?"

Mr. Sullivan said it had been just before seven on Saturday night. "I was coming home with some takeout and a movie. Saturday nights aren't that much fun when you're my age."

"Maybe next week you could ask that young lady over there in the jumpsuit to join you," I suggested, "and it would be more fun."

Mr. Sullivan chuckled. "You took the words right outta my mouth."

"So what did this man do when you saw him?" Rafe wanted to know, yanking the conversation back on track again. "How do you know it was Savannah's friend?"

Mr. Sullivan returned his attention to him. "I may be old, young man, but I'm neither stupid nor blind. I've seen him before. More than once. I recognized him. Besides, he was knocking on her door."

"My door?"

Mr. Sullivan nodded. "Just before seven. Knocking on your door with a bouquet of roses in his hand."

Really? He must have taken those with him when he left, because they hadn't been in the apartment on Sunday morning. Or if they were, I hadn't noticed them.

Rafe kept asking Mr. Sullivan questions, trying to get a firm ID on Todd, but as far as I was concerned, the identification was as firm as it was going to get. Other than Rafe himself, I hadn't been dating anyone but Todd in the time since Bradley and I broke up. And the roses clinched it. Todd has no imagination whatsoever. He always brought me roses.

Not that there's anything wrong with roses, but sometimes it's nice to get something else, too. Some sign that the guy bringing you the flowers hasn't just picked up the standard male-to-female gift, but has actually put a little thought into the giving.

"This is depressing," I told Rafe when the conversation was over and we were on our way toward the back of the room and the door to the outside.

He looked down at me. "Why?"

"I don't want Todd to be guilty of murder. My mother would never forgive me."

"If Satterfield's guilty of murder, it ain't your fault," Rafe said.

"Tell that to my mother."

Rafe shuddered. "Let's hope it don't come to that. Your mama gives me the heebie-jeebies."

Me, too.

"Let's just get outta here. I'll text Tammy when we're in the car and tell her where to meet us."

I nodded.

"What d'you wanna eat?"

"A cheeseburger," I said. "And fries. And maybe a milkshake."

Fattening comfort food. Before getting pregnant, my standby would have been a salad and Diet Coke. The fewer calories, the better. Gotta keep that Southern Belle wasp waist. Occasionally, when I went somewhere fancy, I'd have Chicken Marsala and a glass of Chardonnay, but I'd make damned sure I said no to dessert, even though I have a real weakness for cheesecake.

Now that I had an excuse, I was making up for lost time. If I wanted a hamburger, I had a hamburger. If I wanted dessert, I had dessert. We kept ice cream in the freezer, and sometimes I had a bowl at eleven o'clock at night, without feeling guilty. Or at least without feeling a whole lot of guilt. I was creating a baby, and whatever my body and the baby demanded, the body and baby got. The last thing I wanted to do, was anything that might in any way impact my chances of carrying this baby to term. If I gained seventy pounds, but had a healthy baby at the end of it, it would be worth it, even if I had to spend the rest of my life on a diet.

We had escaped the meeting room and were just a few feet from the exterior door and freedom when a voice rose behind us. "Miss Martin! Please wait!"

Uh-oh.

I thought about pretending I hadn't heard it, in the buzz of voices now emanating from the meeting room, but it wouldn't have worked. The comer kept calling as she hustled toward us.

"Just a moment, Miss Martin!"

I turned, with the front door at my back—*so near, yet so far*—and smiled graciously. Or as graciously as I could manage under the circumstances. "Of course, Miss Duncan. What can I do for you?"

"We're on our way to dinner," Rafe added, driving the point home. He knows me well enough to know what was going through my mind at that moment.

Shannon Duncan glanced at my midriff and then back to my face. "Then I won't keep you. Maybe I could buy you lunch tomorrow?"

"Oh." I hesitated. "Um..."

But it wasn't like I had anything else to do, was it? I had no job anymore. Or at least no office in which to ply my trade. I could sit at the kitchen table at Mrs. Jenkins's house and write a bodice ripper longhand, I suppose, since Grimaldi had taken my laptop into evidence.

Although free food is always nice. And if she was offering to feed me, the conversation probably wouldn't be that bad. Most likely she just wanted to revoke my rental agreement with Fifth and Main early, and at this point I wasn't sure I cared. I'd never sleep in that apartment again anyway. And if I lost what was left of my security deposit, I'd consider it a small price to pay.

Besides, I was curious. What if she knew something about the murder, or the victim, something she wanted to share with me? Something she didn't feel she could share with Detective Grimaldi or Rafe?

So I smiled. "Sure. That would be lovely."

Shannon smiled back. "Great. Would 11:30 suit you?"

I told her that 11:30 would suit me just fine, and we settled on meeting at one of the restaurants that occupied the first floor of Fifth and Main. Once that was done, Rafe whisked me out the door, while Shannon headed back to the meeting room, sensible heels clicking on the floor.

"Do you think she might know something about Jolynn?" I asked when I was installed in the front seat of the Volvo and Rafe was manipulating the buttons on his phone to tell Grimaldi where to meet us.

He shrugged. "Dunno. She was here. She might."

"Think she'll yell at me?"

"If she's buying you lunch, I don't imagine it can be too bad. Do you?" He dropped the phone into a compartment in the console and turned the key in the ignition.

"Where are we going?" I asked, since we hadn't discussed where we'd be having dinner yet.

He named his favorite burger joint. "That OK with you?"

His favorite restaurant is a little dinky hole-in-the-wall just on the cusp of the gentrified parts of East Nashville, where he feels a lot more comfortable than I do. They do have the best burgers on this side of the river, though, and besides, I'd be there in the company of a TBI agent and a MNPD detective, so I figured I'd be safe.

"Has Grimaldi been there before? Will she have a problem finding it?"

"She's a detective," Rafe said and put the car in gear. "I imagine she can figure out the way."

Ten

By the time Grimaldi walked in the door, my cheeseburger was on the table and I was in the process of filling my stomach. My mother had taught me better manners—I was supposed to wait for all members of the party to arrive before starting to eat—but Mother wasn't here and the baby demanded sustenance. Besides, the whole restaurant smelled great, and my stomach was growling so loudly it was embarrassing. Between that and the fact that the detective took a really long time in coming, I figured having something to eat was the lesser of two evils. Tamara Grimaldi isn't the kind of person to stand on ceremony, and my mother, who is that kind of person, would never know.

The detective stopped just inside the door and looked around. And I guess she looks enough like a cop that people noticed her standing there. There wasn't a mass exodus or anything, but a few people shifted somewhat uncomfortably in their seats and made a point of ducking their heads and evincing a passionate interest in whatever was on their plates. Rafe's favorite place is just shady enough that I guess some of the criminal element may be spending time there. Maybe that's why he likes it. It reminds him of old times.

Grimaldi didn't notice, or more likely—since she's trained to notice things—didn't let on that she noticed. She spied the two of us over in the corner and headed our way. As soon as she had passed a table near the entrance, three young men slid out of the booth and headed for the door, with a deliberate nonchalance that didn't fool any of us.

"I guess they were doing something they shouldn't be?" I asked Rafe. He grinned. "Why didn't they leave when you came in?"

He was just as much a member of law enforcement as the detective, after all.

"Guess I don't carry that official smell." He got up to greet Grimaldi as she came closer.

"Are you going to tell her?" I asked.

The detective stopped beside the booth. "Tell me what?"

"Couple kids up near the front booked it when they caught the smell of cop."

Grimaldi glanced over her shoulder, to where the front door was still vibrating from the young men's passage. "What were they doing?"

"Looked like bookmaking," Rafe said.

The detective shrugged. "Not my field."

I scooted farther into the booth so she could slide in beside me. "I was just asking why they didn't leave when Rafe walked in."

Grimaldi looked him up and down, as he took his seat across the table. "He doesn't smell like cop."

Rafe's grin widened. "Told you, darlin'."

Yeah, yeah. I turned to Grimaldi. "I'm sorry we started eating. But I was starving." I picked up my sandwich again, since I was still hungry.

"We got you a burger," Rafe added. "They're keeping it warm. Should be out any minute now that you're here."

And indeed, the waitress was on her way across the floor as he spoke, weaving through the tables with Grimaldi's plate in her hand. She deposited it in front of the detective and took a step back. "Something to drink with that?"

Grimaldi glanced at the table. I was drinking milk and Rafe beer. Light beer, that wouldn't be a problem when it was time to drive me home later. "I'll have what he's having."

The waitress nodded and sashayed off, gum snapping. Rafe did not watch her go. Instead he watched me, and grinned when he caught me watching him.

Grimaldi watched both of us, eyes rolling. She refrained from comment, though; just picked up her burger and took a bite.

We spent a few minutes in silence, eating. It was late for dinner, by anyone's standards, and I guess the detective was hungry, too. We didn't pick up the conversation until after she'd finished more than half her burger and had leaned back in the booth, signaling that the floor was open for business. "Tell me what happened this afternoon."

"Nothing happened," Rafe said. "Other than that he identified his ex-wife."

Grimaldi looked satisfied. "I was wondering if he would."

"He didn't have much choice," Rafe pointed out. "Her brother," he nodded to me, "looked at the picture first. After he recognized her, there wasn't much Satterfield could do but admit it."

"Did he cop to the murder? Or say he didn't do it?"

"He said he didn't do it," Rafe said.

"Well, of course he didn't do it!" Todd was many things, but not a murderer.

They both glanced at me, but neither spoke.

"He said he wasn't in Nashville on Saturday night," Rafe told Grimaldi.

Grimaldi tilted her head. "How'd he explain the email?"

"Said he got it," Rafe said. "Said he had other plans, so he ignored it."

"Sure."

"But that don't matter. Because we have a witness who puts him outside Savannah's door just before seven."

He told Grimaldi about Mr. Sullivan.

"So we can place him in Nashville at the time of the murder. Outside the apartment. But we can't place him inside."

Rafe shook his head. "Not unless your crime scene crew came up with anything."

Grimaldi shook hers right back. "Any idea where he spent the night?"

"He didn't wanna say."

Grimaldi arched her brows, and Rafe said, "The man's a lawyer. Ain't like I could force it out of him. He knows his rights."

Only too well, I could imagine.

"But that doesn't make any sense!" I objected. "He has to realize he's on the suspect list. If he was somewhere else, why wouldn't he admit it?"

"Guess that'd depend on where he was," Rafe said.

Well, yes. But... "What could be worse than being arrested for murder?"

"If it came to that," Rafe said, "I imagine he'd prob'ly come clean."

I looked from one to the other of them. "So will it come to that?" If it was the only way to get Todd to tell them where he'd spent Saturday night, I wouldn't put it past the two of them to arrest him. Or at least threaten to arrest him.

It was Grimaldi who answered. Her case, I guess. Rafe was just, in this instance, her errand-boy. "It might. But it won't be right away. First I've got another job for you."

"Here we go again," Rafe said, resigned.

"You've spent some time in Atlanta."

"Sure." Rooting out Hector Gonzales and his organization.

"You have contacts with the police down there."

Rafe nodded.

"I need you to go to Atlanta tomorrow and try to get a handle on Satterfield's relationship with his ex-wife."

I blinked, disconcerted. "But..."

They both turned to me. "Problem?" Grimaldi asked.

"Well..."

"It'll only be for a couple days," Rafe told me. "I'll be back Wednesday night."

Grimaldi looked doubtful, like she wasn't sure he should be promising me something that specific. I wasn't sure, either. How could he know exactly how long it would take? Wouldn't it depend on the people he had to talk to and what they said, and how many more interviews piled on while he was down there?

"You could come along."

And sit in a hotel room all day? Or wait in the car while he talked to people? It wasn't like I could go along on his interviews, after all.

Unless he tried to pass me off as his stenographer, I suppose, the way detective inspectors in old mysteries did. They always had a young whippersnapper tagging along to take notes of any interviews they conducted.

"No, I can't. I'm having lunch with Shannon Duncan tomorrow."

"You could call and cancel."

I could. But I didn't want to. "What if she knows something about the murder?"

Grimaldi wrinkled her brows. "This is the HOA treasurer, right? From the meeting? She didn't say anything to me."

"She probably doesn't," I admitted. "But she asked to talk to me. She's buying me lunch tomorrow. She has to want something."

"So have lunch with her. And let your boyfriend go to Atlanta and do his job. Surely the two of you can do without one another for forty-eight hours."

Honestly, since we moved in together at Christmas, we hadn't done without one another more than twenty-four at a time. That wasn't the problem, though. I could make do without Rafe for two days if he had to drive to Atlanta to work. True, the prospect was a bit scary. He'd spent undercover time in Atlanta, infiltrating Hector Gonzales's organization. And while he had contacts in law enforcement down there, he probably also had enemies. Not every single soul Hector knew had been swept up with him. And I lived in fear that one of these days, one of those enemies would crawl out of the woodwork to take a potshot at Rafe.

In this instance, though, I was more concerned about my own safety than his. He can take care of himself. He can also take care of me, but not if he's in Atlanta.

"What're you thinking?" He was watching me from across the table. Grimaldi was watching, too, a wrinkle between her brows.

"About what you said earlier. That until we know what's going on, you don't want me to be alone."

Grimaldi glanced at him, and then back at me. "Something you're not telling me?"

I shook my head.

"No shots in the night? Nobody breaking windows or cutting the brake cables on your car?"

"Nothing like that." Not this time. Although all of that had happened at various times in the past. "Just a dead woman in my apartment. A woman who looked like me."

"I think," Grimaldi said, "that that was a coincidence."

"She wasn't killed because somebody thought she was me?"

"I don't think so," Grimaldi said.

"But you aren't sure."

She hesitated. "I believe that Jocelyn Rivera was killed because someone wanted her dead. Her, not you. The fact that she was in your apartment when it happened, was bad luck. Or maybe a contributing factor. But you're right, I don't have any proof of that. It's what I believe based on working a lot of homicide cases and seeing a lot of victims.

But we are approaching this case from the standpoint that the right person was murdered."

I'm sure she didn't mean to make it sound the way it did, and since I assumed it wasn't deliberate, I didn't say anything about it. I had more important things on my mind, after all. "So you think I'm safe. Even without Rafe around to make sure nothing happens to me."

She hesitated. "I think it's always good to be careful. And I think you have more than a normal propensity for getting yourself in trouble. But until we have some sort of evidence that you were the intended victim, or that anyone other than Jocelyn Rivera was, I don't think you have to worry."

"So I'll be OK on my own if Rafe goes away." In Mrs. Jenkins's big house in a part of town where gunshots were such commonplace that people didn't do much more than look around for any dead bodies and then dismiss the incident if they didn't see anyone bleeding to death on the sidewalk.

"Maybe you should go see your mama for a couple days," Rafe suggested. "Go have your lunch tomorrow, and then head down to Sweetwater for a visit."

"I was in Sweetwater yesterday."

"You didn't see your mama."

No, I hadn't. And by now, she had probably heard about Rafe driving down to interview Todd. By now, the incident would have taken on mythic proportions, with Todd cowering in a corner of Dix's conference room while Rafe stood over him swinging the proverbial rubber hose like a lasso. My mother would be fit to be tied.

On the other hand...

"I could do that," I said, pretending reluctant agreement. "My mother's probably heard we were in town yesterday." Audrey had told her, for sure. And Todd must have told his dad what had happened, and Bob had surely passed the news on to my mother by now, too. "She's probably upset that I didn't stop in to see her. If I come down and spend the night, it might make her less upset."

And while I was there, maybe I'd have a chance to talk to Todd about exactly where he'd been on Saturday night, and the importance of coming clean. Being arrested, even if only so he'd spill the beans, wouldn't look good on his résumé.

While this was running through my mind, Rafe watched me suspiciously from across the table. "Stay away from him," he told me.

I tried to sound innocent. "Who?"

"I can read you like a crystal ball, darlin'. You're thinking Satterfield will talk to you when he wouldn't talk to me."

"He might talk to me," I said.

"Or he might wrap his hands around your throat and squeeze." His voice was grim, as if he might just want to wrap his hands around my throat and squeeze, too, if I didn't listen.

"That's ridiculous," I said. "Even if he killed Jolynn—and I don't think he did—he has no reason to kill me."

"If he killed his ex-wife because she couldn't give him what he wanted, he might kill you for the same reason."

I scoffed. "And what reason would that be?"

"You," Rafe said.

"Excuse me?"

"If he went to your place expecting to find you, and he found her instead, he mighta snapped and killed her because she wasn't you. Especially if she shot her mouth off. And she mighta done that, since she prob'ly had some hang-ups about him marrying her and trying to turn her into you. And since you're not about to give him what he wants, either—"

He paused for long enough to make it abundantly clear to me that I'd better not even think about that, "—he might could lose his temper and decide that if he can't have you, I damn well won't."

"That would mean he's insane," I said. "He's not."

During this exchange, Grimaldi hadn't said a word, had just followed the conversational ball being batted back and forth across the table while nibbling on her food. Now she spoke. "I don't much like the idea of you confronting a suspect in a homicide case either, Ms.... Savannah."

"I wouldn't be confronting him," I protested. "We're friends. Or at least we used to be friends. You know, before." Before I turned down Todd's proposal of marriage and started shacking up with Rafe instead.

And yes, maybe they did both have a point. Not about Todd strangling me. I couldn't make myself believe he'd killed Jolynn, and I could even less make myself believe he'd hurt me. But maybe I wasn't the best choice of person to talk to him about where he'd been on Saturday night. I certainly wasn't the right person to ask him whether he'd gone to my apartment hoping to find me there, waiting for him, and when I wasn't, he'd murdered the woman who was there instead.

"Maybe he's told Dix where he was on Saturday," I said. "Maybe I can get Dix to tell me."

"Attorney-client privilege," Grimaldi answered sourly. Maybe she'd tried to get that same information out of Dix, too, and such had been his excuse for not being able to tell her anything.

I couldn't imagine that would have gone over well, if so.

"Trouble in paradise?" Rafe asked, with a quirk of his lips that threatened to turn into a grin.

"Professional conflict." Grimaldi's tone was quelling.

I giggled. The detective's eyes narrowed, at the same time as her cheeks flushed.

"Awww," I said, delighted. "You're blushing!"

She muttered something. I didn't ask her to repeat it.

By now, Rafe was grinning. "Savannah may be right," he told her. "Her brother might tell her things he won't tell you."

Yes, he might. With Grimaldi, he'd be very aware that she was on the opposite side, the side investigating Todd for murder, while he was representing Todd's interests. And while not a criminal attorney, my legal eagle brother is too good of a lawyer to let slip any information, even to the woman he's wooing. Assuming he's wooing her, and they're not just good friends.

Anyway, I wasn't surprised that he'd refuse to talk about the case to Grimaldi. Hopefully he'd be more forthcoming with me.

And hopefully the fact that he wouldn't talk to her, hadn't set their budding romance back any. Surely Grimaldi would understand that it was just business, and ethics.

There were probably a lot of things she couldn't really talk to him about, too. Including what evidence, if any, they had against Todd.

For a second I amused myself by imagining the detective and my brother both assiduously trying to pump the other for information while in the middle of… well, whatever they usually found themselves in the middle of. And then the mental pictures became too uncomfortable and I shut them down and looked up. "I don't want Todd to go to jail for a crime he didn't commit."

It was Rafe's turn to mutter something. I didn't ask him to repeat it, either.

"Nobody wants to send the wrong man to jail," Grimaldi said. "I try very hard not to arrest anyone unless I can prove that they're guilty. But if you can get Mr. Satterfield to provide an alibi so I don't have to start playing hardball, I wouldn't say no. Just be sure you're not putting yourself in danger."

Rafe scowled.

"I won't," I said. "If I talk to him, I'll make sure there are other people around. Either Dix, or someone else. Or that I'm in a public place."

Rafe scowled harder. Maybe he imagined Todd taking me to dinner in a public place. The thought had crossed my own mind, too. But then food crosses my mind an awful lot these days.

I held his gaze across the table. "Nothing's going to happen to me. I promise."

"See that it don't. Or I'll take Satterfield to pieces with my bare hands when I come back."

"I'm sure he already knows that," Grimaldi said drily. "So you'll go to Atlanta tomorrow?"

"Do I have a choice?"

"I'm not going to force you. I can send someone else. It's just that you have the contacts and the experience there."

Rafe sighed. "Yeah, I'll go to Atlanta. And if something happens to Savannah while I'm gone, I'll take you apart when I come back, too."

"Nothing's going to happen to me," I repeated, while Grimaldi seemed amused.

"Threatening a fellow law enforcement officer, Agent Collier?"

"Grrr," Rafe said, or something like it. I giggled. After a moment, his lips curved, reluctantly. "I just wanna keep you safe, darlin'."

"I know," I said. "And I will be. I don't want anything to happen to me, either. I'll be careful."

"See that you are. Cause if I come back and find out that you've been careless and you've gotten yourself hurt, I might just kill you myself."

Good to know.

Eleven

Rafe set out for Atlanta at seven the next morning. The way he drives—like a bat out of hell—that would put him there around nine-thirty or ten, I figured. A full hour before I'd get there, if I were the one behind the wheel.

After waving him off, I took my time getting ready for the day and my own trip to Sweetwater. I took a leisurely shower and washed my hair. I packed an overnight bag, with a couple of extra changes of clothing just in case I ended up staying longer. If Rafe stayed in Atlanta an extra day, I'd stay in Sweetwater until he got back. I dressed and put on makeup for my lunch with Shannon Duncan.

By then, it was after nine o'clock, and I still had two hours to kill before I could head out. Since Tamara Grimaldi had impounded my laptop as evidence, I couldn't work—not that I had any work to do.

Truth be told, the real estate thing hadn't worked out the way I had hoped and planned a year ago, back when my license was brand new and shiny.

Or more accurately, a year ago I hadn't even received the license yet. I'd just been finishing up my real estate courses and studying for the final exam. But I'd been excited by the potential ahead of me. I'd envisioned myself rocking and rolling, juggling listings and buyers and making a nice salary by now. Instead of which I'd be living on the streets if it hadn't been for Rafe.

And now I didn't even have a place to hang my shingle.

Damn Tim, anyway. It wasn't like he hadn't ever created controversy for LB&A. Or like Walker hadn't. What I'd done—which wasn't much at all, and an honest mistake—couldn't compare at all.

Maybe I could sue for wrongful termination. I could probably talk Dix, Catherine, or Jonathan into taking the case for me, *pro bono*. Isn't that what family's for?

Or I could accept Tim's decree and go look for somewhere else to hang my license. There are plenty of other real estate companies around. Given my track record—a half a dozen sales in a year—nobody would be fighting over me, but I'd probably be able to find someone to take me on. Real estate is full of people who only practice part-time and who only sell a house every once in a blue moon. Some people—real estate developers, for instance—only keep current licenses to buy and sell their own properties, so it wasn't like there wasn't precedent.

My last option—if I wanted to keep doing real estate at all—was convincing Tim that he was wrong and that he should give me another chance. The murder would be solved soon—already it was off the evening news and the front page of the paper—and I had every confidence in Tamara Grimaldi and Rafe to figure out what had happened. So any notoriety I'd brought down on myself would soon fade, too. And anyway, notoriety isn't necessarily a bad thing. Tim has always adhered to the old chestnut that there's no such thing as bad publicity. He'd certainly put himself in front of the cameras often enough after Brenda was killed. Really, the whole thing was very hypocritical of him.

Or maybe the murder was just an excuse. Maybe he just wanted to get rid of me because I wasn't pulling my weight.

Getting a foothold in real estate had turned out to be a lot harder than I thought it would be, entirely apart from the fact that I've kept getting sidetracked by murders almost since I started. I enjoy houses. I like to see them all decrepit and run down, yet oozing potential from tiled fireplaces and transom windows, and I like to see them all fixed up and pretty, ready for someone new to fall in love with them and turn them into a home. I like them when they're lived in and comfortable, full of the personality of the people who own them. I even like them when they're a little neglected and sad, squalid and dusty, because I can imagine what they could be like if only someone moved in who'd care.

Houses are great. I really like houses. I like buying them and I like selling them.

What I don't like, is having to sell myself. It doesn't come naturally to me, or if it once did, Mother trained all of it out of me by insisting that a lady doesn't put herself forward. When you've been taught to sit demurely on a tuffet while things are brought to you by admiring swains, self-promotion is something of a foreign concept. I just don't have the necessary cutthroat instincts, it seems.

I leaned back on my chair and sighed. (I was sitting at the kitchen table with a pad of paper and a pen in front of me, in case something occurred to me that I should be writing down. So far nothing had.)

And I still had more than an hour until I had to leave for lunch. Rafe must be getting close to Atlanta by now—

No sooner had the thought crossed my mind, than the phone rang. Too soon for it to be ESP, alas. He must have been dialing even as I thought about him.

"Morning, darlin'."

"You wished me good morning before you left," I said. "Very nicely, too."

Not as nicely as he might have done, had we had more time to spare, but between the morning sickness still plaguing me, and the fact that he had to hit the road, we hadn't had time for a full-out session between the sheets today. I'd had to settle for a couple of kisses, which had to tide me over until he came back. It couldn't be too soon for me.

"I'm here," he told me.

I glanced at the clock. "That was fast."

"I didn't get pulled over." I could hear the smile in his voice.

"If you had, it would have slowed you down. Is that what you're saying?"

He didn't bother to answer. And he must have averaged ninety most of the way. But as long as he hadn't gotten a ticket—or been in an accident—who cared? Certainly not me. The sooner he got to Atlanta, the sooner he'd come home again.

"Where are you starting the day?" I asked.

"With the local cop shop," Rafe answered. "I'm on their turf; I gotta tell 'em I'm here. Then I'm gonna talk to Satterfield's old colleagues, the people he worked with when he was married to Jolynn. Try to get an idea of what their marriage was like. After that, I'll have to see who I can rustle up from her life these days."

Sounded fun. And I wasn't being facetious. "I'm just sitting here waiting for it to be time for me to go to lunch."

"Good," Rafe said callously. "Stay outta trouble."

"Unless one of the pipes bursts, there's not a lot of trouble I can get into just sitting here."

"You keep telling yourself that." He didn't wait for me to respond, just continued, "I gotta go, darlin'. I just wanted to let you know I got here."

"I appreciate that."

"Have a nice lunch. Drive carefully. Make sure you lock up the house before you go."

I promised I would. "You be careful, too. Keep an eye out for bad guys with scores to settle."

"Always. Love you, darlin'. Take care of my baby."

"Always," I said. "See you tomorrow." God willing.

"See you then." He hung up without reminding me that there was a chance he might not make it home by tomorrow night. I put the phone down with another sigh, and picked up the pen again. Thirty seconds later, Rafe's name inside a heart decorated the pad in front of me. Shades of high school.

It would have been fun to go to Atlanta with him. I understood why I couldn't, but it would have been fun. We'd never gone away anywhere together. Spending a night or two in a fancy hotel would have made for a nice change. And I was curious about his interviews. I knew Todd's version of the story—he'd told me about his marriage to Jolynn, and the many flaws that had made him divorce her—but I also knew the poor girl had never really had a chance. I couldn't help but feeling a little sorry for her. From being married to Bradley, I know all about feelings of inadequacy.

Was it possible that Todd had killed her?

I hauled the thought into the light and squinted at it. Not full on, but sort of sideways. Furtively.

Part of me said no, impossible. I'd known him for as long as I could remember. He'd been Dix's best friend since they were both kneehigh to a grasshopper. He'd been my boyfriend in high school. I'd come close to becoming the second Mrs. Satterfield last year. If it hadn't been for Rafe, I probably would have said yes.

Was it possible, in light of all that, that he could be a murderer, and I'd never noticed? Was I clueless enough—or self-centered enough—to overlook something like that?

Was Dix? Was Todd's dad, the sheriff?

It didn't seem likely. My mother, sure. She'd give an axe-murderer leeway if he was polite and nicely dressed. But the rest of us are, hopefully, a little more discerning.

On the other hand, who else could have killed Jolynn? No one else knew her. No one else had a motive.

Except me, I suppose. Or I would have, if I had realized she was a prostitute and that she had tricked me into renting my place to her. If I had confronted her, and she refused to leave, I might have killed her in a fit of anger. Or someone else might, in the same situation. But since I hadn't, obviously no one had. Not for that reason.

Maybe she had come up here to see someone. Someone other than Todd. But someone she knew.

Or maybe her murder was random. Maybe she'd gone out and met someone and brought him back to my apartment, and he had killed her. Just some stranger she'd picked up in a bar.

I liked that explanation the best.

However, if she expected Todd to show up at seven o'clock on Saturday, she wouldn't have gone anywhere else that night.

Maybe the killer was someone she'd met earlier. Friday night, maybe. Or Saturday afternoon. Long before Todd was due to arrive. Maybe Jolynn had gone out during the day and had met someone, and had brought him back to the apartment. They'd done their thing—in my bed; my nose wrinkled—and then she had asked him to leave, because she was expecting someone else. And the guy had realized he was just one of many, and had snapped and killed her.

Not much of a reason for murder, but I suppose some people are unhinged. Someone might possibly kill over something minor like that.

Or maybe she'd blackmailed him. Maybe that's what the camera setup was for. The camera setup Rafe said had been there, but that wasn't there anymore. She'd taped him, and confronted him with the tape—"I'll give it to your wife if you don't pay me!"—and instead of paying, he'd strangled her and walked off with the camera.

I sat back on the chair and looked at the page in front of me. Rafe's name had turned into a doodle of magnificent proportions. There was a noose, and a camera, and a shoe with a high heel, and a blob that might have been my bed... luckily without a corpse on it.

I reached for the phone and dialed. "Detective?"

"Ms.... Savannah? Something wrong?"

"Nothing at all. Rafe's made it to Atlanta. I'm just sitting here waiting for it to be time for me to go to lunch."

"And you thought you'd kill some time talking to me?" Her voice was sweet. Sugary, in fact. So saccharine my teeth hurt.

"Of course not," I said. "I know better than to waste your time when you're in the middle of an investigation."

The gall of that statement must have taken the detective's breath away, because she didn't respond immediately. I took advantage of her silence to continue. "Listen. I had a thought."

I laid out my case for her, and then waited.

"It's a possibility," Grimaldi allowed.

Yes!

"We're looking into it."

"You thought of it already." At the last second, I managed to turn my question into more of a statement. And to eradicate the pout.

The detective's voice was patient. "It's my job to think of the possibilities, Ms.... Savannah. Nobody's railroading Mr. Satterfield."

Of course not. "So you think it's possible? Someone killed her before Todd got there?"

"Anything's possible," Grimaldi said. "We're tracing Ms. Rivera's movements during the time she was staying at your place. We'll see what we come up with."

"Did she come here on Thursday, like she said she was going to? Or did she come earlier?" So she'd have had more time to meet someone else, someone who might have murdered her.

"That's something your boyfriend will have to look into," Grimaldi told me. "If he learns that she left Atlanta prior to last Thursday, we'll have to set wheels in motion to find out where she spent those days.

But for now, we're assuming she left Atlanta when she said she did, and that there's no extra time to account for."

That made sense. Time enough to look into it when we knew—or they knew—there was something to look into.

"Did you ever find out about the other people who stayed in my apartment? The Ericksons? Grant Howard? Wendy Morgan and Shauna Bangs?"

Grimaldi's lips twitched. I couldn't see her, but I knew they were. Her voice was uninflected, however. "The Ericksons were just what they said they were. A nice couple on vacation. Same for Howard and Morgan. He did do work with Dickinson, Durham and Associates, and her husband was offered a professorship at Vanderbilt. I told her you sell real estate, in the event they decide to buy a house when they move here."

"Thank you," I said, touched. "So... um... I guess Shauna Bangs was no better than she ought to be, as my mother would say?"

"I have no idea what Shauna Bangs is, or was," Grimaldi said grimly. "Best as I can figure, she doesn't exist. The email address she used to contact you is a dead end. The phone number she gave is for a disposable cell. Her name and address are bogus."

"Her check cleared," I said. And then added, "Never mind. It wasn't a personal check. It was a money order. She could have put anyone's name on it."

And there was me, thrilled because I didn't have to worry about a bounced check, the way you do when someone gives you money from a personal account.

"Did you happen to meet her?"

I grimaced. "I'm afraid not. She'd sent me a check for the whole stay up front. That indicated to me that she didn't want to be disturbed. Unlike the Ericksons, you know, who wanted to hand over their check in person. So no, I never met her."

"We'll have to do another canvass," Grimaldi said. "See if any of your neighbors can give us a description. See if it was Jocelyn Rivera using yet another name, or someone else. Maybe a friend. Maybe the person who told her about the place."

"I'll ask Shannon Duncan whether she saw Shauna Bangs when I see her for lunch," I said. "Unless you'd rather I didn't?"

"Go ahead. Let me know what she says."

I promised I would, and didn't bother to ask her to return the favor. When I called her later, I'd just ask for an update then.

By now, it was actually getting close to time for me to go, so I walked through the house from top to bottom, making sure all the windows and doors were securely closed and locked, and that all the taps were turned off, none of the toilets were running, and that everything was as it should be for when we got back. I didn't want us coming back to any kind of surprise.

Mrs. Jenkins's house is a grand old Victorian lady. Not painted, like the wooden houses. Mrs. J's house is built of brick, but it has the standard gingerbread trim on the porch, created on a scroll saw almost a hundred and fifty years ago, and painted a gleaming white. It looks fantastic against the red of the brick. The house is three stories tall, with a round tower on one corner, and the entire third floor is taken up by one giant ballroom. When the leaves are off the trees in the winter, it's possible to see the Nashville skyline in the distance.

The second floor consists of all bedrooms and bathrooms, all renovated by Rafe last fall, and downstairs are the common rooms: kitchen, dining room, library, parlor, and of course the entrance foyer with the grand staircase. Rafe did a really nice job of fixing it all up, and if he ever decides he is tired of working for the TBI, I'd totally try to talk him into doing home renovation full time. In fact, I had tried to do just that in January, after he finished putting Hector Gonzales behind bars, and before the TBI came through with the new job offer.

Everything looked just as it should, safe and secure, and I grabbed my overnight bag and purse from the floor of the hallway and headed out, locking the carved front door behind me before dumping the bag in the trunk of the car. The Volvo started up without demur, and navigated the graveled drive without giving me any indication that anything was wrong. I took a left onto Potsdam and headed for Fifth and Main, with no one, as far as I could tell, following me.

Twelve

Shannon was already there when I walked into the restaurant at eleven-thirty sharp, waiting at a table by the window. Like last night, she was dressed in a simple business dress with a jacket, with soft blond hair tucked behind her ears.

She got up when I approached the table. "Thank you for coming."

"Of course." She was paying for lunch, for one thing. And I wanted to pick her brain about Jolynn—Jocelyn—and Shauna Bangs, for another. And then there was the fact that she'd wanted to talk to me, and I was curious.

Yes, I was probably just about to be told to get out and never to darken the doorstep of Fifth and Main again... but just in case it was something else, I didn't want to miss it.

We spent the first few minutes getting situated at the table, ordering drinks, and perusing the menus. After we'd ordered—soup and salad for Shannon, turkey sandwich for me—she leaned back on the chair. "I wanted to apologize for Prisca."

"Oh." That was the last thing I had expected, frankly. "That's OK. You're not responsible for what she does."

Shannon made a face. "I had to apologize to the detective yesterday, too. She shouldn't have gone out publicly with the news about the prostitute before the police had cleared it."

No. Although I hadn't gotten the impression that Grimaldi was all that upset. At least not when I saw her last night. "I'm surprised someone who looks like Prisca would be so uptight," I said.

Not that there's anything uptight about minding prostitution taking place under your nose, I suppose. But Prisca looked and dressed so provocatively that it seemed a bit hypocritical that she should object to someone else using sex to get what she wanted.

Shannon just shrugged, so I guess maybe she didn't feel right about criticizing her fellow HOA officer. I didn't pursue the subject. "You live at Fifth and Main, right? Did you see the... um...?"

"Victim?" Shannon said. "Briefly."

I sat up straight. "When was that?"

It had been Thursday night. Shannon had been on her way home from work around six, and Jolynn had been on her way out. "I stopped to say hi," Shannon said, "and she told me she'd sublet your apartment for a few days. Short term rental. Said it was much nicer than renting a motel room." She wrinkled her nose. "I didn't realize at the time what she meant."

"I'm so sorry. I had no idea what she was, I swear. I'd never..."

Shannon waved it away. "That's when I left that note in your mailbox, asking you to come to the meeting last night. I wanted to talk to you about it."

"I'm really sorry," I said again. And then I stopped apologizing instead of trying to extract information. "Did she... um... look like she was going out to work?"

"She looked nice," Shannon said. "Pretty dress, high heels, pearl earrings. If she was going out looking for business, she wasn't planning to walk the streets."

Right.

"She said she was going to dinner."

I blinked. "Really? I don't suppose she said where? Or with whom?"

"A man in a dark car," Shannon said with a shrug.

Man? "Did you see him? What did he look like?"

But Shannon must be either wholly unobservant or half blind, because the best she could come up with was, "He was wearing a suit."

"Was he blond? Dark? Young? Old?"

"Sort of..." She fluttered her hands around her own head. "Medium. Maybe more blond than brown, but I'm not sure. He was inside the car. And he might have been in his thirties, maybe?"

That could describe half the men in Middle Tennessee, including Tim Briggs, my brother Dix, and Todd Satterfield. Or my ex-husband Bradley, except he was in jail.

I thanked the waitress with a smile as she put my lunch down, and went back to interrogating Shannon as soon as the waitress walked off. "Would you recognize him if you saw him again?"

"Probably not," Shannon said, lifting her spoon. "He stayed in the car. I didn't get a good look at him."

"What about the car? What did that look like?"

"Dark," Shannon said. "Black or blue or maybe brown or green. An SUV."

So that took Tim out of the equation. He drives a baby blue Jaguar. Not that I thought it was Tim picking up Jolynn on Thursday night.

"Did you ever meet any of the other people I rented my apartment to?"

But Shannon shook her head, already forking up shreds of lettuce. "I didn't know you were doing it until this weekend."

Hence the strongly worded invitation to attend the HOA meeting. Right. I grimaced and devoted myself to my own food.

"I wanted to talk to you about it," Shannon said again.

Certain I knew what was coming, I took a breath and launched into my apology. "I'm sorry. I won't do it again. Obviously. I mean...

after what happened, it isn't like I'm going to want to risk renting my place to anyone else, is it? Or like anyone would want to rent it, after a murder took place there."

Shannon chewed and swallowed. "That isn't…" she began.

"I mean, I know some people are ghouls." The first time I'd had an open house at Mrs. J's place after Brenda Puckett was murdered last August—before we realized that Brenda had broken a ton of ethical and legal rules, and the house had to come off the market—this woman showed up who settled down cross-legged in the library and tried to reach Brenda's wandering spirit. "But it isn't like I'm going to advertise the ability to sleep where the dead prostitute slept."

"That isn't…" Shannon tried again.

I barreled right over her, determined to get everything I wanted to say out before she interrupted me. "And anyway, there's no telling how long it'll be until the police release the place. It's still a crime scene. Besides, my lease runs out the end of the month. I was just trying to pick up enough money to pay the rent for the last little bit that I had it."

"That…"

"But I won't do it anymore. Not after what happened. I'll just wait until the police release it, and then I'll get my furniture out and let it sit empty until the end of the month."

"That's not what I wanted to talk to you about," Shannon said.

I blinked. "It's not?"

She shook her head. "It's terrible about the murder, of course. And about the prostitution, too. Was she really using your apartment to entertain johns?"

"I'm not sure," I admitted. "Detective Grimaldi said she was a prostitute. Or a call girl. Escort. Whatever. But she was also my ex-boyfriend's ex-wife, and I think that's the reason she was here."

Or maybe it was a little bit of both, but why spell that out?

Shannon nodded. "What I wanted to talk to you about," she said, "before we knew any of that, was the whole short term bed and breakfast thing. It's become very popular, and I understand it's possible to make a lot of money at it."

That was my understanding, too, and why I had decided to give it a try. Needless to say, I hadn't made a fortune, but then I hadn't had all that many guests, even before the murder. Although it was certainly possible to make a lot more than one could leasing the apartment to a regular renter, who paid regular rent. The short term B&B thing fell under the same guidelines as hotels and motels, so the nightly and weekly rates were almost the same as a monthly rate for a regular apartment.

Shannon nodded when I said as much. "It seems like we could make a lot more money doing the short term B&B thing. I thought maybe, since you'd already been doing it for your own apartment, you might be willing to take on the leasing of the others, as well."

I blinked, my mouth dropping open. There was a bite of turkey sandwich inside, and Mother would have been horrified. I snapped my teeth closed as quickly as I could, and masticated furiously.

After swallowing, I croaked, "You're offering me a job?"

It was Shannon's turn to blink. She looked a bit nervous. "Um... not so much a job. You're a real estate agent, right? I'm offering you the chance to manage the rental units here at Fifth and Main. For a fee, of course."

"So you're offering me a job."

She blinked again. "If you want to look at it like that. I guess."

I did want to look at it like that. I was already envisioning walking into Tim Briggs's office to tell him I had found a new job. It was a glorious vision. Or at least a very satisfying one.

"I accept," I said.

"You don't want to think about it?"

"I don't have to think about it. It'll just be an extension of what I do already, right?"

Shannon nodded. "You can work out of the rental office on the first floor. Or from your other office. Or from home. You'll be responsible for promoting the units, and booking them, and keeping the schedule, and coordinating with the cleaning service to come in and clean them between guests."

"Pretty much the same thing I've been doing for my own apartment." Minus the cleaning service. I did my own cleaning. And unlike selling houses, where you sell it once and it's sold, I could keep renting the same apartment over and over again. For a lot less money each time, sure. But over and over.

"I'll handle the financial end," Shannon said. "You just make sure you get a credit card and forward it to me, and I'll take it from there."

Sounded fair. "One problem," I said. "I'm going out of town this afternoon. Down to Maury County to spend the night with my mother. I should be back tomorrow night."

"That's fine," Shannon said. "Why don't we make an appointment for Thursday morning? Eleven o'clock? I'll show you around the office and the empty units, and let you know what's available."

"Sounds good." Detective Grimaldi hadn't given much credence to the theory that I might be in danger, so if Rafe wasn't back from Atlanta by then, it probably didn't matter.

"Good," Shannon said and went back to eating. I did the same thing.

We parted ways at the end of lunch: Shannon back into the bowels of Fifth and Main, and me out to the curb and into the Volvo. I was tempted to swing by LB&A on my way out of town to rub Tim's nose in the news that I'd landed another job, and so soon too, but I thought I should probably refrain, at least until I knew that nothing was going to go wrong. So I turned the Volvo's nose toward the interstate instead, and headed south on I-65.

An hour later I was approaching Sweetwater and the Martin Mansion. But it wasn't until I pulled up in front of my childhood home and saw Sheriff Satterfield's red truck parked at the bottom of the stairs, that it occurred to me—belatedly—that maybe I should have called and warned Mother I was coming.

By then it was too late, of course. My mother has some kind of built in radar for when one of her children approaches the nest. (Wonder if I'd have the same thing when my baby was born?) No sooner had I turned off the engine and opened the car door, than the door into the mansion opened, too. Mother stood there, with the sheriff a foot or two behind.

They were both fully dressed, thankfully, and looked surprised to see me. "Savannah?" Mother said.

"Rafe went to Atlanta for a couple of days. I didn't want to be in Nashville alone."

I didn't wait for her response, just ducked into the car for my overnight bag. If she and the sheriff exchanged words, or even a glance, I didn't see it.

"You don't mind, do you?" I added, once I had straightened again.

"Of course not, darling." Mother smiled, and it looked genuine. "There's plenty of room."

"That's what I figured." The mansion has something like five thousand square feet. "Although if it's a problem, I could always stay with Dix or Catherine. They both have guest rooms."

"No," Mother said firmly, "that won't be necessary."

She took a step back, and the sheriff did, too. I took one forward, across the threshold and into the two story foyer that makes up the front of the mansion.

My ancestral home was built between 1839 and 1841, with tall, white pillars holding up the roof, and a breezeway that runs from the front door all the way through the first floor to the back door; a lifesaver during those early years before air conditioning. The downstairs consists of formal rooms—various parlors, dining room, kitchen, that sort of thing—and the upstairs has five bedrooms. Mine hasn't changed much in the ten years since I moved out, other than that the lowbrow posters I had tacked to the wall at that time are gone. The furniture was always antique, and still is. Mother does occasionally rent the place to people shooting interior scenes for costume dramas or music videos, or to photographers from fashion magazines wanting their thoroughly modern models to pose in juxtaposition to the old slave cabin and smokehouse of a hundred and fifty years ago.

I dumped my overnight bag in my old room, made sure my face looked all right in great-great-maybe-another-great-aunt Suzanne's dressing table mirror, and headed back out. By the time I got downstairs, Mother and the sheriff had retired to the kitchen.

I was a bit surprised to see Sheriff Satterfield still there, to be honest. I had thought he might have pushed off now that I had arrived. Especially considering what had happened yesterday with his son and my boyfriend.

Yet here he was, sitting at the kitchen island with a glass of orange juice in front of him, while Mother was pouring another for herself. When I came through the door she lifted the pitcher—because yes, my mother decants orange juice from the cardboard carton into a glass container before depositing it in the fridge. "A glass of juice, darling?"

"Don't mind if I do," I said, and took a seat next to the sheriff on the far side of the island while Mother pulled out another glass from the cabinet next to the fridge, and proceeded to fill it. "Thank you."

"Of course, dear." She put the juice back in the fridge and took a dainty sip from her own glass. "What brings you to Sweetwater, Savannah?"

"I told you," I said. "Rafe had to go to Atlanta."

They didn't do anything so obvious as exchange glances, nor even look at each other. Nonetheless, I could feel my mother's mental nudge of the sheriff loud and clear.

He cleared his throat. "Business?"

"What...? Oh, you mean Rafe? Yes. He went down to check on your ex-daughter-in-law's movements over the past few weeks."

The sheriff blinked. "My...?"

"Jolynn? Jocelyn Rivera? Todd's ex-wife?"

"What about her?" the sheriff said.

It was my turn to blink. "Todd told you that Rafe came down to talk to him yesterday, right?"

"Of course," Sheriff Satterfield said, while Mother sniffed.

"Really, darling, how could your boyfriend even think that Todd would have had something to do with a murder?"

My mother has this idiosyncrasy where she won't use Rafe's name unless there is no other choice. I guess she thinks it's too personal, or something. Or she just doesn't like the way it fits on the tongue. So she tries to maintain distance by referring to him in other ways. I suppose calling him my boyfriend was better than calling him LaDonna Collier's good-for-nothing colored boy, which was how he'd spent most of his life until he went to prison.

It irked me, though. As did the implication that he was being unreasonable in suspecting Todd of any wrongdoing.

Sure, I'd told Rafe myself that I couldn't imagine Todd as a murderer, but my mother didn't get to disparage my boyfriend for that reason.

"It was his ex-wife who was killed," I said. "In my apartment. You may think Todd is incapable of having had anything to do with killing her, but you can't tell me Rafe doesn't have good reason to talk to him."

Mother had turned a shade paler. "*Your* apartment?" she said faintly.

I nodded. "She rented my apartment for the weekend. And then she used my computer to send Todd a message to stop by for a visit."

Mother turned to Bob Satterfield. "Did you know about this?"

He squirmed. "I knew about the murder. Saw it on the news. Didn't think it had nothing to do with us."

And why would he? It was just another dead body up there in the big scary city. Nothing to do with life in peaceful Sweetwater. And Detective Grimaldi hadn't mentioned my name, nor for that matter Jolynn's, in the news clip.

Bob Satterfield continued. "When Collier walked into the courthouse in Columbia yesterday, I gotta call from the receptionist there. But there wasn't nothing I could do about it. Wasn't like I could refuse to let him talk to the boy."

No. Not when the boy was thirty years old and an assistant District Attorney, not to mention very well aware of his rights. For Bob to come running to the rescue would only make things look worse.

"But he didn't say nothing about it being Jolynn got herself killed," Bob added.

He must have struck my mother speechless, because all she did was gape at him.

"I'm sorry for your loss," I told him formally. "Were you and your daughter-in-law close?"

"They weren't married long, and all of it in Atlanta."

"So you didn't really get to know her?"

Bob said he hadn't. "I don't know that I met her above a half a dozen times. They stayed in Georgia, mostly."

"I guess you don't know what their relationship was like."

He squinted at me. "That what that boyfriend of yours is doing in Atlanta? Digging around in my boy's past?"

"I'm afraid so," I admitted. "He's probably talking to people who knew them both when they were married. And he's also trying to find out what Jolynn's been up to since the divorce."

Bob shook his head. "Can't help you there. Never heard from her again after they split up. Don't think Todd mentioned her again."

"There's a reason she came to Nashville and rented my apartment," I told him. "If all she wanted to do was see Todd, she could have come to Sweetwater and knocked on his door." Or to Columbia, if she hadn't wanted to risk running into her ex-father-in-law. "Rafe's in Atlanta trying to figure it out."

Because that couldn't be a coincidence. Someone had gone to the trouble to figure out who I was and where I lived, and that someone knew me—or Todd—well enough to be able to guess, with a reasonable degree of certainty, that if I emailed him, he'd drop everything and come running.

"He lied," I told the sheriff. "He told Rafe he hadn't been to my apartment on Saturday." On record, too. During a formal interview. "But last night, one of my neighbors said he'd seen him there, knocking on the door."

The sheriff didn't answer, just shook his head. Not in a disbelieving way; more like he couldn't believe how stupid Todd had been.

"If he lies," I continued, "he can't expect Rafe or the Nashville PD to work with him."

Mother sniffed. Eloquently. She didn't have to speak; I knew what she was thinking. That they weren't inclined to want to work with him anyway.

"Rafe's a professional," I told her. "He won't try to railroad Todd if he isn't guilty. No matter what his own feelings are. Although as far as I'm concerned, he doesn't have a problem with Todd. It's more that Todd has a problem with him."

"And why is that?" Mother asked snidely.

"You know why." And I wasn't about to spell it out, especially in front of Todd's daddy. "In any case, Rafe isn't in charge of the investigation. Detective Grimaldi is. It's the Nashville PD's case. She just sent Rafe down here because it's out of her own jurisdiction and she couldn't involve Bob."

Bob Satterfield grimaced, but didn't tell me I was wrong.

"Rafe and Detective Grimaldi think he might be guilty," I said. "Because he was there and lied about it. And because it's Jolynn who's dead, and they always look at the significant other." Or in this case the former significant other.

"She sent him a message telling him to come see her. And he came. And then lied about it. If it were your case, you'd look at him, too."

I waited for the sheriff to nod. Which he did, if reluctantly.

"Has he said anything to you about it?"

I glanced from Mother to the sheriff. She shook her head.

"No," Bob said. He didn't add, "and if he had, I wouldn't tell you," but he didn't have to. I already knew that.

Thirteen

headed out shortly after that, leaving the two of them alone in the kitchen. I have no idea whether they stayed there, or whether they headed upstairs for some private time in my mother's bedroom once I was gone. Nor did I care. That was their business. I had my own business to worry about.

By now it was the middle of the afternoon. Lunch with Shannon had taken time, and then the drive from Nashville to Sweetwater had taken more time. I hadn't called Rafe to tell him what Shannon had said. I wanted to share the news with him, and I was positively agog to hear what he'd discovered, but I didn't want to disturb him, and anyway, I was a little worried about what he might have found out.

So while I thought about calling him as I maneuvered the Volvo through the streets of Sweetwater, from the mansion to the town square, I didn't actually do it. Too much of a chicken.

Walking into Martin & McCall again was like wiping away the last twenty-four hours. Darcy sat the desk in the lobby twirling a brown curl around her finger, and as soon as he heard my voice, Dix's head popped out of his door farther down the hallway.

"Sis?"

I gave him my best smile. "Hiya, Dix."

He closed the door behind him and eyed me suspiciously as he came closer. "What are you doing here?"

"Rafe's in Atlanta," I said, thinking as I did it that I was getting sick of explaining this. "He didn't want me to be in Nashville alone. Just in case the murderer got the wrong victim on Saturday, and it was supposed to be me."

"That's ridiculous," Dix said.

"Not according to Rafe." Although granted, he can be a touch overprotective at times, and especially now, when I had a baby onboard. "I don't think Grimaldi agrees with him," I added, fairly. "Anyway, I came down here for a couple of days while he's away."

If I had hoped that this little speech would make my brother more kindly disposed toward me, I was disappointed. He was still scowling.

"What are you doing *here?*"

"Can't I stop by and visit my favorite brother without you getting all suspicious that I have ulterior motives?"

"No," Dix said. "And besides, I'm your *only* brother."

"That's probably why you're my favorite." I smiled at Darcy, who had followed this exchange. She probably wondered what I was doing there, too. But since it wasn't any of her business, I turned back to Dix. "Do you have a minute?"

"No," Dix said. "But I don't suppose that'll make a difference to you."

"Not really. Shall we?" I gestured down the hallway in the direction of his office.

Dix sighed. "Hold my calls, Darcy."

"Yes, Mr. Martin," Darcy chirped. I wished Brittany at the LB&A office was as efficient. And then I remembered I didn't have to worry about Brittany any more.

"I got fired yesterday," I told Dix when we were sitting on opposite sides of the desk in his office. "I was thinking of suing for wrongful termination. But then I got a new job today and changed my mind."

He leaned back. "What are you going to be doing?"

"Short term rental management. For the building where my apartment is."

"They hired you after you rented your apartment to a call girl who got herself murdered?"

Well, yes. "It surprised me, too."

"Talk about your ulterior motives..."

I tilted my head. "Really?" I hadn't considered that.

Although if Shannon Duncan had an ulterior motive in asking me to take on the job, what could it be?

"No idea," Dix said when I asked out loud. "But if you brought prostitutes and murderers into my apartment building, I wouldn't offer you a job that would allow you to bring more."

When he put it like that... "I'll ask her," I said. "Although she probably won't tell me."

"I don't imagine she will," Dix answered.

"And speaking of not admitting things..."

He rolled his eyes. "Here we go."

"You sat in on that interview with Todd yesterday. You were his representative."

"That's right," Dix said. "And you went through enough of law school to know I can't tell you about that. Attorney-client privilege..."

"I understand Tamara Grimaldi isn't real happy with you."

He grimaced. "There's nothing I can do. Privileged information is privileged information."

Right. "I was told that in the interview, Todd said he hadn't gone to my apartment on Saturday night. That he got the email, the one that was supposed to be from me, but he didn't go to the apartment."

"You know I can't tell you..." Dix began.

"Last night, one of my neighbors told me he'd seen Todd there. On Saturday night. He wondered whether my friend had found me."

There was a pause. "I don't suppose..." Dix said.

I arched my brows and he added, reluctantly, "I guess there's not much chance he'd be lying?"

Probably not. "I don't see how he'd have any reason to lie. I doubt he knew Jolynn. I doubt even more he had anything to do with killing her. He's a nice, old guy in his sixties."

Although the police were probably looking into connections like that. Just in case anyone at Fifth and Main—someone other than me—had a previous knowledge of Jolynn.

If I hadn't been living with Rafe and hadn't been friendly with Grimaldi, would the police have suspected me of doing away with her?

Of everyone at Fifth and Main, I was probably the only one with any connection to Jolynn. Someone could argue that if I'd realized that she was using my apartment for entertaining johns, I might have been angry enough to kill her. I had the means to get inside—it was mine, so I had the key—and it isn't hard to find something to strangle someone with. A belt, a pair of nylons, a rope... or if you're a man, a tie.

There'd been nothing around her neck when I found her, apart from bruises. So either whoever killed her had used his hands—or her hands, if a woman was capable of strangling another woman; I'd have to ask Rafe or Grimaldi about that—or he had taken whatever he'd used with him.

I imagined the scene: Jolynn lounging on the bed, maybe smiling invitingly or else smirking knowingly, depending on how the meeting up until then had gone.

At the foot of the bed stood a man in a suit, and as I watched, he undid the knot in his tie and pulled it slowly from around his neck. I imagined Jolynn's smile widening, as she thought she was getting what she wanted. Until he wrapped the ends of the tie around his hands. And by then it was too late.

"Savannah?" Dix's voice said, and I wrenched my thoughts back to the present with an effort. I hadn't pictured the man's face, but the suit looked an awful lot like something Todd would wear. I had sat across from that suit at dinner a few times.

My brother looked worried. "You OK? You turned pale."

"Fine," I said, forcing a smile. "Just thinking."

"Not about anything good."

No. "I'm worried about Todd." Dix didn't say anything, and I continued. "I trust Grimaldi not to try to pin a murder on him that he didn't do, but he was there that night. And he lied about it. It looks bad."

Dix nodded, his lips tight.

"If he didn't do it, they won't find proof that he did, but if he won't cooperate, they may find enough circumstantial evidence to arrest him anyway."

Dix nodded. "Does Collier know you're doing this?"

"Doing what?" I said. "I'm just talking to my brother. And anyway, he's the one who wanted me to go to Sweetwater."

"But not so you could interfere with his investigation."

"Who's interfering? The more real information we have, the better Grimaldi and the police will be able to determine what really happened."

I looked at him across the table. "How is this affecting the two of you?"

Dix winced, and then tried to pretend he hadn't. "We're fine."

"Sure," I said. "Only, I had dinner with the detective last night. And she seemed annoyed with you."

Dix sighed and closed his eyes. I contemplated him for a moment and then decided to bite the bullet. I'd been wondering for a while, and now might be a good time to put him on the spot. "What's going on with the two of you?"

"We're friends," Dix said, without opening his eyes.

"Is that all?"

He squinted at me. "Isn't it enough?"

"Is it enough for you?"

He closed his eyes again. "My wife died recently."

November. Not that recent.

Then again, if Rafe died, I'd probably grieve for more than seven months.

On the other hand, if I were grieving, I didn't think I'd start hanging out with Todd Satterfield right away, the way Dix had started spending time with Tamara Grimaldi.

That was assuming Todd was around to be hung out with, and not in jail for killing his ex-wife, of course.

And I was getting way off the subject. Again.

"You like her, right?"

"Tamara?" Dix said. "Of course."

"She likes you, too."

"She tell you that?"

"She didn't have to," I said. "I know her. She's upset about the fact that you're on opposite sides on this case."

"Can't be helped," Dix said. "Todd asked me to represent him. I have to."

"But you're not even a criminal lawyer!"

"I'm his best friend. If it goes to trial, he'll get someone else. Someone better." He shook his head. "He knows criminal law better than I do. He'd be more capable of representing himself than I am of representing him. But it's never a good idea to talk to the police without someone to guard your back."

I'd have to remember that.

"I want to talk to him," I said, and Dix opened his eyes wide to stare at me.

"Are you sure that's a good idea, sis?"

No. To be honest, I had rather avoided Todd since Christmas, when Rafe and I worked things out between us. The situation was awkward.

But someone had to impress upon him the necessity of being honest with Grimaldi and with Rafe, and who was in a better position than me? I wasn't on anybody's side. I just wanted the case solved as quickly as possible, with minimal trouble to myself or any of my friends.

And then it occurred to me to wonder whether my brother suspected—or knew—that Todd had kill Jolynn.

I couldn't ask him, though. He wouldn't tell me. Although I would hope, if he did know that such a thing had happened, that he'd make sure I wasn't in any danger.

"Did you ever meet Jolynn?"

Dix nodded. "Sure. I was best man at the wedding."

"You were?" He had always been Todd's best friend, so I guess maybe I shouldn't have been surprised, but... "I wasn't even invited."

"You were busy playing the newlywed game," Dix said. "It was just a few months after you married Bradley. And I'm sure Todd didn't want to watch you cozying up to your husband through the whole ceremony."

He was busy cozying up to Jolynn, so I wasn't sure it mattered, but OK. "What did you think of her?"

"Jolynn?" Dix shrugged. "I hardly ever saw her. They lived in Atlanta, and I don't think Todd brought her home more than a couple times during the year or two they were married."

"Why not?" Atlanta isn't very far away, and Todd had always had a good relationship with his dad, not to mention Dix.

"My opinion?" my brother asked. I nodded. "I think he figured out pretty quickly that he shouldn't have married her. And if he brought her here, the rest of us would be able to tell, as well. Although to be honest, I could have told him that at the wedding."

"That's awful."

Dix shrugged. "It probably wasn't true love for her, either."

Maybe not. Although— "What makes you say that?"

"She wasn't exactly his type, you know? I could see what he saw in her—she was hot, and she looked like you, especially after she lightened her hair—but her background…" He trailed off without finishing the sentence, and for a moment he looked and sounded amazingly like Mother.

"Common as dirt?" I suggested.

He colored. "Something like that."

After a second he added, "Let me guess. Mother's description?"

I nodded. "She said Todd married her because he couldn't have me. I guess she was right."

"Pretty much," Dix agreed.

We sat in silence a few seconds.

"Did you like her?"

"Jolynn? I didn't know her well enough to like or dislike her. I'm not sure any of us did. Maybe not even Todd."

Ouch. I'd never felt sorry for Jolynn before—except for when I'd found her dead, of course, but that was for a totally different reason, and anyway, I hadn't known yet that she was Jolynn then. But now I felt a stirring of pity. Even if she hadn't married Todd because she thought he was Prince Charming, but just because he'd asked, and because he was fairly good-looking and well-off and a lawyer, no woman should have to live with knowing she doesn't measure up in her husband's eyes. I'd dealt with that for the two years I'd been married to Bradley, and I didn't wish it on anyone. Even Jolynn.

It was funny, in a way. She'd probably resented me, assuming she'd known I existed. I was the woman Todd compared her to, and in her place, I would have resented the heck out of me. And all along, unbeknownst to her, I'd been dealing with the same thing she'd been dealing with: the knowledge that my husband found me lacking.

"Do you know anything about the divorce?" I asked Dix. "And what happened afterwards? Did Todd have any contact with Jolynn these days? Did he know what she did for a living?"

Dix hesitated, but I guess he must have decided that this wasn't privileged information, or wasn't incriminating, because he answered the question. "He said he didn't. He said he hadn't seen her since the divorce was final and he moved back here. He gave her a fair settlement, and she agreed not to bother him again. She didn't."

"Until now."

"Right," Dix said.

"I wonder what changed."

Dix didn't answer, and I added, "Something must have. Maybe she needed money. Or maybe something happened. Or maybe she just decided she'd waited long enough."

"Who knows?" Dix said.

"Not me. But I'm sure Rafe will find out. That's what he's in Atlanta for."

Dix leaned back in his seat. "Does he know you're here?"

"In Sweetwater? Of course. It was his idea."

"Here," Dix repeated. "In my office. Asking questions about Todd."

Oh. Um... "No," I admitted. "I didn't tell him I was going to get involved."

"Shit."

It's not a word I often hear from my brother, who was brought up to be a Southern gentleman. And he shot a guilty glance at the door after he said it.

"Afraid Mother is listening at the keyhole?" I asked maliciously.

He sent me a quelling glance. "I have kids. I try to watch what I say."

Couldn't fault him for that. I could only imagine how Mother would react if six-year-old Abigail or four-year-old Hannah suddenly blurted out a resounding 'shit.'

"And anyway," Dix added, "Mother would never stoop to listen at keyholes. That would be unladylike."

Indeed. "She was talking to the sheriff when I left. I was kind of surprised to find him there in the middle of the day. In civvies, too."

Unlike Rafe and Tamara Grimaldi, who always wear civilian clothing, Sheriff Satterfield usually wears his uniform on duty. But not today.

"I think he took the day off," Dix said.

Yeah, I guess it didn't look so good for the sheriff's son to be involved in a murder investigation.

Hell, it didn't look so good for the assistant DA to be involved in a murder investigation, either.

"I assume word got out. How?"

"I don't know," Dix said, sounding disgruntled. "I certainly didn't say anything to anyone. I don't think Todd did."

"He had no reason to." And every reason not to say anything.

"I don't suppose Collier...?"

"I don't suppose he did," I said coldly. "First of all, we went back to Nashville directly from here yesterday afternoon. He didn't have a chance to talk to anyone. And it's not like he has a lot of friends in town he'd gossip with. If he never has to come back to Sweetwater at all, it wouldn't be too soon for him."

Dix nodded.

"I don't know what he said, or might have said, to the people at the District Attorney's office when he went in there looking for Todd, but I doubt he said any more than what was necessary. He isn't the type to talk about other people. So many people have talked about him his whole life that he knows what it's like. And anyway, he's a professional. He doesn't talk about his cases. Usually not even with me."

"Sure," Dix said. "But this is Todd. And given his and Todd's history..."

"He still wouldn't gossip." At least I was fairly certain he wouldn't. If Todd got himself in trouble on his own—as he had—Rafe might secretly rejoice in the fact, although I wasn't even sure of that. And anyway, outwardly, I was pretty sure he'd hide it. "You were there with them yesterday, during the interview. Was Rafe gloating?"

"No," Dix said. "He was professional. Very professional. If anyone was snide, it was Todd."

So the admiration was due to Rafe keeping his temper under trying circumstances, instead of lowering himself to Todd's level. "This is kind of a tough situation for you, isn't it? With your best friend on one side, and your sister's boyfriend on the other. Not to mention your own... um..."

"Yeah," Dix said. "I've been in more comfortable positions. Especially now that I have your boyfriend to look forward to."

"I thought you liked Rafe."

"I like him just fine. But he won't be happy when he figures out what you're up to down here. And he'll want to blame somebody. It'll probably be me, since I'm the head of the family."

I sniffed. "Don't be ridiculous. We're not the mafia. We don't have a head. And he won't blame you. If he blames anyone, it'll be me."

"Make sure that he does," Dix said, "because I have kids counting on me."

"If he damages you, I'm sure Grimaldi will hurt him. You don't have to worry."

Dix didn't answer that, although the tips of his ears turned pink. "I'm having dinner with Todd tonight," he told me instead. "If you're serious about wanting to talk to him, you could join us."

It was tempting. Very tempting. "Where are you going to eat?"

"The Wayside Inn," Dix said.

Of course. The nicest restaurant in Sweetwater, and also where Todd had taken me the night he proposed (and I said no). That particular memory wasn't likely to make things any easier. However...

"He probably wants to talk business, don't you think? Won't it freak him out if I'm there when he walks in?"

Dix allowed as how it might.

"Maybe you could bring him by the house afterwards. For a nightcap or whatnot."

Dix arched his brows at me.

"At least I didn't suggest that you invite him home to see your etchings," I told him. "Tell him it would be better to talk in private. Tell him anything you want. Just bring him by the house. And when you do, I'll be there."

Dix's eyebrows rose again. "How do you plan on making that work, with Mother? You know she'll be all over Todd the second she sees him."

I rolled my eyes. "You don't bring him to the mansion. You bring him to your house."

"You're going to be at my house?"

Sheesh. He was usually quicker on the uptake than this. Or maybe I was confusing him with Rafe, who doesn't need every little detail spelled out for him. "Someone has to babysit your kids, right?"

"I was planning to give them to Catherine," Dix said. "Two more won't bother her."

"Now you don't have to. I'll stay with them until you get home. It makes for a perfect excuse. Just forget, conveniently, to mention it to Todd. That way he won't refuse to go."

Dix promised he wouldn't. He seemed a bit reluctant, or maybe he just wasn't looking forward to the awkwardness of the situation, but he agreed.

"I should let you get back to work," I said, pushing the chair back. "Sorry for taking so much of your time. Is it a busy day for you?"

Dix got to his feet, too. My mother raised a gentleman. "No more than usual. We have enough to do to keep the kids fed."

I wrinkled my brows. "The firm isn't in trouble, is it?"

Dix grinned. "Not at all. You know how it is. Small town. Small client pool. But we're fine."

"You could always marry Tamara Grimaldi. Get a second income."

"If I marry again," Dix said, with rather undue—I thought—emphasis on the first word, "it won't be for the money."

He reached for the doorknob and twisted it, but then seemed to change his mind before actually opening the door. "I'm glad you and Collier are happy together, Savannah."

"Thank you," I said, touched. Outside the door, something made a slithering sound. Or maybe it was just my imagination. If something slithered, it was lost in Dix's next words.

"But stay out of my love life. I'm not ready to get involved again."

"If you have a love life," I said, "you're already involved."

"You know what I mean."

Right. "I just like Tamara Grimaldi," I said. "I never, in a million years, would have put the two of you together, but it works, somehow. But if you're not ready for anything official, that's fine. Take your time. I don't think she's going anywhere. Just try to make sure this thing with Todd doesn't come between you."

"It won't," Dix said. "If you're babysitting, be at the house at six o'clock tonight." He pulled the door open.

I told him I'd be there and passed through into the hallway. If something had slithered past, I didn't see any sign of it. Jonathan's door, on the other side of the hallway, was closed, and I could hear the murmur of his voice through the wood. He either had a client in with him, or was on the phone. And Darcy was sitting where I'd left her, at the desk in the front room. She was on the phone, too, saying things like, "Uh-huh," and "Of course," and "Right away." I gave her a fingerwave on my way past, and headed out into the humidity of the afternoon.

Fourteen

With nothing left to do but wait for evening, I ended up driving down to the Bog, the trailer park where Rafe spent his formative years. I usually end up there at least once every time I visit Sweetwater—except for yesterday, since Rafe had been with me and he only goes there when he absolutely has to.

The truth is, I felt out of sorts. Here I'd been, all gung-ho to prove Todd's innocence, and after just an hour in my hometown, I had exhausted all avenues of investigation.

Dix couldn't talk to me. The sheriff wouldn't talk to me. And I had to wait until tonight to talk to Todd. If Darcy hadn't been on the phone, I might have asked her if she had happened to overhear anything yesterday, after Rafe left, anything Todd and Dix said to one another... but since she'd been on the phone, I couldn't. And she probably hadn't heard anything anyway. And if she had, as an employee of Martin & McCall, she was probably bound by the same confidentiality agreement that Dix was.

So now I had to wait until tonight and see what I could get out of

Todd himself. Which left me with several hours to kill before I had to be at Dix's house to babysit.

The last time I was in Sweetwater, for my ten year high school reunion at the beginning of May, a company named Stonegate Development had, once again, been ready to start developing the Bog. The land had been bought a year ago, slated to become a subdivision of so-called 'affordable'—read non-luxury—housing, but one thing after the other had happened to halt construction. First there'd been LaDonna Collier's death—or murder, as we now knew.

Rafe's mother had died of an overdose in July last year, in her trailer in the Bog, and the sheriff had kept investigating for several weeks after that, before finally concluding, none too happily, that because he couldn't prove it was murder, it must have been an accident.

Then in September, Marquita Johnson's body had been found outside that same trailer, and a week or two later, Jorge Pena was shot inside. By then, the powers that be at Stonegate Development must have decided to give up for the time being. Winter was coming, and I guess maybe it was too late in the year to start breaking ground.

Then, last month, Rafe's old nemesis Billy Scruggs had been shot in LaDonna's old bedroom, just as construction was slated to begin yet again, and things had been pushed back once more while the police strung crime scene tape and went to work.

Not that I'm particularly superstitious, but to be honest, sometimes it felt almost as if the Bog was cursed and that nothing would ever change there.

It was a depressing, gloomy place, the very air itself somehow permeated with despair. When I went there, it was at least partly to shudder at the awfulness of it, and to marvel that Rafe had managed to survive a childhood spent there, in the company of Old Jim Collier, his maternal grandfather.

Today, I expected to find the same rundown, derelict piece of ground with the same decrepit singlewide trailers and leaning clapboard shacks as had been there every other time I'd taken my car down the rutted track that led down from the Pulaski Highway into the trees.

Imagine my surprise when this time, something had actually changed. The trailers and shacks were gone, and the earth had been turned, the ground divided into building lots with stakes and strings. One, two... best as I could tell, twelve of them, in three rows of four.

"Wow!" I stepped on the brakes, quickly enough that I was thrown forward against the seatbelt and then back against the seat. I didn't even notice; I was too busy gawking out the windshield.

Not that it looked particularly good. I mean, there wasn't anything to look at. Not really. It was an empty patch of dirt, a construction zone. Or not even; it was what would become a construction zone once someone got around to actually starting to construct something. But just the fact that the trailers were gone, and the shacks, and with them the miasma of depression and despair that used to overhang the Bog like a raincloud, made an enormous difference. The sun was shining, and although it had probably shone on the Bog before, the light felt different today. Brighter and cleaner. Even the little tributary of the Duck River that runs through the Bog—the one where Old Jim Collier had drowned the year Rafe was twelve—looked a little less sickly and sluggish than it used to. I wouldn't want to dangle my toes in it, but at least it no longer looked like it was carrying the Ebola virus.

It wasn't until now, after I'd had a good look around, gaping at everything, that I realized I wasn't alone. There was a vehicle parked off to the side, a red truck, double-cab, and a man with a clipboard walking through the dirt toward me.

I got out of the car to meet him.

"You can't be here," he began, "this is private—"

He stopped before he got to the word 'property.' I have no idea why. I'd never seen him before, so there was no reason why he'd be struck dumb at the sight of me. I didn't even look that good. By now, I was carrying ten extra pounds in my stomach, in addition to the ten I'd been carrying in my butt before I got pregnant, and by this time of day, most of the gloss had worn off, anyway. My feet hurt, and I was tired.

"I'm sorry," I told him, dredging up my best smile. "My boyfriend grew up here. I just wanted to see what was going on." I extended a hand. "I'm Savannah Martin."

It looked like he hesitated a second before taking it. Or maybe it was just my imagination. "Ronnie Burke."

"Nice to meet you." He squeezed and released; didn't hold on to my hand an uncomfortably long time, but didn't act like he couldn't let go fast enough, either. Although he didn't tell me it was nice to meet me, too.

"I'm sorry, Ms. Martin, but you can't be here. This is a construction zone."

"I can see that," I said. "It looks very different from the last time I was here."

He looked like he would like to physically shove me into my car and push me out of there, but he answered predictably. His mother must also have raised a Southern gentleman. The Burke name was familiar to me, although I'd never come across Ronnie before. He was maybe ten years older than me, stocky and with touches of gray at the temples, so we were too far apart in age to have gone to school together. But there are Burkes all over Maury County. Like the Martins, they're one of the early families. Mother probably knew Ronnie's mother. Who had brought him up not to be rude to a lady. He sighed, but asked, "When was that?"

I smiled brightly. "Last month, when I was here for my high school reunion. I was the one who found Billy Scruggs's body in the Colliers' old trailer."

"Of course." He smiled back, although it looked automatic. "I knew your name was familiar."

"Do you work for Stonegate Development?" Or was he, perhaps, the surveyor or the representative for the county water and sewer authority, looking into the building permits?

"I own Stonegate Development," Ronnie Burke said, and I don't think I imagined the arrogance in his voice.

I resisted the temptation to tell him that that was certainly nice for him. A gentleman shouldn't brag, no, but a lady shouldn't be rude, either. I smiled instead. "I'm a real estate agent. Maybe you could keep me in mind if you need someone to list the houses you're building." I dug a business card out of my purse and handed it to him.

"My fiancée is a realtor," Ronnie said, but pocketed it. "Who do you work for?"

If he'd just looked at the card before shoving it in his pocket, he would have known the answer to that already, but I didn't mind telling him. I fudged the truth a little, though, and pretended I still worked for Lamont, Briggs & Associates. Then I told him I also do property management for the Fifth and Main condo development, although I hadn't started yet. "But I grew up in Sweetwater. And my boyfriend grew up right here in the Bog. I know the area well."

"You mentioned that," Ronnie nodded. "Who's your boyfriend?"

I had thought everyone in town knew who I was and that I was slumming with Rafe Collier. Guess not.

I watched Ronnie Burke's face closely when I told him who I was shacking up with, but his expression didn't change. He just nodded. "I know the name. He's in law enforcement of some kind, right?"

"As a matter of fact, he is." And color me surprised. Most people in Sweetwater prefer to cling to the belief that Rafe's a criminal, even after it's been proven, conclusively, that he's not. Point to Ronnie for acknowledging the truth. "He works for the Tennessee Bureau of Investigations."

Ronnie nodded. "Wasn't he here recently?"

"Yesterday. And last month, when Billy Scruggs died." Since he and Billy had had a set-to thirteen years ago, one that had left Billy with a taste for prescription drugs and sent Rafe to prison for two years, Sheriff Satterfield had, quite naturally, wanted to talk to him about the murder.

"Thought I caught a glimpse of him yesterday," Ronnie said.

"You may have." Although if he had, I hadn't seen him. Ronnie, I mean. "Do you know Rafe?"

"Just to look at," Ronnie said. "Like everyone else in town."

Right. I suppressed a grimace.

"I thought I saw him at the law office on the square. That's your family's business, right?"

"My brother and brother-in-law." And if he'd been hanging out on the square yesterday afternoon, I hadn't seen him. Then again, I hadn't been looking for him, either.

"Driving my mother around," Ronnie said with a grin. "Shopping and tea."

So maybe the lady who had been in Audrey's boutique yesterday was Ronnie's mother. She'd been the right age, anyway. Older than Audrey and Mother, but then Ronnie was older than me. Older than Dix and Catherine, too.

"Tell your boyfriend good luck with the investigation," Ronnie said, winding up the conversation and nudging me on my way without actually telling me I needed to leave.

I told him I would, and accepted defeat. "I guess I should go. It was nice to meet you. Keep me in mind if you need a realtor."

Ronnie said he'd do that, and I got back into the Volvo, did a sixteen point turn in the dirt, and headed back up the gravel road past the sign that said *Future Home of Mallard Meadows, Homes from the $180s.*

BY THE TIME I GOT BACK to the mansion, the sheriff was long gone. Mother was still there, though, sitting at the counter in the kitchen with a glass of Chardonnay, leafing through a magazine. I wasn't sure what to think when I saw that it was a wedding magazine, full of women in white dresses with poufs of tulle and rhinestone tiaras on their heads.

I stopped, staring. I could choose to ignore it, of course, but it was right there; kind of hard to overlook. Or I could make a comment. But what would I say? And who knew what would happen if I asked what my mother was doing?

Mother looked up, and saw me eyeing the magazine. She closed it and slid it into a drawer in the island. "Hello, darling."

"Hello," I said, watching the glossy cover disappear.

Mother shut the drawer with a definite click and waited for me to meet her eyes. When I did, her face gave nothing away. I opened my mouth, and then thought better of it. What if she told me that she was planning my wedding to Rafe? I'd probably fall down in a dead faint.

Or worse, what if she said that the sheriff had proposed, and she was planning her own wedding? Todd and I would be half-siblings, which would be beyond awkward.

No, much better not to know.

I pulled out a stool and seated myself. "Did the sheriff leave?"

"At least an hour ago," Mother said primly. I guess she wanted me to know that they hadn't had time to get up to any hanky-panky in the time between when I left and when the sheriff did.

"It was nice to see him." The sheriff and I had had a strained relationship for a while, since Bob Satterfield naturally wasn't happy that I had turned down his son's offer of marriage. When a son proposes, his father likes to see things work out. And the fact that I chose to get involved with Rafe, of all people, only added insult to injury. The sheriff had spent thirty years firmly convinced that Rafe was up to no good, and that he was responsible for anything that went wrong anywhere in Maury County. It wasn't until the reunion, just a few weeks ago, that they'd finally seemed to work things out. The sheriff had even apologized for the way he'd treated Rafe all these years.

Of course, this new development wasn't likely to help. And I couldn't expect the sheriff to side with Rafe against his own son, even when the evidence against Todd—if largely circumstantial—was so compelling.

"I won't be around for dinner tonight," I said. "I'm babysitting for Dix. He and Todd are going somewhere."

Mother nodded.

"You met his wife, right? Jolynn?"

"At the wedding," Mother said.

"What did you think of her?"

Mother sniffed. "No better than she ought to be."

My jaw dropped, and I had to hike it up quickly. "She's dead!" And we all know you aren't supposed to speak ill of the dead.

"That doesn't change the fact that she was common as dirt," my mother said tartly. And added, piously, "Bless her heart."

Fat lot of good my mother's blessing did now. "What about her gave you the idea that she was no better than she ought to be?"

Not that I needed confirmation of that, I suppose, considering how she'd died.

"It was obvious," Mother said. "She got drunk at her own wedding reception, can you imagine? And her dress... you can't even begin to imagine what it looked like! Strapless, and cut up to there...!"

It sounded modern. Sexy, even. While I'd gotten married in the approved hoop-skirted monstrosity so voluminous I'd only barely managed to squeeze through the double doors into the church. I swear my dress kept knocking the flower arrangements off the ends of the pews as I headed down the aisle.

Would Rafe want a church wedding when we got married?

He had proposed, just about a month ago—in front of my mother and the sheriff, no less. So he did want to marry me, and had made it official. But would he want to marry me in a church, or would he prefer less hoopla and a quick stop at the county clerk's office?

It would be my second marriage, and a big church wedding with the white dress and veil is considered tacky the second time. Especially when the bride is visibly pregnant.

On the other hand, it would be Rafe's first time, and if he wanted the church and the gown and the tuxedo and the wedding march, how could I refuse?

I'd hear about it for the rest of my life, of course, whenever Mother decided to throw in my face how I had disgraced her in front of the whole town, but it would be worth it if it made Rafe happy. And considering that I'd married Bradley in front of God and all of Sweetwater, how could I do less when I married Rafe? If there was any justice in the world, I should be marrying him on satellite television, so the whole world could see what I was doing.

"Darling?" Mother said, a little wrinkle between her brows.

"I'm fine." I smiled to prove it. "Just distracted."

She didn't look convinced, but she also didn't argue. "Can you tell me more about what's going on, darling? With Todd and Rafael and everything?"

I blinked. She sounded almost humble, a rarity for my mother. And because she did, and because she'd used Rafe's name without being prompted, I answered more nicely than I might have otherwise. "I don't know everything, but I'll tell you what I can."

"Please."

OK, then. "It all started when I moved into Mrs. Jenkins's house with Rafe. I still had my apartment for another couple of months, and rather than letting it sit empty, I decided to try to make a little bit of extra money renting it out. Short term B&Bs are very popular right now—Nashville hotels are fully booked most of the time, so individuals with room to spare pick up the slack—and I figured it made sense to try. So I've been advertising the apartment for daily and weekly rentals on various websites."

I went on to describe some of the people who had stayed with me—the legitimate ones; I left out Shauna Bangs—and then explained about Jocelyn, or Jolynn. "I had no idea who she was. It didn't even cross my mind. Why would it? She said she was coming in for a job interview, and I had no reason to doubt her."

"You didn't recognize her?"

"I never saw her," I said. "Not until I found her dead on Sunday morning. And anyway, I wasn't invited to Todd's wedding."

Mother let that one pass without comment. Good of her.

"None of us knew who she was. Rafe called Detective Grimaldi with the Nashville PD—the same detective who handled Sheila's case, remember?—and she found out that the victim's name was Jocelyn Rivera, but I still didn't put it together with Jolynn. And then, on Monday morning, Liz, the new agent in my office, told me that my sister had stopped by to see me on Saturday morning."

"Catherine?"

"I checked. She said she hadn't been in Nashville this weekend."

Mother shook her head.

"So we discovered that someone had used my computer and my email program to send a message to Todd, asking him to come see me on Saturday night. And that's why Rafe came to Sweetwater yesterday, to talk to Todd."

Mother was quiet for a moment after that. "And—?" she said eventually.

"Todd denied going there. He said he had other plans Saturday night."

"And he might have," Mother said. "You can't expect him to sit around and wait for you forever, Savannah."

"Of course not." In fact, he could stop waiting for me anytime he wanted. "If he had other plans, he ditched them, though. One of my neighbors saw him."

Mother had no response to that.

"For what it's worth," I said, "I don't think he killed Jolynn. I don't think he had a reason to kill her. Even if she fooled him into thinking she was me, and made him come all the way to Nashville under false pretenses. Normal, sane people don't kill other people over something like that. But he also isn't helping himself by lying about it."

"Perhaps he feels your boyfriend can't be trusted to conduct a fair investigation," Mother suggested. A bit pointedly, I thought.

"Then he's wrong. Rafe's been accused of things his whole life that he didn't do. He won't do that to someone else."

And besides, he'd know that everyone would suspect him of wanting to railroad Todd, so he'd make doubly sure he didn't. If he ended up arresting Todd—with the proper arrest warrant, of course—it would be because a judge thought there was enough evidence to sustain the arrest. It wouldn't be because Rafe wanted to take Todd down a peg or two.

Mother didn't look convinced. "Do the police have any other suspects?"

Good question. If they did, Grimaldi hadn't shared the information with me. I hadn't asked, either. It hadn't occurred to me to ask. But— "They seem to be focusing on Todd. Once he comes clean and tells the truth, they'll be able to focus on other people."

"What other people?" Mother wanted to know.

I told her my theory that Jolynn had met someone earlier on Saturday, and had taken that someone back to my apartment, and then that someone had killed her and walked off with the camera that could prove he'd committed murder. Mother seemed to like the idea.

"How do we find out who it was?"

"Detective Grimaldi's looking into it," I said. "They've been interviewing my neighbors, and trying to figure out how Jolynn spent the rest of the time she was in Nashville. I'm sure they're going through her phone records and credit card receipts and putting together a timeline. And then they'll be talking to the people in the places she went to see if anyone remembers her." Similar to what Rafe was doing in Atlanta, tracing Jolynn's life prior to going to Nashville. Police work can be very tedious at times.

I scooted back off the stool. "If you don't mind, I think I'll go lie down for a bit before I have to go to Dix's house."

"Of course, darling." Mother glanced at my stomach. I waited to see whether she'd ask me any questions about it—*I hope everything is going well, darling?*—but when she didn't, I headed down the hall and up the stairs. And although I tried not to feel resentful at my mother's lack of interest in my pregnancy, I couldn't help but feel a little hurt.

Sure, she had grandchildren from before: two from Dix and three from Catherine. It wasn't like this was her first, or even anything especially new or exciting. And it was Rafe's baby, which I'm sure didn't make her happy. But I'd had two miscarriages already. Surely it had crossed her mind that I might have a third. Shouldn't she be just a little bit worried?

Unless, in her heart of hearts, she was hoping I'd lose this baby, too.

Not maliciously, of course—my mother loves me—but because she truly believes she knows what's best for me, and having Rafe's baby doesn't fall into that category.

I put a protective hand over my stomach as I reached the top of the stairs and headed down the hallway to my room.

Fifteen

By the time I reached his house in the Copper Creek subdivision, Dix was ready to go. "The girls are eating," he told me. "Cheese sandwiches."

I nodded, and watched as he brushed past me toward the door.

"After they eat, they can watch TV or play. Abigail may have some homework, although I asked and she said she was finished."

"OK."

"They can have dessert if they want. We have fruit, and ice cream, and Oreo cookies."

I nodded.

"They get one," Dix said. "Not all three."

"Of course not." I tried to look like I hadn't considered the idea of mixing the Oreos with the ice cream.

"They go to bed at nine," Dix added, "if I'm not back."

"I know that," I told him. "It isn't the first time I've babysat your kids. Do you expect to be late?"

"That depends on how easy it is to talk Todd into coming over,"

Dix said grimly. "If he wants to sit at the Wayside Inn drowning his sorrows all night, there isn't much I can do about it."

I lowered my voice. "He doesn't have a drinking problem, does he?" I'd never noticed one—when we'd gone to dinner together, he'd always stopped after a glass or two of red wine—but I suppose under the circumstances, a man might be excused for having a little extra to drink.

"Not usually," Dix said. "At the moment, who knows?"

"Just do your best. If you can't get him over here so I can talk to him, try to convince him to talk to Rafe."

Dix looked at me.

"Or Grimaldi. Get him to talk to Grimaldi."

"I'll try," Dix said, but not like he felt very positive about the outcome.

He headed out, and I headed into the kitchen to the girls.

Dix has two: Abigail, who's six, and Hannah, who's four. They're two little tow-headed blondes, like both their parents. I could see Dix in their faces, but I could see Sheila, too, in the pointy little noses and rosebud mouths.

It had been hard for them when she died. Hannah, especially, had regressed back into sucking her thumb and refusing to speak. Even Mother had been worried. They were doing better now, though. They still missed Sheila, of course, but they'd come to terms with the fact that she was in Heaven with Jesus, and not down here with them.

They were adorable, sitting side by side at the table in the kitchen nook, with their cheese sandwiches and bowls of tomato soup. One curly head—Hannah's—and one straight. The curls must be coming from the Martin side of the family, because Sheila's hair had been straight as water, a sleek pageboy. Mine's wavy, though, and Catherine's kinky and curly, a legacy of our great-great-a-few-times-more-great grandfather William, who was born during the War Between the States, a product of great-great-etc-grandmother Caroline's affair with one of the grooms while her husband, the current Martin, was off defending the slavery and the old Southern way of living.

My baby would look nothing like this. He or she would have Rafe's dark hair and eyes, and darker skin than mine. Although he, or she, would probably have curly hair. Rafe's hair wasn't straight, nor was mine, and anyway, Rafe's son David—Elspeth's son, too—had curly hair and skin the color of *café au lait*. He looked so much like Rafe at that age it was a bit scary.

Not that I'd known Rafe at that age. David was thirteen. At thirteen, Rafe had been living in the Bog and going to the middle school on the south side of town. I'd been ten and going to the middle school on the north side of town. It wasn't until four years later that we'd ended up at Columbia High together for a year, until Rafe graduated and then went off to prison.

But I digress. I looked at Dix's girls and thought about the baby growing inside my stomach. Mother adored the girls. She liked Catherine and Jonathan's three kids, too: Robert, Annie and Cole. But would she like mine? Or would she hold the baby's skin color, and who his or her father was, against him or her?

"Are you sick, Aunt Savannah?" Hannah asked.

I blinked and focused on her. "No. Why?"

"You're holding your tummy." She pointed down the hall to the half bath. "The bathroom is that way. I had to throw up last week."

"Thank you," I said, dropping my hand and sliding onto the bench next to her. "But I'm fine. I'm sorry you had to throw up, though."

Hannah shrugged and spooned up more soup. "I ate too much candy," she informed me.

Ah. "I didn't eat too much of anything." In fact, I hadn't had dinner yet. And I was starting to get hungry. "I don't have to throw up. But thanks."

"Are you having a baby, Aunt Savannah?" Abigail wanted to know.

Oh. Um... We'd originally planned to keep quiet about it until the first trimester was safely over, just in case something went wrong, but when I was down here at the beginning of May, someone had figured it out, so the cat had slipped out of the bag a little early. "Did your daddy tell you that?"

Abigail shook her head. "Kayla's mom's having a baby. She throws up a lot."

"Is Kayla one of your friends from school?"

She nodded.

"Yes," I said, "I'm having a baby."

"Kayla's mom's having a baby boy," Abigail said. "What are you having, Aunt Savannah?"

"I don't know yet," I told her. "It's too soon to tell. Another month, maybe. By the Fourth of July picnic, I might know what kind of baby it is."

"I'd like a puppy," Hannah said.

"A puppy would be nice," I agreed. "You could talk to your daddy about that."

"What's the baby's name?" Abigail asked.

"I don't know that, either. We haven't talked about it yet." I had an idea, but I didn't know whether Rafe would go for it. He probably had his own ideas. And he'd been deprived of any say at all in David's birth, name, and everything else.

"I like Max," Hannah said.

For a dog. Although I guess it would make an OK name for a boy, too. Or a girl, if it happened to be short for Maxine. Not that I planned to name a girl Maxine. Or a boy, for that matter.

"Max is nice," I said diplomatically.

"I like Tommy," Abigail said.

"Tommy's good." Although for some reason I didn't think my kid would turn out to look like his name should be Tommy.

"I'm finished, Aunt Savannah," Hannah said. "Can I go play?"

"Sure."

She squirmed off the chair and disappeared. Abigail slurped a bit more soup and then put her spoon down. "I'm finished, too. Can I go watch TV?"

"Your dad said you could. Just don't watch anything inappropriate."

She rolled her eyes and walked off. I stared after her. Eye-rolling at six? Surely that was a bit young to start with the teenage drama?

But they were Dix's kids, not mine, so if she rolled her eyes at him, I'd let him deal with it. I busied myself cleaning up after dinner instead, and pouring myself the bowl of tomato soup that was left in the pot on the stove. I paired it with some crackers I found in the cabinet, and a glass of milk from the fridge. Calcium is important for healthy bones, and a healthy baby.

I ended up on the floor with Hannah for a while, playing veterinarian. She really did seem serious about wanting that puppy. And then both of us ended up in the bonus room with Abigail, watching the latest Disney movie to be released on DVD.

It was fun to see how different they were. Both of them looked like the other, and looked like a combination of Dix and Sheila. But where Abigail was all girl, excited about the pretty princess and handsome hero, Hannah liked the reindeer and the animated snowman.

My stomach did a little flip, and I put a hand on it. Wonder what my baby would be like? A girly-girl, like me, or a tomboy, like her father? Or a smaller version of David, hooked on basketball, video games, and bicycling?

Whatever he or she turned out to be, I made a vow then and there to let him or her develop into the person they were intended to be. I'd spent too many years trying to live up to my mother's expectations of what a Southern Belle should be, and I was damned if I'd lay those kinds of pressures on my own child. If I had a boy, I'd do my best to teach him to be a gentleman, to respect women and to treat them well, but I'd make sure he knew not to wrap them in cotton wool and protect them to such a degree that they never got to do anything. And if a girl, I'd make damn sure she knew that she could be anything, and do anything, and we'd support her, no matter what it was.

Within reason, of course—her father would crack down on anything illegal. But apart from that, anything she wanted to be or do, was fine with me. If my daughter wanted to be a welder, or the first woman to walk on Mars, she could do it with my blessing.

Dix wasn't back by the time nine o'clock rolled around, so I coaxed the girls into pajamas and into bed. Tomorrow was a school day, so they couldn't stay up extra late, even if I was there instead of their dad. I promised I'd have him stop in and kiss them when he came home, and they went off to bed, if reluctantly. When I checked on them twenty minutes later, Abigail was sound asleep. Hannah was wide awake, waiting for her daddy.

"You'll be tired tomorrow if you don't go to sleep now," I told her. "I'll make sure your dad comes in and says goodnight when he comes home."

She nodded and closed her eyes, but I'm sure, as soon as I shut the door behind me, they were wide open again.

If I had a little girl, would she lie awake until Rafe came home from work to kiss her goodnight?

Would she like him better than me?

And if she did, did it matter? If anyone deserved the unconditional love of a baby, after not being part of his son's life for twelve years, it was Rafe. If we had a girl, and she turned out to be a daddy's girl, I could live with that.

I HEARD THE BUZZ OF THE garage door a few minutes before ten. Then I heard Dix's car drive inside, and the buzz of the garage door closing again behind him. A minute later, the door from the garage to the kitchen opened. "Sorry I'm late," my brother said.

"It's no problem. Abigail's asleep. Hannah's probably still awake."

"I'll go up and see her." He headed up the stairs without another word. I began the process of cleaning up my ice cream dish—dairy is an important component in making a baby!—and prepared to leave.

"I guess you weren't successful in convincing Todd to talk to me," I said when Dix came back into the kitchen again.

He sighed, and slumped onto one of the stools at the breakfast bar. "I tried. He told me you're the last person he wants to see."

Ouch. "I'm trying to help him!" I said.

He ran a hand down his face. "I know that. I think even he knows that. He just can't face you right now."

"That's ridiculous," I told him. "I'm on his side."

"Sure. But you also found his ex-wife naked and dead in your bed."

Well, yes. "Did he tell you she was naked? How did he know?" That tidbit of information hadn't been on the news, had it?

"That's privileged information," Dix said.

"He admitted he was there, didn't he? He wouldn't have known she was naked otherwise." Unless it was just a good guess, of course. Prostitutes spend a lot of time naked, I suppose. "Did you talk him into telling Grimaldi? It looks worse for him if he won't admit it."

"I tried," Dix said. "I don't think I succeeded."

"He's being stupid. They'll arrest him."

"Not without evidence."

"There's enough circumstantial evidence to make a case."

"Tamara won't arrest him until she's sure," Dix said. "By then, maybe another suspect will have come along."

I put my hands on my hips. "Like who? If it was random, just some guy she picked up along the way, the police might have a hard time tracking him down. While they know just who and where Todd is."

Dix shook his head. "I tried, Savannah. I swear. But he doesn't trust Collier, and I can't say I blame him, and he doesn't know Tamara, and he's scared. He knows how bad it looks. But he's afraid that if they know he was there, they'll arrest him. He thinks the only reason they haven't, is because they can't prove that he was."

"They can prove that he was! Or at least they have Mr. Sullivan willing to swear to it." I shook my head. "Where did he spend Saturday night, anyway? Surely not in my apartment with the corpse?"

"He said he was driving around," Dix said.

"For twelve hours?"

He shrugged.

"I'm going to have to talk to him myself."

"Not tonight," Dix said.

No, I wouldn't go to Todd's house at ten-thirty at night. That wouldn't be a good idea. "Is he working? Or has he taken time off?"

"He's working," Dix said. "He's working on a big case and getting very close to filing an indictment. He said it's keeping him busy, and besides, he hasn't been charged with anything, so he doesn't have to take a leave of absence."

"Good." Then I'd know where to find him in the morning.

"Have you spoken to Collier?" my brother wanted to know.

"Um... not recently. Not tonight."

I'd been feeling too guilty, to be honest. I'm a poor liar, and I know he can see right through me—even from several hours away. He'd hear it in my voice that something was going on. And since I'm not good at keeping secrets from him, he'd soon worm exactly what was going on out of me. And then he'd be upset that I was getting involved in the case and putting myself in danger—as he'd see it—by meeting Todd. Especially after he told me not to.

No, much safer to keep everything to myself.

"Aren't you curious what he's found out?"

Of course I was. But I couldn't call without tipping him off to what I was doing—or planning to do.

"Won't he think it's strange that you're not calling?" Dix asked.

He probably would. I'm usually more on the clingy side. But— "I'll call him when I get home. Back to the mansion. He might still be working."

"It's after ten o'clock at night," Dix said.

"If he was finished for the night, he'd be calling me. If he isn't calling, that means he's still busy and hasn't had time to think."

Dix nodded.

"I'll talk to you tomorrow," I said. "Thanks for trying to talk sense into Todd."

"He's my friend, too. I don't want anything to happen to him." He walked me to the door.

"Hopefully nothing will." I took my leave and headed home.

When I got back to the mansion, Mother was still up, watching the late news. "Anything new?" I wanted to know.

Her lips were so tight that the words sounded as if they were squeezed out between two rocks. "The police are getting closer to making an arrest."

Uh-oh. "Did they say who they'll be arresting?"

Mother shook her head.

"I'm going up to bed," I said.

She nodded and turned her attention back to the screen.

RAFE DIDN'T ANSWER WHEN I called, by which I deduced that I had told Dix the truth, and he was still working in spite of the late hour. This was confirmed ten minutes later, when he called back.

"Evening, darlin'."

"Evening," I said, listening to the buzz of voices behind him. "Bar?"

He chuckled. "Can't put much past you, can I? You home and in bed?"

"In bed, in my room in the mansion. I miss you."

"I miss you too, darlin'. We've had some fun in that bed."

Yes, we had. But I hadn't called to talk about that. "How's it going? Are you finding out anything?"

He sighed. "A lot of nothing so far. It don't seem like she had any contact with Satterfield in the couple years since they broke up.

Everyone says she was OK with it. Not happy that he dumped her, but tired of feeling like she didn't measure up."

I could relate. I hadn't been happy when Bradley informed me he wanted a divorce, either. But at least I knew it meant that I wouldn't have to deal with him and his disapproval every day anymore.

"Did you figure out when she came to Nashville?" Thursday, like she'd said? Or earlier?

"Friday," Rafe said.

Friday? "She booked the apartment from Thursday."

"I guess she changed her mind."

Maybe so. But... "Are you sure?"

"The doorman saw her walk out Friday morning around ten. With an overnight bag."

That seemed pretty conclusive, then. "So who was there on Thursday?"

"Nobody," Rafe said.

"Shannon Duncan told me she saw Jolynn—or someone she thought was Jolynn, except obviously it wasn't Jolynn—leaving the apartment Thursday night."

"No kidding?"

I shook my head. "She said hello, and Jolynn—or whoever it was—said hello and that she'd rented my apartment for the weekend. She got into a car—a dark SUV—with a man who might have had middling to fair hair and might have been in his thirties."

"Satterfield?"

"Don't know," I said. "I guess someone will have to find out where Todd was on Thursday night. I'll ask around tomorrow."

"You're being careful, right?"

"Of course. So far, I've seen my mother and the sheriff, Dix, Abigail and Hannah. Oh, and the guy who owns Stonegate Development." I'd forgotten all about him until now. "They've pulled all the trailers out of the Bog. And razed the shacks. They're starting to build next week."

"Good," Rafe said. "The sooner that place turns into something else, the better."

"Other than that, I haven't seen anyone." Except Darcy, Dix's receptionist.

"Satterfield hasn't come knocking to explain himself?"

"He doesn't seem to want to talk to me," I said. "He and Dix had dinner. I took care of Abigail and Hannah while Dix was gone. I told him to bring Todd back to the house if he wanted to talk, so I could convince him to come clean with you and Grimaldi. But Dix said he didn't want to see me."

"Good," Rafe said. "I don't want him looking at you, either."

"He won't hurt me."

"That ain't what I'm afraid of," Rafe said.

"What? You think I'm suddenly going to decide I like him better than you, and leave you for him?"

He didn't answer, so maybe that really was what he was thinking. Ridiculous, if so. Not even worthy of comment.

"The news said the police are getting closer to making an arrest," I said. "Are they talking about Todd?"

"I imagine they are." He didn't sound upset about it.

"You haven't spoken to Grimaldi?"

"Not since this afternoon. She's busy, too."

Right. "So what are you doing tomorrow?"

"More of the same," Rafe said with sigh. "You?"

"More of the same, as well. Eating, sleeping, relaxing." Bearding Todd in his den at the DA's office. But Rafe didn't need to know that.

The smile was back in his voice. "Don't do anything I wouldn't do."

"Of course not."

"Baby OK?"

"Seems to be," I said, probing inward. "Everything feels the same."

"Make sure you get enough sleep."

I promised I would. "I'll call you tomorrow morning. How much longer do you think you'll be down there?"

"Tomorrow, at least. I got an appointment with the service Jolynn was working for. They wanted to lawyer up before they talked to me, so I had to wait."

Made sense. "Is it legal to run an escort service?"

"As long as they don't facilitate prostitution," Rafe said.

"Isn't that what an escort service does?"

"Not on paper. On paper they provide escorts for events."

Of course they did. "So what kind of event was Jolynn hired for in Nashville?"

"I'll tell you tomorrow," Rafe said, "when they tell me."

"I guess that's it, then."

"Yep. Sleep tight, darlin'. Dream of me."

"Always," I said, and hung up the phone.

Sixteen

It was past nine-thirty when I stumbled into the kitchen the next morning, with my eyes still at half mast and my hair looking like birds had nested in it overnight. Mother was back at the counter, sipping coffee and making her way through that same bridal magazine as yesterday. She looked up when she heard me come in, and frowned. "Darling…"

As always, she looked like she'd come straight from the day spa. Her hair was perfect, champagne colored and sleek; her makeup was elegantly understated, and she was dressed in a gorgeous raw silk dress that had Audrey's Boutique written all over it. Her toes, peeking out of a pair of slingback sandals, were freshly manicured in a melon shade.

"You look great," I said, dropping down on a chair and closing my eyes, knowing I looked anything but.

"Thank you, darling," Mother's voice said. "Is everything all right?"

"Fine." I didn't bother opening my eyes. It would take too much effort. "Just a pregnancy thing. I sleep a lot."

Mother didn't respond to that, but I heard the sounds of the bridal magazine disappearing into the drawer. "Are you getting remarried?" I asked.

"Of course not, darling." She sounded funny.

"Is someone else getting married?" Not Dix, or I would have heard about it. Catherine and Jonathan were already married. And Mother wouldn't be planning my wedding to Rafe. Especially not from a bridal magazine. If anything, she'd be looking into the most unobtrusive instant wedding chapel in the state, as far away from Sweetwater as it was possible to get.

"No one you know, dear. A friend has rented the mansion and grounds for her son's wedding next month."

Ah. Nothing personal, then. And since I'd been pretty sure of that, there was no reason why a little part of me should be disappointed.

"Coffee?" Mother asked brightly.

"No. Thank you. Pregnant."

"Some orange juice, then." I could hear her slide off the stool and then the clicking of her heels on the floor.

"Milk. Please. The juice is too acidy."

"Heartburn?" Mother said, accompanied by the sound of the fridge door opening.

"Uh-huh."

"They say that means the baby will have a full head of hair." I heard her rummage.

Considering that the baby was roughly the size of a kiwi at the moment, and probably didn't have any hair at all, it seemed a bit early for a pronouncement like that, but what did I know?

"Did I have hair when I was born?"

"No," Mother said. "You and Dix both had just peach fuzz. Catherine was the one with the hair."

"She takes after the Martins." Including great-great-great-etc-grandma Caroline and her son William, the child of the groom. All of them with thick dark hair.

But according to my Aunt Regina, my mother didn't know about that, and I was keeping it in reserve for sometime when she was giving me a hard time about marrying Rafe. At the moment, she was almost pleasant, so now clearly wasn't the right time to say anything. I'd leave it for sometime when she wasn't being nice.

"Here you go, dear." She put a glass of milk in front of me. It clicked against the granite.

"Thank you." I lifted it and took a sip.

"I'm going to lunch with Audrey in a couple of hours." She slithered up onto the stool again. "You're welcome to come along, if you'd like."

"Oh." I had thought I might go to Columbia this morning, to corner Todd. But it was nice of her to invite me. And I could always see Todd in the afternoon instead. "Sure. Why not?"

"Wonderful," Mother said. "We'll be leaving at eleven."

"I'll be ready." And since getting ready—not to mention presentable—would take some doing when I looked like I'd been dragged backwards through a hedge, I excused myself and headed upstairs to get started.

A leisurely bubble bath came first, and while I waited for my hair to dry into loose curls, I called Atlanta, and caught Rafe on his way to Jolynn's workplace. Or the place that put Jolynn to work.

"Are you hoping to find anything exciting?" I wanted to know.

"No," Rafe said, "but it still needs doing." After a second, he added, "If I get lucky, maybe I'll find out if going to Nashville to meet Satterfield was her idea, or his idea, or if somebody else hired her and sent her up there."

"Who would that be? And what do you mean, *his* idea? Todd wouldn't do that."

"Someone knew your place was empty and available," Rafe said. "I don't believe Jolynn just happened to come across it when she was looking for somewhere to stay in Nashville. Whoever suggested that she make a trip there, probably suggested the apartment, too."

"So someone told her about it."

"I don't see how else she could have known," Rafe said. I could hear traffic noises in the background, the humming of cars and the occasional blasting of horns. "Too much of a coincidence otherwise."

"That takes Todd out, though. I didn't tell him. I haven't spoken to Todd for months."

"Did you tell your brother? He mighta told Satterfield."

I thought back. "I'm not sure I did. It was none of Dix's business."

"Somebody knew," Rafe said. "I mighta mentioned something to Tammy, and she mighta told your brother, and your brother mighta told Satterfield."

"I suppose." It was possible, if a bit convoluted. But it wasn't important enough to argue over. Especially as I could hear an edge creeping into his voice. "I'm going out to lunch with my mother and Audrey in an hour."

"Good for you," Rafe said, in a tone of voice which expressed, eloquently, how happy he was that the invitation hadn't extended to him. Not that it would have. If he'd been in Sweetwater, Mother wouldn't have asked me to join her.

"I just came out of the tub. Now I'm waiting for my hair to dry."

"Uh-huh," Rafe said. "What're you wearing?"

I looked down at myself. "Panties and a bra." Since I hadn't gotten around to picking out a dress yet.

"Lace?"

As a matter of fact. He made an appreciative little sound, and I asked, "What are you wearing."

"Too much." But there was amusement in his voice, so I wasn't too worried.

"Any chance you'll be back tonight?"

"A chance, but I wouldn't count on it. Tomorrow, though. Prob'ly."

"Guess we'll have to wait until then."

"I'll call you tonight," Rafe said. "At least we can have phone sex."

"We can have phone sex right now." I wasn't doing anything else, and it would help to pass the time until my hair was dry.

"No, we can't. I gotta leave the car in a minute, and I ain't stepping out in front of the Atlanta PD looking like my pants are too tight."

No, I could see where he might not want to do that. "Tonight, then."

"It's a date. Take care of my baby."

I promised I would, and hung up. Bless his heart, and his libido: talking to him never failed to make me feel sexy and desirable—and loved—even with my stomach sticking out above the waistband of the lavender panties and below the matching bra.

It wasn't hard yet. The stomach, I mean. With the baby inside still so tiny, I guess I shouldn't be surprised. But I was definitely getting bigger around the middle. My skirts and pants—the ones with buttons and zippers—were all pinching.

Sliding off the bed, I padded over to the mirror and examined myself, twisting from front to side and back.

My stomach was rounder than it used to be. You're not supposed to gain a lot of weight in the first trimester—and with the morning sickness, you aren't likely to—but I'd managed to pack on a few pounds. I didn't look pregnant, though. I looked puffy, as if someone had stuck an air pump in my belly button and given a few squeezes.

I stuck my tongue out at my reflection and went to find a dress that would minimize the effect. It's better not to take any chances around my mother. Being pregnant is no excuse for looking frumpy.

I drove the Volvo into town to meet Audrey, with Mother in the passenger seat. My plan was to go straight to Columbia after lunch, to see if I could corner Todd. Naturally I didn't tell Mother that, but I made sure she knew I might not be able to drive her back to the mansion after we ate. She informed me that she'd get Audrey, Dix, or Jonathan to do so.

When Audrey and Mother meet for lunch, they always go to the Café on the Square, halfway between Audrey's boutique and Dix's office. I prepared myself to eat salad, since that's what ladies who lunch do. The Café on the Square has some lovely rolls, though, moist and dripping with butter, and I ignored Mother's frown for long enough to stuff two in my mouth.

Not at the same time, naturally.

"Eating for two," I reminded her when I'd swallowed.

"That's no excuse to get fat, darling."

"I'm not fat. I'm pregnant." I liberated a third roll from the basket and put it on my plate. For later.

Mother didn't respond, just looked up. "There's Frances." She lifted a hand.

"Who?" I looked over my shoulder. In time to see the lady from Audrey's shop two days ago pause inside the door to look around. "Frances... Burke?"

Mother sent me a surprised look, in the process of waving Frances down.

"How do you know Frances?" Audrey wanted to know.

"I saw her in your store the other day. And I ran into her son in the Bog yesterday."

"He's a land developer," Audrey nodded. "His mother has leased the mansion for the wedding next month."

"So it's Ronnie who's getting married?"

"He's the last Burke," Mother told me, as Frances made her way toward us, edging around the glass-topped tables. "Of course, he's been married before..."

And that was all she had time for before Frances reached us and slid onto the chair directly opposite me. "Margaret Anne. Audrey." She air-kissed them both before facing me. "You must be Savannah."

Her tone indicated that she'd heard about me, and not good things.

"Nice to meet you," I said pleasantly. And insincerely, because I didn't like the way she talked, nor the way she looked at me. She was seated, and so was I, but she still managed to give the impression of having to look down to see me.

Like Mother and Audrey she was well past middle age. I'd put her in her early sixties, although of course she didn't look it. Her hair was nut brown and elegantly styled, with chunky streaks from the crown to the razored edge. She was dressed in a silk blouse and an A-line skirt, that did what it could to minimize the fact that she was a bit broader in the beam that maybe she should have been.

Then again, at 60+, she could be excused for not looking like a girl anymore.

"Did you find a dress?" Mother wanted to know.

Frances nodded, grabbing her napkin and spreading it across her lap with a snap of fabric. "Pewter satin and lace. Very elegant."

Audrey nodded, too, looking pleased. It must be what Frances had picked out at the boutique the other day. I bet it was expensive.

"I understand your son's getting married again," I said.

She looked at me down the length of her nose. "Do you know Ronnie?"

"Not well. I ran into him in the Bog yesterday, though. We had a nice talk."

The nose crept another inch closer to heaven. At this rate, I'd be able to inspect for boogers soon. "Don't you mean Mallard Meadows?"

"I suppose I do. Although the Bog has been the Bog as long as anyone can remember, so I don't think calling it something else will change anything." At least not in people's minds.

Frances sniffed.

"My boyfriend grew up in the Bog, you know," I added, sweetly.

Frances glanced at my mother, sympathy etched on her face. I did the same, in time to see Mother do her own elegant version of the eyeroll.

"So I hear," Frances said. "And really, my dear, why that's something you would want to go around telling people...! Have you no shame?"

I pretended to think about it. "Not much, no. But then I've mostly stopped caring what a lot of people think of me. It's amazing what falling in love with the town screwup can do for a girl."

Frances sniffed.

"I don't suppose your son's fiancée is from around here?" I added.

"Franklin," Frances said.

Franklin is a town about halfway between Columbia and Nashville. It's located in Williamson County, which happens to be the wealthiest county in Tennessee, and also one of the 25 wealthiest counties in the whole USA, according to Forbes. A lot of country stars and record company executives live there, which drives the per capita wealth up. And then, of course, there are the horse ranches.

"Elizabeth is a lovely young woman," Mother said approvingly.

Frances nodded. "Oh, yes. So much better than the tramp he married the first time."

I waited for the obligatory 'bless her heart,' but it didn't come. So I picked up the third roll from my plate and took a bite. A big bite. "I'm eating for two," I informed Frances when she looked at me. "Knocked up, you know. By my no-account boyfriend. And out of wedlock, too."

I waited a second for that to sink in before I added, "In fact, I should probably start thinking about planning my own wedding. Before I get too fat to fit into a proper wedding dress."

I glanced at my mother. She seemed too stunned to speak.

"I realize having a big wedding the second time around is a bit tacky," I continued, all the while munching on my roll, "but Rafe's never been married before. And I've never seen him in a tuxedo. I'd take almost any opportunity to get him into one." And to get him out of it later. With my teeth.

Maybe I should say that out loud, just to see what kind of reaction it would get...

Before I could, Mother spoke. "He probably doesn't own a tuxedo, darling."

"Maybe not. Or at least we don't have one in the closet at home." I addressed myself to Frances. "We're living in sin, you know. No better than we ought to be."

She blinked. Probably speechless. Mission accomplished.

I turned back to my mother. "Maybe we could just do the whole ceremony on the grounds of the mansion, along with the reception afterwards. After all, marrying Rafe in the same church where I married Bradley would definitely be a little bit tacky. We just have to make sure that we schedule it for one of the other weekends in June, and not the weekend when Ronnie's marrying Dear Elizabeth. I'm sure she wouldn't appreciate the competition. Especially since my wedding to Rafe is likely to be the event of the summer."

Nobody managed to come up with a response to that, and I finished, triumphantly, "And the best thing is that if I could pull it off in a month, I'd still look halfway decent in a white gown."

Mother blinked. She opened her mouth, but no words came out. Meanwhile, Audrey was vibrating, making a sort of a noise like a teakettle coming to a boil. Her face was mostly expressionless—other than her eyes, which bulged slightly, and looked weirdly shiny—but she made this sort of leaky hiss, like steam was escaping through her ears. And she was flushed from the neckline of her dress up to her hair.

Hot flash?

It was a bit strange, but she didn't seem to be suffering, so I returned my attention to Mother, and to Frances Burke, who was staring at me from across the table as if I'd grown a second head. "I should probably go and get started on the preparations. It won't be easy, planning a whole wedding in a month."

"Darling," Mother said plaintively, but I pretended I couldn't hear her as I got to my feet.

"I'm sorry about lunch. I'll catch something to eat somewhere else. But if I'm getting married in June, I have a lot to do. I'm sure you understand."

"But your salad..." Mother said.

"Have them pack it up and take it next door to Darcy." I swept out of the café without looking back, still clutching my sweet roll, my head held high.

By the time I got to the car, I had walked off a little of the steam, and to be honest, I wasn't entirely sure what had possessed me to go off like that. It wasn't as if I was serious. I didn't want a big white wedding, and I certainly didn't expect Rafe to get married on the grounds of the mansion, with all of Sweetwater in attendance. I might want to marry him in front of God and everybody, but he wouldn't think that was necessary, and if it would make him feel uncomfortable, then I definitely didn't want to do it.

It had just annoyed me when Frances Burke insisted that the Bog was Mallard Meadows, not the Bog.

I understood why Ronnie had renamed the place. Really, I did. The Bog had been there forever, and had bad feelings attached to it. The murders, of course, plus, for as long as I could remember, and for a long time before that, the Bog had been where the underprivileged of Sweetwater lived. Keeping the name would stigmatize Ronnie's new subdivision.

But Frances's insistence on the new name translated, somehow, into an effort to erase the past, which developed—in my mind—into a refusal to accept Rafe. And then, when she told me I should have the decency to be quiet about him having grown up there...!

Besides, there was the way she was planning her son's second nuptials, as if it was OK for him to have a big wedding the second time, while it wasn't OK for me to think about doing the same thing. Like I should be ashamed, and should be hiding.

Pushing back had felt good. And—bonus—it had had the additional benefit of scaring my mother into fits.

Although now, as I made my way to the Volvo and climbed in, I did feel a bit ashamed. I wasn't really thinking of using the mansion for my wedding, so it wasn't very nice to threaten my mother's peace of mind with it.

On the other hand, I knew they were back there talking about me—and Mother was surely not standing up for me and my decision to marry Rafe. So I couldn't feel too bad. Besides, I could always apologize later. If I felt like it.

The three buttered rolls had filled my stomach nicely, and I was revved up from the confrontation and ready to kick someone else's derriere. So I didn't bother stopping for lunch on my way to Columbia. Twenty minutes later, I had found a parking spot on the square and was ready to beard the Assistant DA in his den.

The front office was guarded by a dragon in brown polyester. When I asked to see Todd Satterfield, she looked at me like I was something that had arrived in her reception stuck to the bottom of someone else's shoe, and asked whether I had an appointment.

"No," I said, "but he'll want to see me."

She sniffed. "Mr. Satterfield is very busy."

"Believe it or not, so am I. I have a wedding to plan, and a murder to solve, and a real estate career to salvage, so I can afford to pay for the wedding... At any rate, he'll want to see me."

The nostrils flared. "Your name?"

"Savannah Martin," I said.

She didn't do anything so gauche as gasp, but her expression changed just enough, for just long enough, that I knew she'd recognized my name. I wondered how much she—and everyone else at the District Attorney's office—knew about me and Todd and the marriage that wasn't.

"One moment," was all she said, before she pushed buttons on her desk phone and lifted the receiver. She spoke in a murmur, as if hoping if she were quiet enough I couldn't hear, but of course I was standing three feet away; there was no way I could avoid catching her side of the conversation.

"Mr. Satterfield? A Miss Martin to see you."

Todd said something, and then, "Miss," the receptionist said.

I guess maybe Todd had wondered whether it was my mother coming to say hi. Or maybe my brother.

Todd spoke again, and the receptionist glanced at me. "I don't think that'll work, Mr. Satterfield."

No, I wouldn't believe her if she suddenly told me he wasn't available.

"I just want to talk to him for a minute," I said. "It won't take long."

She relayed the information, then listened for another few seconds. "Yes, Mr. Satterfield." She hung up the phone. "You can go on back, Miss Martin. Last door on the right." She nodded down the hallway behind her.

"Thank you." I smiled prettily and headed past the desk.

As I walked, I realized—of course—that I was walking the same path that Rafe had taken two days ago. Did anyone put two and two together? Did the receptionist know, or guess, that I was here on the same errand, more or less, that he had been? Did they know what was going on? Or hadn't Todd mentioned anything about it?

The last door on the right was closed, and I knocked twice and twisted the knob. When I pushed the door open and peered in, Todd was standing behind his desk with his hand on the knot of his tie. Hard to say whether he was adjusting it to make sure it was perfect, or whether he felt like it was choking him and he couldn't breathe.

I took a breath of my own, and stepped across the threshold.

Seventeen

This was, pretty much, the first time I'd spoken to Todd since Christmas. We'd found ourselves in the same places occasionally since then—he'd been at Abigail's birthday party in February, for instance—and we had pretty studiously ignored one another whenever we found ourselves in the same room at the same time. The situation was awkward, to say the least, and if it hadn't been for this new development, I would have been happy to continue to stay away from him. Out of courtesy more than for any other reason, to be honest. What had happened had to be worse for him than for me, and I felt bad about putting him on the spot.

My smile was probably more like a grimace than anything friendly. "Todd."

"Savannah." His wasn't any better. He glanced past me to the door. "Are you alone?"

I nodded. "Rafe's in Atlanta."

"Digging around in my past?" His voice was bitter.

"Not yours so much as Jolynn's," I said, "although I'm sure he's probably talking to people who knew you both."

He didn't respond, and I added, "I'm sorry for your loss."

He looked up at that, and I continued, "I know you weren't married anymore. But she was your wife once. You shared your bed and your life with her. You must have cared."

Todd didn't respond to that either, although his face quivered, maybe with grief, or maybe just with relief.

"May I sit?" I asked, putting a hand on the back of one of the visitor's chairs.

"Of course. Please." Todd ran a hand down his face. "I'm sorry. It's just..."

All a little too much.

I didn't say it, though; just sat down and put my purse on the floor next to me. "I won't stay long. Dix said you're busy. Some big investigation you're trying to finish?"

Before he got arrested and charged with murder himself...

"Real estate fraud," Todd said, taking the seat on the other side of the desk. "Blockbusting. With conspiracy to commit murder."

Goodness. "Anyone I know?"

He hesitated. And I'm sure he probably shouldn't have been telling me, but he said, "It's a continuation of the serial murder case from last month. Your high school reunion."

When some of my classmates had viciously attacked others of my classmates over something that happened a dozen years ago. Right.

"Does it have anything to do with Stonegate Development and the Bog? The new Mallard Meadows subdivision?"

One of my former classmates, now languishing in jail right here in Columbia, had worked for Ronnie Burke and Stonegate.

"As a matter of fact," Todd said, and then seemed to decide that there was no point in being coy. He leaned forward across the desk and lowered his voice. "We've got Hollingsworth dead to rights for Underwood, Perkins, and Gunther, and the attempted on Danny Emerson. She's going away for a long time. Probably the rest of her life."

And no more than she deserved, if he asked me. She'd tried to kill my old friend Charlotte, too, although it sounded like that particular attempted murder wasn't part of the charges. Maybe Todd didn't think he needed it.

"And she confessed to shooting Scruggs," he added, "and to ordering the murder of LaDonna Collier."

I nodded.

"We still have the death penalty in Tennessee. And with that many murders, she's looking at it. Even if she is a woman. So in an attempt to get the death penalty taken off the table, she offered me a deal. Evidence against Burke."

"Ronnie?"

Todd nodded. "You know him?"

Not really. "I ran into him yesterday. I wanted to see if anything was going on in the Bog, and he was there. They're starting construction next week. And his mother is having lunch with my mother and Audrey right now. Apparently they've hired the mansion for Ronnie's wedding next month."

Todd muttered something.

"Let me guess," I said. "There won't be a wedding next month."

"We haven't filed charges," Todd began.

"But you will?"

He hesitated. But I guess after telling me everything he'd already told me, there wasn't any point in holding back the rest. "It looks that way. Hollingsworth implicated him in the Collier murder-for-hire. Apparently the order to get rid of LaDonna Collier came from him— Hollingsworth was just handling the details."

"Do you believe her?"

"She has no reason to lie," Todd said. "She's going to spend the rest of her life in jail either way. And Burke is the one benefitting financially from the Mallard Meadows development."

True. Depending on how much he'd paid for the land—and I imagine he'd probably paid very little, since no one else was likely to want it. The handful of residents who had still been living there last year, when he started to buy up the lots, probably hadn't had the sense to consult a real estate agent to find out how much their properties were worth, so he might have gotten them dirt cheap... Anyway, depending on how much he'd paid for the land and how much it cost to develop it, and then how much he sold each property for, I imagined he stood to make a very tidy profit. Millions, possibly. Well worth a little trickery.

"If he ordered the hit on LaDonna Collier," I said, "I want him to swing."

Other than Tondalia Jenkins, who didn't recognize him half the time, LaDonna had been the only family Rafe had. If Ronnie Burke had had her killed for money, just so he could take her plot of land and build on it, he deserved to swing.

We sat in silence for a moment.

"You didn't come here to talk about that," Todd said finally.

I shook my head. "I came to talk about Jolynn. Although now that I know about it, it's interesting."

Todd shrugged. He must not see the implications. Maybe the implications were imaginary on my part. Which was a possibility, I suppose.

"I spoke to Dix last night," I said. "He says you won't admit that you went to my apartment on Saturday night."

Todd opened his mouth, but nothing came out.

"My neighbor, Mr. Sullivan, saw you. He recognized you from before. When..."

Oops. Before, when Todd used to come by to pick me up for dinner. BR—Before Rafe.

Todd's cheeks flushed. Mine did, too. "I'm sorry things worked out the way they did," I said. "I just..." *Just fell in love with him and not you.*

But you can't say that. Especially to the guy you didn't fall in love with. Talk about rubbing salt in the wound.

I let the silence lie heavy for another second, and then I said briskly. "Rafe's in Atlanta talking to Jolynn's friends. Detective Grimaldi is in Nashville talking to my neighbors. I'm here, because neither of them want me underfoot. If they can't come up with another suspect, they'll arrest you. You were there. She was your ex-wife. And she got you there under false pretenses. The fact that you won't admit to being there makes you look guilty. The best thing you can do is come clean."

Todd sneered. I didn't think he had it in him, to be honest, but he managed a creditable curled lip. "With Collier?"

I kept my voice even. Just because he sneered, didn't mean I had to. "It doesn't have to be Rafe. You could talk to Tamara Grimaldi."

"She's hand in glove with Collier," Todd said. "Are you sure they aren't sleeping together?"

"Positive." Eight months ago that possibility might have worried me. Now it didn't. "Neither of them would do that to me. Besides, she's more or less dating Dix. Or spending a lot of time with him, anyway. And she's not really Rafe's type. Nor he hers."

Todd didn't answer, and I added, "That was a low blow."

He looked a bit guilty. "Sorry."

"That's OK. I forgive you." I knew where it had come from, after all. "Please talk to somebody, Todd. Or have Dix talk to Tamara Grimaldi. Or tell me what happened so I can tell Rafe. I don't want them to arrest you." My mother would never forgive me.

Todd hesitated. I could tell he was thinking about it, so I pressed what I saw as an advantage. "Just tell me what happened. You got the email. You went to my apartment at seven o'clock."

"I thought it was from you," Todd said, without looking at me.

Of course he had. No reason to suspect otherwise. He'd probably been hoping for something just like that to happen. Which made the trick even crueler. Although I doubted Jolynn had considered that when she sent her email.

"So you went to see me. What happened when you got there?"

"I knocked," Todd said. "And then I tried the doorknob. When I discovered that the door was open, I walked in."

So whoever had strangled Jolynn—since we were going on the assumption that it wasn't Todd—had left the door open. Did that mean he knew Todd was expected, and wanted Todd to walk into the crime scene, or had he been in too much of a hurry to even think about locking up behind himself?

"Did you see anyone?"

"There were people outside. Coming and going on the street. Parking their cars. Going into the restaurants. Upstairs, there was an older man—"

"Mr. Sullivan," I said. "He told me he'd seen you."

Todd nodded. "A couple of women were standing outside one of the townhouses, talking; one of them had a red dress on —"

"But nobody suspicious? Nobody looking like he was trying to run away?"

Todd shook his head.

"So the door was open. And you went in."

He nodded. "The kitchen and living room were empty. The light was on in the bedroom. I walked in there and saw her—you..."

"Her," I said firmly.

He swallowed. Audibly. "I thought it was you. I thought that Collier..."

That was another low blow, although I don't think that's why he said it. But I didn't expect it, so it literally took my breath away for a second. And my voice was none too steady once I found it again. "He'd never... Rafe would never..."

"And then I realized it wasn't you after all," Todd said. "And I realized who it was."

"Your ex-wife."

He nodded. He had turned pale. I probably had, too. All I had to do was close my eyes, and I could still see Jolynn sprawled there, across my sheets and comforter, with those dark bruises circling her throat.

"Did you touch her?"

"Yes," Todd said, his voice half-choked. "She was still warm."

So she hadn't been dead long. I don't know a lot about forensics, but I do know that much. And speculating about body temperature and time of death was easier than dealing with the fact that Todd was close to tears. I felt for him, really I did... but I didn't want to act too comforting, since that might open up a can of worms I didn't want to open.

"Why didn't you call 911?" I asked.

I mean, here was a dead woman—a dead woman he knew; a dead woman who still made him choke up when he thought about her death—and instead of calling the police, he left her there?

"Do you know who I am?" Todd asked when I said so. He sounded a bit arrogant, to be honest. "I'm the assistant DA of Maury County. She was my ex-wife. Can you imagine the uproar if I called to report her murder?"

Actually, I could. Only too well. "But surely you had to realize that the uproar would happen either way. People had seen you get there!"

"I didn't think about that," Todd said. "I just didn't want anyone to see me leave."

"How long did you stay in my apartment, anyway?"

"Until it got dark," Todd said.

Yowch. So an hour, at least. Cooped up with a dead body.

I didn't say anything, but he must have read the thoughts on my face. "I had to wait until there were fewer people on the streets. And I wanted to go through Jolynn's things. To see if she had anything that incriminated me."

"Like the email."

He nodded. "It wasn't on her phone, though."

"No. Apparently she visited my office and used my computer to do that. She told them she was my sister."

"She always did look like you," Todd said. "Even when her hair was dark."

Right.

"So you went through her stuff. Did you find anything?"

"I found out what she did for a living. My ex-wife, the hooker."

I wasn't about to touch that one. This conversation was difficult enough without asking him whether he'd left his ex-wife so badly off that she'd had to turn to selling her body to make ends meet.

"What about the camera?" I asked instead. "Did you take that?"

I hadn't thought Todd could turn any paler, but he exceeded my expectations yet again. "Camera?"

"There was a camera setup in the bedroom. If you didn't take the camera, the killer must have."

Todd shook his head. "I didn't see a camera."

OK, then. "So you waited until it got dark. And then you left. But you didn't go home."

He blinked at me, and I explained. "My mother called me at six-thirty the next morning to ask if I'd seen you."

Todd muttered something. I don't think it was complimentary. Mother would have been devastated. I was secretly pleased.

Naturally I didn't let it show. "Did you stay in a hotel? Or with a friend?" Not Dix, if so. "Or did you drive around all night? What were you doing? And where?"

"I can't tell you that," Todd said.

"It would help if you could." Not that it really mattered, because Jolynn was dead by then anyway and he could have killed her earlier. But if he was going to come clean, he had to come clean all the way and not hold anything back. Otherwise, he'd look just as suspicious as before.

"She's not someone I'm supposed to be spending time with."

O-ho! Todd was seeing someone? And what was wrong with her, that he wasn't supposed to be seeing her?

"If she doesn't have anything to do with anything, I'm sure nobody will make anything of it." And at any rate, Rafe was seeing me and Tamara Grimaldi was seeing Dix, and Dix and I both weren't supposed to be seeing either of them, so it wasn't like we couldn't all relate. "Rafe or Tamara Grimaldi are the safest people you could talk to about something like that."

"I don't know..." Todd said.

"This woman... did you tell her what had happened?"

"No. I just... spent time with her." He avoided my eyes. "Platonic time. Drinking wine and watching TV."

Platonic time... "So she's a friend."

"Yes," Todd said firmly.

"But you didn't tell her about the murder. Or about going to my apartment."

He shook his head. "I couldn't tell her about Jolynn. If something happened, it would make her an accessory after the fact. And she wouldn't understand about..." He trailed off.

She wouldn't understand about him going to see me? Or who he thought was me?

So maybe this woman, whoever she was, didn't feel as platonic as Todd did. For that matter, maybe he didn't feel platonic all the time, either; he just didn't want to admit it. Or not to me, at any rate.

"Well, ask her how she feels about you giving me her contact info. If she's OK with it, I'll tell Rafe. He won't tell anyone else."

Todd looked mutinous, but he didn't actually say anything.

"It will help to clear you," I said. "The more upfront you are about everything, the easier it'll be on you. I promise Rafe is not out to get you. He and Grimaldi want to find who killed Jolynn. If it wasn't you, they won't want you to be arrested for it."

Todd nodded, but I don't think he believed me. If I were him, I'm not sure I would have believed me, either.

"I guess I should go," I said, scooting forward on the chair preparatory to grabbing my purse. "I've taken up a lot of your time."

Todd nodded. Not very flattering, but I couldn't really blame him for wanting to get rid of me.

"I don't suppose you have any idea who might have wanted Jolynn dead."

Todd shook his head. "We didn't talk anymore. I hadn't seen her for almost two years. I don't know the kind of people she associated with these days. And I have no idea why she'd suddenly do this to me."

I didn't, either. "Maybe she just wanted to see you. And she thought if she contacted you as herself, you'd say no."

Todd shrugged. I pushed to my feet. "Good luck with bringing the case against Ronnie Burke."

Todd rose, too. Pauline Satterfield had raised a gentleman. "Thank you."

I turned toward the door. He came around the desk to escort me. I'm perfectly capable of opening my own doors, but I let him. "Does he know?"

He glanced at me, with his hand on the knob. "Who? Ronnie?"

I nodded.

"He's not stupid," Todd said, "so I imagine he does."

"But he's still planning his wedding for next month."

He shrugged. "Maybe he thinks we don't have enough evidence for an indictment. Or maybe he thinks he'll make bail and then he can get married while he waits for the trial."

"Does his fiancée know?"

"I have no idea," Todd said. "I haven't had the pleasure."

Ah.

"I'm avoiding contact to as much of a degree as I can. I don't want to tip him off. Just in case he decides to take an extended vacation to Costa Rica."

"You'd better nab him before he goes on his honeymoon, then."

He nodded and pulled the door open. "It was good to see you again, Savannah."

He actually sounded sincere.

"You, too," I said, a little surprised to find I meant it. But really, this conversation hadn't been as bad as it might have been. As bad as I had expected it to be. "I'll give Rafe a call and tell him what you told me. When he calls you, please try to work with him. My mother will kill him if you go to prison."

Todd's lips twitched. He didn't promise anything, though. "Be careful out there," he told me.

I smiled. "For once, nobody's out to get me. It's a nice change."

Todd blinked, and for a second, a strange look crossed his face. Then he smiled back. "I'll see you around, Savannah."

"See you," I said, and walked out of the DA's office to my car.

Eighteen

It wasn't until I was inside the car, and was rolling down the hill away from the town square, that I realized what I'd said. And what Todd had said.

Nobody was out to get me. It was a nice change.

OK, so there was a slim chance someone was out to get me. It was possible that Jolynn had been killed instead of me. She'd been in my apartment, in my bed. Although nobody who knew me would make a mistake like that. We may have looked alike on the surface, but not so much that anyone who knew me well enough to want to kill me would think she was me, or vice versa.

Of course, it could have been a murder for hire. With some of Rafe's old associates, that wasn't out of the realm of possibility.

Or the murderer—who knew me—could have walked in expecting me to be there, and by the time he or she realized that Jolynn was there instead, it was too late. Jolynn had seen his or her face and could identify it, so she had to go. In which case she wasn't killed because someone thought she was me; she was killed because she'd seen whoever wanted me dead.

Except nobody wanted me dead right now, that I knew about. I wasn't meddling in any of Rafe's cases. And none of his old enemies had come crawling out of the woodwork to settle old scores. We would have heard about it if so.

No, to the best of my knowledge and belief, I was not in any danger from anyone. Rafe was a little worried, perhaps, but that was likely more because I was pregnant. He'd sent me down here because he didn't want me to be alone in case something happened. He'd rather have me surrounded by family if something went wrong.

And Grimaldi didn't think I was in danger. She thought whoever had killed Jolynn had wanted to kill Jolynn.

So no one was out to get me. Nice change.

The real question was, was someone out to get Todd?

He'd said it himself: if he was caught with a prostitute, even one who used to be his wife—maybe especially one who used to be his wife—had I any idea the uproar that would cause?

And I didn't, not really, but I could imagine. Or thought I could.

He wasn't an elected official, so he couldn't be impeached. But he could be fired. And a scandal could do a lot of damage to his reputation, and his ability to bring cases before a judge. A man who sleeps with prostitutes can't stand up in open court and defend the law. He might lose his job over this. And that was if he didn't go to prison.

So if I assumed for a second that Todd had been set up, had whoever done it planned to frame him for murder? Or was it getting a sex tape with a prostitute—a prostitute who happened to be his ex-wife—that was the goal?

And that brought me to another question. Did whoever set the whole thing up know that Jolynn was Todd's ex-wife? Or did that come out later? Had she been chosen because she looked like me, and they'd thought that would help to get him into bed with her? Or had they chosen Jolynn specifically?

Had she been in on it, or had she found out later who her mark was? Had she refused to cooperate? Was that when she was killed?

Or was I going off half-cocked, spinning crazy theories out of nothing but air?

It would depend on what Rafe discovered in Atlanta, I guess, about Todd and Jolynn's relationship. But as I'd said to Todd earlier, they'd shared beds and lives for a couple of years. There must have been something there, between them. Affection, or attraction, if not love. She might have refused to be a party to ruining his life.

Or the whole thing might have been her idea.

The thoughts were coming so fast I couldn't keep my focus on the road and kept drifting into the other lane because I was too busy thinking to keep the car between the yellow lines. The second time it happened, I decided I might as well get off the road. The last thing I needed was to get into a traffic accident. Beulah's Meat 'n Three, a little cinderblock diner that had sat on the road between Columbia and Sweetwater for as long as I could remember, was coming up on the left, and I zoomed into the gravel lot and found an empty parking space. And then I turned the car off and reached for my phone.

Rafe answered on the first ring, and my breathless, "Rafe?" must have scared him, because the first words out of his mouth were, "Everything OK?"

"Fine," I said, taking a calming breath. Sounding like I'd been running for my life wasn't likely to reassure him. "I'm sitting in the parking lot outside Beulah's."

I could picture that single eyebrow arching. "Give Yvonne my love."

Yvonne McCoy is a waitress at Beulah's. She went to school with Dix and Todd—in their year—and she slept with Rafe once. If it had been up to her, it would have been more than once, but he must have scratched that itch and didn't feel the need to scratch it again. She and I get along fairly well, everything considered, although—

"I'm not sure your love is something I want to share with her," I told him, "but I'll tell her you said hi."

I could hear a smile coloring his voice. "That'll work." After a moment, he added, "It's a little late for lunch, ain't it? You not feeling good?"

"I feel fine. Mother invited me to lunch with her and Audrey and a lady named Frances Burke."

"At Beulah's?"

He sounded surprised, as well he might. Mother would never deign to set her designer-shod foot inside Beulah's Meat'n Three.

"No, no. This was two hours ago, at the Café on the Square."

"Ah," Rafe said. "You're eating for two."

It did sort of sound like I was getting ready for a whole second lunch, didn't it? "Not quite. I had a couple of rolls earlier, but Frances Burke annoyed me, so I left before the food was served."

There was a beat while he thought about it. "Do I know Frances Burke?"

"I doubt it," I said. "But her son is Ronnie Burke, and he owns Stonegate Development. They're the company that's turning the Bog into Mallard Meadows."

"Ah." He didn't say anything else, but I knew what he was thinking. His mother had died because of Stonegate Development and Mallard Meadows. He was predisposed to dislike both Frances Burke and her son.

"Todd's getting ready to indict him for real estate fraud and conspiracy to commit murder," I added.

He got very quiet. "You spoke to Satterfield?"

"Yes, and before you start yelling at me, let me tell you what he said."

I heard a very distinct breath. I think he drew it in through his nose. I pictured his nostrils flaring. That's something my mother's nostrils do every time she has to deal with Rafe, but Rafe isn't in the habit of doing it. "Go ahead," he said eventually, his voice carefully controlled.

I went ahead, rushing through what Todd had told me about Stonegate and the plea bargain and how he was getting ready to file charges against Ronnie and Stonegate Development on Friday for LaDonna's murder and the dirty dealings Ronnie had had to go through to get his hands on the deeds for the properties in the Bog.

When I was finished, Rafe grunted.

"This is good," I prompted, "right? We want him to pay."

"If he did it."

"He did it. Todd seems sure he did it."

"Todd sometimes makes mistakes," Rafe said. He doesn't usually use Todd's first name, so I figured when he did it now that he was being sarcastic.

And he was right. Last year, Todd had indicted a woman named Marley Cartwright for her baby's murder when, as it turned out, all along, little Oliver had been alive and well and living with an adoptive family. A family who hadn't realized he'd been kidnapped and sold to them.

But that was an honest mistake on Todd's part, and the only one I knew of. Aside from proposing to me, I suppose, but he really couldn't have guessed that I'd turn him down and go shack up with Rafe instead. That possibility would have been absolutely foreign to Todd. And anyway, I didn't want to believe he was making a mistake about this. I wanted Ronnie to pay for what he'd done.

"I thought I told you to stay away from Satterfield," Rafe growled in my ear.

"You did. But someone had to talk to him. It's not like he'd unburden himself to you."

"I wonder why."

I shook my head, in spite of the fact that he couldn't see me. "No, you don't. You know why. He doesn't trust you. He thinks you're out to get him."

"He's crazy," Rafe said flatly. "I don't wanna get him. Not unless he's guilty."

"He's not."

"Lemme guess. He tell you that?"

"As a matter of fact he did," I said. And since I was feeling a bit annoyed, I added, "Do you have time to listen to what he said? I don't want to interrupt your work."

"Course, darlin'." His voice was so solicitous and reasonable it set my teeth on edge. "I don't want it said I didn't give Satterfield a fair shake, now do I?"

"Grrr," I said.

Rafe chuckled.

I sighed, resigned. "Listen. He said he went there, to my apartment, on Saturday night..."

I recapped everything Todd had told me, and ended with, "He didn't tell me who he spent the night with. Just that it's platonic, and she's someone he shouldn't be spending time with."

"I wonder why."

"Stop saying that. It's annoying. And it could be for any number of reasons. She could be black—"

Rafe hooted derisively, loud enough that I had to remove the phone from my ear. "Satterfield? You're joking."

OK, she probably wasn't black. I couldn't really picture that. It was just the first thing that came to my mind.

"Maybe she's married," I said.

There went Rafe's eyebrow again. I could hear it in his voice. "He the type to go after someone else's wife, darlin'?"

"I wouldn't have thought so," I answered, aware of the fact that if Todd was that type, Rafe might suspect him of behaving inappropriately toward me, which he hadn't been.

"Uh-huh." He made no attempt to sound like he believed me.

"Listen," I said. "He behaved like a gentleman. I got in his face, and made him admit that he'd gone to see me because he thought something had gone wrong with you and me. When he saw Jolynn, he thought it was me, and that you—"

An absolutely blistering expletive cut me off, and it was probably a good thing.

"It was just for a second," I said. "And I told him you wouldn't. Ever. But what I was getting at was that even with all of that, he still behaved like a gentleman. He's stayed away from me for six months, Rafe. He wouldn't have spoken to me today if I hadn't shown up at his office and gotten in his face. And he's afraid of you. He thinks you won't be able to keep your personal feelings separate from your job."

A slightly less blistering version of the same expletive greeted this pronouncement. I heard him breathe. Slowly and carefully, in and out. Then he said, his voice controlled, "If I thought I couldn't, I woulda told Tammy to send someone else."

"I believe you," I said.

"Yeah? Listen, I'm so damn afraid I'm gonna think it's him just cause it's him, that I keep looking at everything I hear two and three times, just to make sure I don't. He's prob'ly safer with me doing this investigation than he'd be with anyone else."

After a second he added, "Lessen it was his daddy, anyway."

Because then Todd would never even be a suspect.

"Right," I said. "I love you."

"Love you too, darlin'." He didn't ask me where the proclamation had come from, right at that moment. Perhaps he knew that hearing him admit weakness, admit that he had to be careful to play fair with Todd because of his own feelings, made me feel all gooey inside. "Call Tammy and tell her what he said, OK?"

I said I would. "What about you? Are you learning anything new?"

He sighed. "She liked him. Wanted things to work out. Took the blame when they didn't. Talked to her friends about how unfair it was that she couldn't be what he wanted, cause he wanted you. They all said she woulda stayed married to him if he hadn't divorced her."

"What made her suddenly decide to go to Nashville and get him in trouble now? Did something happen?"

"Nothing nobody said nothing about," Rafe said. "Why?"

It took me a second to sort through the double and triple negatives. "I was just thinking about that camera setup you guys said was there. Minus the camera. Someone might have wanted to get Todd in trouble. A sex tape of the assistant DA with a prostitute wouldn't do his ability to try cases any good. I'm not sure whether it would make it better or worse that the prostitute was his ex-wife."

"Worse," Rafe said. "You got somebody in mind for this?"

"For the person who wanted to get Todd in trouble, you mean? It might be Jolynn herself, if she suddenly decided to get revenge, two years after the fact. Although I'd like it better if someone had said something about that."

Rafe made an agreeing sound.

"I thought of Ronnie Burke," I said. "If he knows that Todd's working on indicting him, he has a very good reason for wanting to discredit Todd."

There was a beat. "I want you to promise me something," Rafe said.

"OK."

"I want you to stay away from Ronnie Burke. No more side trips to the Bog. No more lunches with his mom."

"No problem." I wouldn't be here next week, when building was set to start in the Bog—excuse me, Mallard Meadows—and according to Todd, neither would Ronnie. And I hadn't liked Frances enough to want to hang out with her again. "You don't want to get married at my mother's house, do you?"

"What?"

"Frances has rented the mansion for Ronnie's wedding to someone named Dear Elizabeth next month. I floated the suggestion that we could have our wedding there, too."

There was a pause. "You wanna get married in Sweetwater?"

"Do you?"

"I just wanna marry you," Rafe said. "I don't care where it is."

"So you wouldn't mind if we got married at the mansion?"

I couldn't see him, but I could feel him squirm all the way from Atlanta. "Is that what you want?"

"No," I said. "I mean, I could want that. If you did. But if you don't—" And it sounded like he didn't. Which was what I had assumed all along, really.

A voice spoke in the background on his end of the phone, and he said, "I gotta go. Can we talk about it later?"

"Sure." Or not, as the case may be. "Take care."

"You too, darlin'. Stay away from Satterfield. And Ronnie Burke."

I promised I would, and turned off the phone. And since I was there, and since I hadn't had any lunch save for those three rolls I'd filched from the Café on the Square earlier, I got out of the car and made my way across the parking lot to Beulah's for something to eat.

By now, the lunch rush was mostly over, and there were several empty tables. Yvonne greeted me with a "Good afternoon, princess!" and escorted me to one of them. "Where's that gorgeous man of yours?"

"Atlanta," I said. "But he said to tell you hello."

"You tell him hello right back." She was practically purring.

I told her I would, while I tried not to grimace too obviously. "I'd like a glass of milk, please. And a chicken salad sandwich. And a side of home fries. And maybe some coleslaw."

"Coming right up." Except she didn't move, just cocked a hip and contemplated me. "Still cooking?"

I put a hand on my stomach. "So far."

"Rafe happy?"

"He seems to be. You saw him just a month ago."

"I know. I just wanna be prepared if you throw him over." She winked at me.

"And here I thought you had your eye on my brother," I said, since Yvonne used to have a soft spot for Dix, too. Not that she'd ever slept with him, of course.

She grinned. "I hear he has a new girlfriend."

Uh-oh. If Yvonne had heard, how long could it be before Mother found out? "Really? Who told you that?"

"There's been a car parked at his place," Yvonne said. "A car with Nashville plates."

"Are you sure it isn't my car? I was there last night. Babysitting the girls while Dix was out to dinner."

Yvonne arched a brow inquiringly, probably hoping for something juicy, and I added, "With Todd Satterfield."

Yvonne grimaced. "Now, there's someone I've seen too much of lately."

"Really?" Was it possible that Todd and Yvonne...?

My mind hiccupped.

I quieted it, and tried to look at the question without prejudice.

They knew each other, obviously. Yvonne had gone to school with Todd, just as she had with Dix. And she was definitely someone Todd shouldn't be spending time with. His father wouldn't approve. Nor would my mother. Dix probably wouldn't either, although he'd become a bit less puritanical since Sheila died. Or maybe since I started bringing Rafe around. Anyway, Yvonne was, not to put too fine a point on it, 'not our kind.' Her main claim to fame in school had been having the biggest breasts at Columbia High.

The rest of us had grown up some since then, of course, and my breasts are nothing to be ashamed of these days, but hers were still exceptional, and at the moment displayed in a skin-tight, low-cut T-shirt. I could see the pink scars from last autumn, when a nutcase obsessed with Rafe attacked Yvonne with a knife for daring to kiss him.

(It hadn't made me happy, either, but it was before we were together in an official way, so I'd kept my feelings to myself.)

Yvonne nodded. "I don't know if you know this, but I've been married a couple of times."

I did know that, since it was part of that 'not our kind' thing. I didn't know the details, though. For most of the past ten years, I'd been living elsewhere.

"My first husband," Yvonne said, "was Ronnie Burke."

My eyes bulged. "You're kidding."

She shook her head.

"But he must be ten years older than you!"

"Eleven," Yvonne said. "I was twenty. He was a real man." She made a face. "It didn't last long. He cheated."

"I'm sorry," I said. "I've been there."

"We were only married a year. He couldn't keep his pants zipped. And it's ages ago. I wasn't able to help Todd much when he came and wanted to talk about Ronnie. He'd barely even started Stonegate Development then."

I nodded sympathetically. "I guess you know he's getting married again?"

"Rather him than me," Yvonne said and tossed her head. "I'll be back with your milk."

She wandered off. I waited for her to put in my order and bring the glass of milk back before I asked what I really wanted to know. "Did you see Todd on Saturday night?"

"I worked on Saturday night," Yvonne said, without even a pause to think about it. And while it wasn't a solid negative—no, they hadn't—it seemed like that's what she was saying.

"Are Saturdays busy here?"

Yvonne shrugged, jiggling her bra straps and setting the girls into motion. "I make most of my money during lunch, but Friday and Saturday nights are OK. The rest of the week not so much."

"And you didn't see Todd."

"Here?" She hooted, loud enough that a couple of people turned around to see what was going on. I flushed and sank down farther in my seat. "Honey," Yvonne said, without bothering to lower her voice, "His Highness doesn't show his face in a place like this. Or talk to the likes of me in public. I had to come to his office so he could interview me 'on the record.'" Her fingers, with long, pink nails, made quotation marks around the last three words.

"But not on Saturday night."

"No," Yvonne said patiently. "I was here Saturday night. Until I went home. I have no idea what Todd Satterfield did. And I don't care."

That seemed to take care of that, then. She wandered off to refill cups of coffee and glasses of sweet tea for some of her other guests, and I sat back and drank my milk while I waited for my sandwich to arrive. When it did, with Yvonne carrying it, I tried again. "Have you met Ronnie's new fiancée?"

"Dear Elizabeth?" Yvonne made a face. "No, I haven't had the pleasure. But Frances makes sure she talks about her, loudly, whenever she sees me. So I won't miss how much more desirable of a daughter-in-law Elizabeth is. Like she thinks I care that Ronnie's getting remarried. Good riddance, I say." She tossed her head again, so the red ponytail bounced.

"Frances said she's from Franklin."

Yvonne nodded. "She's some kind of designer or something, I think. And maybe she's doing something in your line, too."

"Real estate agent?"

"Or maybe that's just in my head. I know Ronnie's working with her. I think maybe she's designing those new houses in the Bog."

"I was down there yesterday afternoon," I said. "Ronnie was there. She wasn't. But all the trailers are gone, and he told me they're starting construction next week."

"He'll be in prison by then," Yvonne said and walked away.

Nineteen

When I walked into the mansion, Mother was back at the kitchen island. For a change, she wasn't perusing a bridal magazine this time; she was looking at... photographs?

I sidled closer and peered down. Definitely photographs. And not of people I know.

Actually, I take that back. They weren't photographs of family, but I recognized Ronnie Burke. And...

"Who's that?" I put out my finger.

Mother sent me a cold look and twitched the photograph out of my reach. "I can't believe how rude you were to poor Frances, Savannah!"

Poor Frances, my posterior!

"She was rude to me first," I said.

"She's old enough to be your mother." She reached up to fluff her hair. Probably telling herself that she's half a dozen years or so younger than Frances Burke and doesn't look her age. "I've taught you to be polite to adults, darling."

"You talk to me like I'm still fourteen," I said. "I'm an adult, too, you know. I'm responsible for my own actions. What I do doesn't reflect on you anymore."

"You'll always be my daughter," Mother said, self-righteously.

For my sins.

I pushed the thought away. "Of course. But it's not like you can ground me if I don't behave appropriately. Frances Burke was rude to me. So I was rude back."

I guess she couldn't argue with that, because she didn't try.

"Besides," I added, "it isn't like you've got room to talk."

"Me?" She looked astonished, as if I had accused her of wearing white shoes after Labor Day. "Darling, I'm never rude."

"You're extremely rude. Poisonously rude. Without ever raising your voice or using a bad word. You just slice people to ribbons and leave them bleeding. It's a good thing Rafe's used to people with no manners, because another man would have left me by now. You're pretty much the mother-in-law from hell."

Mother gasped and pressed a hand to her chest, as if I had mortally wounded her. Or like she was having a heart attack. "How dare you?"

I stuck my hands on my hips. "You twitch your nose like he smells bad. You talk to him like he's one of the servants—when you talk to him at all. If I don't shame you into it, you just look through him, like he isn't even there. Like you can't see him, because he's so far below you. Like somebody's discarded chewing gum stuck to the bottom of your shoe. This is a man who has saved my life two or three times in the past year, Mother, and you can't even bring yourself to look him in the eye when he shows up!"

She had no answer to that, naturally. I don't know why I should have expected anything different. And since I'd pretty much said what I'd planned to say, I turned back to the photographs on the island. "Who's that?"

Mother hesitated. For a moment, I thought she might refuse to talk to me. Then she must have decided that since I was still willing to keep the lines of communication open, she'd be stupid not to go along with me. That way, she could cling to the belief that I was the one who had been out of line and needed to apologize, instead of her. "That's Dear Elizabeth."

"That isn't really her name, is it?" I twitched the photograph closer to my side of the island.

"Of course not." Mother sniffed. "Her name is Elizabeth. But compared to Ronnie's first wife…"

"Funny you should mention that. I ran into Yvonne earlier. At Beulah's. After I left Todd's office."

Mother blinked. And blinked again as she processed the various tidbits of information in that statement. After a moment, she homed in on what she obviously deemed most important. "You went to see Todd?"

I resisted the temptation to roll my eyes. I'd been disrespectful enough for one conversation. "Yes, Mother. I went to see Todd. He's getting ready to indict Ronnie Burke for real estate fraud and conspiracy to commit murder."

Mother's mouth opened, but nothing came out.

"And if you say a word about that to Frances," I added, "I doubt Todd or his dad will talk to you ever again. I certainly won't. So keep it to yourself."

She closed her mouth. And opened it again. Her voice was weak. "Murder?"

"Remember last year, when LaDonna Collier died of an overdose in the Bog, and the sheriff tried to pin it on Rafe?"

She nodded.

"Well, he was right. It was murder. It just wasn't Rafe who killed her. It was Billy Scruggs. Because LaDonna wouldn't leave her trailer and give the property over to Stonegate Development, Stonegate hired Billy to get rid of her. Mary Kelly cut a deal with the DA's office—with Todd—to stay off Death Row, and she gave them Ronnie Burke in exchange. So Todd's getting ready to indict him." Or he would, if I could keep him out of jail for long enough to get the motion filed. Or whatever it was they did at the District Attorney's office.

"But the wedding..." Mother said helplessly, looking at the photographs scattered across the kitchen island. "I was trying to choose the best photograph for the registration table..."

It was almost enough to make me feel sorry for her. "I don't think there'll be a wedding, Mother. Ronnie will probably be in jail by the time his wedding date comes along, and Frances is better off saving her money to pay his bail."

Mother paled. After a second, she asked, "Does Rafael have something to do with this?"

Her nostrils twitched when she said his name. I guess she couldn't help herself.

"Not a thing," I said brightly. "Other than that Ronnie Burke hired a drug dealer to do away with his mother, you know? Although you can't really blame Rafe for that. But other than that, it's all Todd's doing. And Ronnie's, I suppose."

Mother subsided. In the silence, I picked up the photograph of Dear Elizabeth and examined it.

Dear Elizabeth looked familiar.

Not that she was terribly easy to see. Half her face was obscured by flowing, brown hair, and the other half was mashed against Ronnie's beefy bicep. They were somewhere tropical, with azure water behind them. The Caribbean, maybe. Or the Gulf of Mexico.

"Are there any others? I want a better look at Dear Elizabeth."

Mother didn't speak, just pushed the photographs in my direction. I sorted until I found one that looked like I might get a better view of Dear Elizabeth's face.

And then I did, and...

Oh. My. God.

"That's Liz," I said.

"Elizabeth."

"I know that. But she told me her name was Liz. She works at my office. Tim just hired her. She's a brand new agent."

"She's a designer," Mother said. "She's designing Ronnie's houses."

"Be that as it may, Tim wouldn't have hired her without a real estate license. He doesn't need a designer. So she's got one of those, too."

I looked at the photograph again.

Yes, it was definitely Liz. Same light brown hair, same slightly tilted eyes, same wide cheekbones and pointed chin.

But why would a successful designer bother to get her real estate license and start from scratch selling houses?

Unless she'd done it just so she could sell Ronnie's houses, of course. Keep it all in the family, so to speak.

Although she lived in Franklin and planned to work in Maury County. Why would she bother to sign on with a real estate company an hour north, in East Nashville?

And—the biggie—was it just a coincidence that it was Liz who had been doing floor duty on Saturday morning, alone in the office, when my 'sister'—or Jolynn—came into the office to send her message to Todd?

"I have to call Grimaldi," I said, reaching for my purse.

I hadn't called her after I spoke to Rafe, because I'd gone into Beulah's and gotten distracted talking to Yvonne. And I hadn't called her on the way home from Beulah's, because... well, I guess I'd just forgotten. Yvonne hadn't really told me anything I didn't already know, and in addition to the eating and the sleeping, the baby was making me distracted and forgetful, as well.

But I needed to call Grimaldi now. This was an important piece of information. Ronnie Burke's fiancée signing on as a realtor at LB&A just a couple of weeks before Jolynn died—and just as I started renting out my apartment—couldn't be a coincidence.

I had the phone in my grasp when it rang, and startled me. It wasn't Grimaldi. It wasn't anyone else I knew, either. The number was local—a 931-area code; Sweetwater, Maury County, Southern Middle Tennessee—but I'd never seen it before.

I lifted the phone to my ear. "Hello?"

"Savannah?" a voice said. A female voice. Vaguely familiar, in the way of voices you may have heard before, but can't place.

"This is she." I'm usually better about introducing myself when I answer the phone. Usually I mention my name, since the hope is always that some stranger is calling to find out about a house, and he or she deserves to know that they've reached the right person.

"This is Marley." She paused for just a second, and when I didn't immediately say anything, she added, "Cartwright?"

I giggled. I have no idea why. "Small world. I thought about you just a couple of hours ago."

"Really?" She sounded like she wasn't quite sure what to make of that. Then she shook it off and continued. "I heard you were in town. I thought maybe you were free for dinner tonight."

"Dinner?"

Gah. To listen to me, you'd think I'd never heard of the meal between lunch and breakfast.

"I never really had the chance to thank you for everything you did to help me get Oliver back," Marley said. "And if you hadn't been there at the end—" Her voice cracked, "if you hadn't followed me, I wouldn't be here now. I would be dead, and everyone would think I'd killed my baby."

"I pretty much did what anyone would have done," I demurred.

"You did more than that. If it weren't for you, I wouldn't have Oliver. And I'd really appreciate it, if you aren't busy, if you could come over for dinner tonight."

I supposed I could, at that. I didn't have any other plans, and I didn't have to go back to Nashville to start working for Fifth and Main until tomorrow morning.

If Grimaldi arrested Liz, would Tim want me back? I couldn't offer him commissions on a subdivision in Maury County, but at least I wasn't engaged to a real estate criminal.

"Do you still live in the same place?"

Marley said she did. "Six-thirty?"

I told her I'd see her then. And then I finally got around to dialing Tamara Grimaldi's number.

It took quite a long time to explain the situation and recap everything I'd done since I arrived here yesterday. And it didn't help that Mother was sitting on the other side of the kitchen island listening to every word. But I finally got it all out, and waited for the detective's questions. I figured she'd probably have more than a few.

"Are you sure?" was the first one. Not surprisingly.

"About Liz being Elizabeth? Absolutely. I recognize her from the pictures."

"Send me one of those. Take a picture with your phone and send it to me."

"Just a second." I lined up the photo that showed most of Dear Elizabeth's face, snapped its picture, and sent it to Grimaldi. Technology is wonderful. It took just a few seconds before she said, "Hang on."

I waited while she manipulated buttons on her phone. Then she came back. "That's her, all right. Unless she has a twin."

"I don't think she does," I said. "Although I can ask. But the name is the same. Elizabeth. Liz. Common nickname."

"Yes," Grimaldi said. "There's that. And she's engaged to marry Ronnie Burke?"

"Uh-huh."

"A man whom the District Attorney's office in Maury County is planning to indict for real estate fraud and murder."

"Conspiracy to commit murder. Yes."

"That's a hell of a reason to want to embarrass the District Attorney," Grimaldi said. "Or in this case, the assistant DA bringing the case."

"Yep."

"It doesn't explain the murder, though. The sex tape makes much more sense."

Yes, it did. "Maybe she refused to cooperate," I said. "Maybe she discovered what they were trying to do, and she refused to go through with it. Rafe spoke to people in Atlanta who said she seemed to genuinely care for Todd, even after they got divorced."

Grimaldi thought for a moment. "That's possible. I'll have to get onto Sheriff Satterfield, to see if he can help me nail down where Ronnie Burke spent Saturday night. Whether anyone down there saw him at any point. If not, we'll have to start showing his picture around your building. In fact, maybe I should have Spicer and Truman get started on that while we wait."

"Couldn't hurt," I said. "Can you see his face in the picture I sent, or would you like me to send another one?"

"I'll get his official driver's license photo from the DMV," Grimaldi said. "And hers, too. That'll be better."

"Are you sure? A lot of people don't look good in their driver's license photos."

"I know what I'm doing, Ms.... Savannah," Grimaldi informed me, and of course there was no arguing with that. "But you're right. Why leave anything to chance? Take a picture of a photo of Ronnie Burke, by all means, and send it to me. Who knows if it might come in handy."

I'm sure she was just humoring me—she does have a tendency to do that—but I took the picture and sent it to her anyway. While I was in the middle of the process, she asked, "Just for the sake of argument, what are you doing tonight? Not meddling in my case, I hope?"

"I'm having dinner with a friend," I said with dignity—and between you and me, relieved that I had something planned that wasn't meddling in the detective's case. "A female friend. The woman Todd put on trial for infanticide last fall. The one whose baby was stolen and sold to an adoptive couple in Nashville."

"Ms. Cartwright." Grimaldi had been involved in that investigation, too, since it had touched, peripherally, on my sister-in-law Sheila's murder. "Does she have anything to do with this?"

"I can't imagine what," I said. "She said she never thanked me properly for helping her get Oliver back, and for making sure she stayed alive long enough to get exonerated. And she's right. I don't think I've seen her since I got out of the hospital after I got shot. I'm just going to visit for a bit and then come home. And tomorrow morning I'm driving back to Nashville. Shannon Duncan offered me a job handling short term rentals for Fifth and Main. I start tomorrow at eleven."

"Congratulations," Grimaldi said. "Stay away from the real estate office."

"LB&A, you mean? Of course. Tim told me to." Although why would Grimaldi care?

"We may not arrest Ms.... What's Liz's last name?"

I realized I had no idea, and turned to my mother. "What's Dear Elizabeth's surname?"

"Pettigrew," Mother said faintly.

Like the human rat in *Harry Potter*. How fitting.

Naturally I didn't say so to Detective Grimaldi. I just relayed the name.

"Thank you. We may not arrest Ms. Pettigrew tonight. We don't have probable cause. The circumstances are suspicious, but I'll never find a judge to give me an arrest warrant based on the evidence we have. So I don't want you anywhere near that real estate office until you know for sure she's gone."

"No, ma'am," I said. "It's OK for me to go to Fifth and Main, though, right?"

"Of course. Just stay there."

I promised I would. "Anything else, Detective?"

"You called me," Grimaldi said.

And so I had. "In that case, have a good evening."

"You do the same."

She hung up. I dropped the phone back into my bag and turned to face my mother. She looked like all the life had been sucked out of her, like a shadow of her usual self. Old and tired. "Maybe you should go lie down for a bit," I said kindly.

And of course that was all it took for her back to snap up straight and her face to firm. "Nonsense. It was a surprise, that's all."

"You can't tell anyone about it," I warned.

"As if I would do anything to jeopardize Todd's case!" She clicked her tongue. "Really, Savannah, how you could imagine I would do anything at all to interfere..."

"I don't," I said. "I just know how close you and Audrey are. It must be hard for you to keep secrets from her." When what she wanted to do, must be to get on the phone with Audrey right this minute and pour out every last detail of what I'd told her.

"We've been best friends for more than thirty years, darling. She's the one who got me through it when your father died. And of course when we lost dear Sheila..."

She trailed off.

"I've been wondering," I said. "How come Audrey never got married? She hasn't been, has she? Or is there something I don't know about?"

Mother shook her head. "No, dear. Audrey's never been married."

"Not even before you met her? Because you've only known her since you and Dad got married, right?"

"She would have told me," Mother said firmly. "No, darling. I guess she never met anyone who measured up."

"Measured up to who?"

"Whom," Mother said. "The picture in her mind, I imagine."

She thought for a moment, and added, "I believe there was someone at some point, though. Before my time, so I'm not sure what happened. But I suppose I might ask Bob..."

"Or you could just ask Audrey."

Mother looked shocked. "Oh, no, darling. I couldn't do that."

No, of course not.

"I'm sure Sheriff Satterfield would know," I said, resignedly. "He's always lived here. If Audrey ever had a boyfriend, I'm sure the sheriff knows all about it."

Maybe he'd arrested the guy and sent him to jail, and that's why the relationship never developed into anything more.

"You may not be tired," I added, scooting off the stool I'd been sitting on, "but I've had a big day so far. And if I have to go out tonight, I should probably rest a little bit this afternoon."

Mother glanced at my stomach and nodded. I gathered up my purse and phone and headed out, leaving her to her photographs of Ronnie Burke and Elizabeth Pettigrew.

Twenty

Last year, when I first met her, Marley Cartwright lived in the Copper Creek subdivision, just down the street from Dix's and Sheila's house. She'd lived there when little Oliver was born, too, and on the day a few months later when someone stole him out of his baby swing on the back deck. And of course she hadn't moved after that: she spent every day in the hope that whoever had taken him, would come to their senses and bring him back. So she had to stay in the same place, so they'd know where to find her.

At this point she had Oliver back, and I think, if it had been me, I might have wanted to get out of the house where all the bad stuff had happened. But I wasn't familiar with Marley's situation. I knew her ex-husband, Oliver's father, had written her off as a murderer, and I'm sure she'd spent a lot of money looking for Oliver and also on defending herself against the murder charge. Maybe she couldn't afford to move. Or maybe she simply didn't want to.

Whatever the reason, she was still there. But the house looked like a whole different place now. Then, the landscaping had been untended and all the curtains had been drawn, because Marley was sick of people pointing at her and staring. And the inside had been a mess, with overflowing ashtrays and the scent of stale cigarette smoke everywhere. Marley was chain-smoking, drinking too much, and as far as I knew, addicted to sleeping pills and antidepressants. I didn't even know that I could blame her.

Now, the ashtrays were gone, and so was the smell. The furniture was new, or if not, it had been cleaned to within an inch of its life. The carpets were shampooed and the walls freshly painted to get rid of the stench. The curtains were open, letting the early evening sun in. And there were toys scattered across the floor throughout the first floor.

But with all that, the biggest change was in Marley herself. In November, she'd been skinny, almost gaunt, with cheekbones that stood out sharply against the skin. Her eyes had been huge and haunted, her pale face surrounded by stringy, dark hair. And she'd looked years older than her real age as she sucked on cigarette after cigarette, her cheeks hollow.

When she opened the door for me, I almost didn't recognize her. She must have gained twenty five pounds, and on her it looked good. Her cheeks had filled out and her lips plumped up. Her hair was cut shorter, just brushing her shoulders, and it was soft and shiny, bouncing around her ears. She was wearing makeup, but even without it, I could tell that her skin was glowing with health. And she was smiling, her eyes clear and unshadowed. "Savannah!"

"Hi, Marley." I returned the hug a little less enthusiastically—we weren't that close—and handed her the bottle of wine I had brought for a hostess gift. "Here you go."

"Thank you." She took it, and looked at it, biting her lip, before looking back up at me. "To tell you the truth, I've quit. I drank so much for so long—trying to drown everything that was going on, you know?—that once I got Oliver back, I decided it would probably be best if I just went cold turkey. Sorry."

"That's OK," I said. Goodness, it wasn't like she had to apologize for something like that.

"I'll pour some for you for dinner, though."

"That's not necessary. I'm not drinking alcohol either, at the moment."

She looked surprised for a second, and then her gaze dropped to my stomach. "Are you…?"

"Pregnant. Yes." Perhaps I should have used the more polite euphemism 'expecting,' but to tell the truth, I was pretty tired of worrying about choosing the politest word in everything I said.

"Congratulations." She waved me in and closed the door behind me. "I'm so glad you could make it. I know I should have tried to track you down sooner, to thank you for everything you did for me, but first all my effort was focused on proving that Oliver was mine, and on getting him back, you know? Proving that I could provide a stable, caring home for him. And things were looking kind of bad around here then, so it took some doing."

"But you're his mother," I said, following her through the house, looking left and right. The place looked great. "You shouldn't have to prove you're fit. He was stolen from you!"

"Yes, but he didn't know me. He knew his other mother. Taking him away from her was going to be traumatic for him, and for them, as well. They had no idea he hadn't been given up for adoption legally."

What a nightmare that must have been. For everyone involved.

"And the judge is supposed to look at the welfare of the child first. I had a good case, but if I couldn't prove that he'd be safe and taken care of with me, she had the option of ruling that it would be better for Oliver to stay with his adoptive parents. I would have gotten visitation rights, maybe…"

She ran down, for a second, nobody spoke. I had nothing to say, nothing that wouldn't sound clichéd, and Marley was obviously lost in the past. A shadow of that past self crossed her eyes, the haunted despair.

Then she did a little shake, throwing it off. "And I was a pretty big mess then, you know. Between the drinking and the pills and the fact that the house wasn't really fit to be lived in, plus Sheila's murder on top of it. The one person who believed in me!" She shook her head. "I had a lot of work to do."

She put the bottle down on the kitchen counter and turned to me. "I hope you like Italian."

"I love Italian," I said. And I do. Only not at the moment, since the tomato sauce gave me heartburn and would make it hard to sleep tonight.

"Chicken Marsala," Marley said, indicating the oven. "I know it's fattening, but I can still gain a couple of pounds and be OK. And you're eating for two."

"Fine with me." I like Chicken Marsala. Like it a lot, in fact. Before Rafe, when Todd would take me out to dinner, he'd invariably take me to this Italian restaurant on the west side of Nashville called Fidelio's. And I would always order the Chicken Marsala. Todd would order the Alfredo and finish up with cheesecake while I savored—sarcasm totally intended—a cup of black coffee.

"I bought a cheesecake for dessert," Marley added.

I squinted at her—maybe Sheila had mentioned what I like to eat, sometime before she died?—and she turned away, toward the double doors to the deck and the back yard. "Oliver's playing in the back. I'll get him."

I followed her over to the doors and onto the deck, looking around while she called her son in for dinner.

Here was another change: the back of the property was completely fenced, with an eight foot tall privacy fence enclosing every blade of grass. There was no way in or out, apart from scaling the bare planks, which thoughtfully had been left rough and full of splinters. Since Oliver's kidnapper had come and gone this way—had, in fact, lived just on the other side of the line of trees—I didn't blame Marley at all for wanting to make the place Oliver played as safe as possible.

He came running when she called, a little towheaded boy in jeans and a striped shirt. He must be three years old now, but I recognized him from the photograph I'd seen last year. The one that had tipped Sheila off that Oliver was still alive and well, and his mother really hadn't killed him and disposed of the body.

He looked like Marley. Her coloring was darker while his was fair, but he had the same little elfin face with the same tilted eyes and pointed chin. He was clearly his mother's son. And he ran up to her babbling and smiling, so whatever he had felt at the time when he left his adoptive parents, the only parents he could remember having, he was over it now.

Marley scooped him up and carried him inside, her face glowing with love as she smiled back and listened to him jabber. Here was one mother who'd never take her kid for granted, anyway.

Oliver dominated dinner, of course. Kids usually do. Abigail and Hannah are the same way. Whenever they're around, the adults can forget saying anything meaningful. So we made small-talk over Chicken Marsala and milk, while Marley focused most of her attention on Oliver. It wasn't until he had finished eating, and had squirmed off the chair and headed for the TV in the family room, that we were able to get back to anything resembling adult conversation.

"He's adorable," I said.

"Thank you." She glanced in the direction of the family room, where the TV was now blaring. Even though she couldn't even see Oliver through the wall, adoration was simply pouring from her. "Do you know what you're having?"

Her gaze landed on my stomach again for a second before glancing off.

I shook my head. "It's a little too soon. I'm just coming up on the end of the first trimester. We might find out in another couple of weeks, I guess."

"Weren't you pregnant last fall, too? When Sheila..." She shook her head. "What happened?"

I swallowed. I still have to, every time I say the words out loud. "I lost the baby." The miscarriage has gotten easier to think about over time, and the hope that I'll get to carry this baby to term helps, but it's still not an easy thing to talk about. Especially because it also meant that Rafe walked out of my life for a couple of months, thinking it had been Todd's baby and not his, and that I hadn't told him.

Marley's life wasn't the only one that had been a bit of a mess during that time.

"I'm sorry," Marley said. "Sheila had a couple of miscarriages, too."

I nodded. I knew about that. "The miscarriage last fall was my second. I'm just doing everything I can to hang onto this pregnancy. Not that there's much I can do, really."

Marley shook her head. "There isn't. I'll keep my fingers crossed for you."

That was nice of her. "I've lasted longer this time than either of the other two times, so I'm hopeful this one will stick." I wasn't quite sure what I'd do if it didn't. Well, other than survive and try again, I guess. But it would come close to killing me, emotionally.

I shook my head. "This is a gloomy topic for conversation. Let's talk about something better. It was nice of you to invite me for dinner."

"It's the least I could do," Marley assured me. "After everything you did for me and Oliver. You risked your own life to save me. You got shot!"

Well, yes. But it wasn't like I could have stood there and watched her being killed without trying to stop it, now was it?

Marley ducked her head. "And Todd told me you'd argued with him that I wasn't guilty, even before then. You'd tried to get him to drop the case."

"Todd?"

I didn't realize I'd said out loud until Marley answered.

"He stopped by after it was all over, to apologize. He even went to the family court judge, and told her that she should give me custody of Oliver."

"That's... nice." And surprising. When I'd spoken to Todd about Marley before the trial, he'd been almost vitriolic about how guilty he thought she was.

"He's a nice guy," Marley said.

"Right." That came out sounding more sarcastic than I'd intended. "I mean..." I cleared my throat, "Of course he is."

She was fiddling with her spoon, using the end of the handle to draw lines on the fabric of her placemat. Two horizontal, two vertical, in a pound sign. Hashtag. Whatever. She didn't look at me, except for a quick glance once in a while.

"He told me he proposed to you."

Had he really? "That was a long time ago. Before everything happened with Sheila." Before I was pregnant with Rafe's baby the first time.

Hell—excuse me, heck—before I even slept with Rafe the first time.

Marley nodded. "He said you turned him down."

"Flat. I like him. He's my brother's best friend. My mother adores him. We even dated for a year in high school. But you couldn't pay me enough to marry him."

Marley looked taken aback at my vehemence. Truth be told, I had taken myself aback just a little.

"I was married once before," I said, trying to explain. "To a man very much like Todd. A Southern gentleman, wealthy and well-bred. Another lawyer. And he cheated on me."

"Todd wouldn't cheat on you," Marley said.

"Oh, I know that." Without a question. "But he wouldn't make me happy, either. I like him, but not for my husband. Anyway, when Bradley dumped me, I guess I decided it was time to see who I was. On my own. I'd spent my whole life trying to be who my mother wanted me to be, and then who my husband wanted me to be, but I'd never figured out who I wanted to be." I shrugged. "It turns out that who I want to be, isn't someone either of them would approve of."

There was a pause while we both digested this.

"I know who your boyfriend is," Marley said.

"You and everyone else in Sweetwater."

She shrugged, acknowledging the truth of that. "Does he approve of who you want to be?"

Good question. "I guess he does. Or at least he wants me to be whoever I want to be; he's not trying to turn me into someone else."

Marley nodded.

"I love him," I said. "I know that shocks all of Sweetwater, including my mother. Margaret Anne Martin's perfect daughter and LaDonna Collier's good-for-nothing colored boy." I shook my head. "Believe me, my life would be a lot easier if I hadn't fallen in love with Rafe. If I had fallen in love with Todd instead, and I wanted to be his wife. Nobody would have said a word about that. But you can't choose who you fall in love with. Nor who you don't."

Marley nodded.

"And anyway, he's worth it. All of it. I'd deal with a lot worse for the chance to be with him."

"That's nice," Marley said.

I suppose it was. 'Nice' was perhaps a bit inadequate, but whatever.

We sat a moment in silence while the TV played music in the other room and Oliver's little boy voice sang along.

"About Todd..." Marley said.

Here we go. "If you want him, he's all yours."

She looked shocked. "Oh, no. I mean... No, that's not what it's about."

"Oh." I could have sworn there was a little more than just interest in her voice and on her face when she talked about him. "What's it about?"

Marley squirmed. "I like him. He's been nice to me. You know, after he stopped trying to prosecute me for murder."

Right.

"We've become friends. Sort of."

OK.

"He'll come over and hang out sometimes, you know. Watch TV and share a bowl of popcorn. Talk."

Huh.

I must not be catching on as quickly as Marley wanted, because she blew out a breath. "He told me what happened on Saturday night."

Ah! Suddenly the pieces came together, and the light was blinding. I couldn't believe how slow I'd been. "This is where Todd spent Saturday night!"

Marley nodded, flushing. "On the sofa. We're not... we didn't..."

No. Platonic, as Todd had said. Except the look on Marley's face wasn't platonic. They may not have gotten physically intimate yet, but I was willing to bet there was some emotional intimacy in their relationship, and a romantic attachment on Marley's side, at least. Todd... well, he was a man, and might not notice emotional intimacy until it reared up and bit him.

Then again, he'd thought enough of her to want to protect her from my questions. Unless he'd only been trying to protect himself.

"He's still a little hung up on you," Marley confessed. "That's why he didn't tell me everything on Saturday. He just showed up and asked if he could come in."

"And you didn't think to ask any questions?"

"I asked," Marley said. "He told me he'd gone to Nashville to see you. I didn't ask anything after that."

"I'm sorry." It wasn't my fault that she liked Todd while he liked me—even if that was probably just habit by now—but I still felt bad about it.

Marley shrugged. "Like you said, you can't choose who you fall in love with, or who you don't. Anyway, we watched a movie, and then I went upstairs and to sleep. When I got downstairs in the morning, he was gone. I didn't think anything of it."

"So when did he tell you about Saturday?" Or had he really only told her that he'd gone to see me? If so, I had just stuffed my foot in my mouth in a big way.

"This afternoon," Marley said. "He called and told me everything. About Jolynn and the murder and that your boyfriend is going to arrest him if he can't prove where he was on Saturday night."

"Rafe is not going to arrest him!" *Sheesh*. And I had taken such pains to explain that to Todd, too. "You're not just saying this because he asked you to, are you?"

Marley shook her head. "I figured you'd ask that. But he really was here. He got here late—maybe around ten. Oliver was in bed and I was headed that way, too. But when Todd showed up, I stayed up and watched a movie with him instead. Until midnight. Then I went upstairs and he stayed here on the sofa. I swear."

"I believe you," I said. She certainly seemed sincere. "I'll have to tell Rafe. And you'll have to talk to him or Detective Grimaldi."

Marley nodded. "I don't want him to get arrested, Savannah. Not even for something he didn't do. I've been arrested, and it wasn't any fun."

I nodded. "I don't want him to get arrested, either. And for what it's worth, I don't think anyone wants to arrest him."

Marley looked like she wasn't quite ready to believe that, and I added, "Between you and me, the police are thinking that maybe they know who killed Jolynn. They still have to come up with proof before they can charge anyone, but they're leaning in a certain direction. And while it's a direction that impacts Todd, it has nothing to do with arresting him."

Marley was silent for a moment. "Someone trying to frame Todd?" she asked.

"Um... Sort of. In a way."

"The camera setup. Someone trying to make him look bad."

"Um... yeah." She was quick on the uptake. Then again, I'd been known to have the occasional flash of brilliance, too, especially when Rafe's safety was on the line. Something to do with threats to people you care about putting you on high alert, I guess. And then she'd been framed for murder once herself. Maybe that had made her extra sensitive, or something. "Nothing's going to happen to him, though. Just hang in there. He'll come around."

I had no idea whether he would or not, although the fact that he'd gone to her on Saturday night, after what happened, was pretty significant, I thought. He could have just gone home and to bed. Or he could have gone to Dix's house—his best friend, the one with the confidentiality agreement—and unburdened himself. Or he could have come clean with his dad, who certainly would have done a lot to protect Todd.

But he hadn't done either. He'd come to Marley. Someone he could talk to and be himself with. Someone who knew how badly he could screw up—like, when he prosecuted her for a murder that she not only didn't commit, but that never happened—and forgave him for it. Someone who liked him anyway, in spite of the fact that he wasn't always perfect.

A refuge.

And boy, did I know the power of those.

"I should go," I said, getting to my feet.

"But the cheesecake..." Marley glanced over her shoulder at the kitchen counter.

"I don't really need the cheesecake. If I don't watch out, I'll be as big around as I'm tall by the time this is over." I pushed my chair in. "Give Todd a call and ask him to come over. He likes cheesecake. And red wine."

I headed down the hall toward the front door.

"But..." Marley said behind me.

I pretended I didn't hear her as I closed the door behind me and started down the steps to the street and the Volvo.

I DROVE HOME BEFORE I CALLED Rafe. It necessitated waiting a few minutes, but I didn't want to drive and talk at the same time.

And by a stroke of luck Mother was gone when I got there: having dinner with the sheriff, maybe, or—if he was working on trying to discover where Ronnie and Dear Elizabeth had spent last Saturday night—unburdening herself to Audrey and lamenting the fact that she couldn't trust anyone anymore. Even her old friend Frances, from one of the founding families of Maury County, had skeletons on her family tree.

As if we don't all have skeletons on our family trees.

Anyway, the house was empty. I locked the door behind me, climbed the stairs to my room, kicked off my shoes, and curled up on the bed with the phone. "You'll never guess who Todd spent Saturday night with," I told Rafe when he answered my call.

"Hello to you, too," was his answer.

"I'm serious."

"So am I. Who?"

I paused for added suspense. "Marley Cartwright."

Rafe paused too, but I don't think it was for suspense. "Who?"

I deflated. "Marley Cartwright. Sheila's friend. The one Todd tried to prosecute for killing her baby, when the baby had been stolen and adopted by that couple in Hermitage. Or Mount Juliet or wherever."

"Dunno if I ever met Marley Cartwright," Rafe said.

Well, no. Now that I thought about it, he probably hadn't. The few times Marley's and my paths had crossed, he hadn't been around. He hadn't come to Sheila's funeral at the mansion, and by the time Marley and I had had our encounter with a kidnapper and murderer, I'd recovered—physically—from my miscarriage and he was off in

Atlanta infiltrating Hector Gonzales's SATG, firmly believing that the baby I'd lost had been Todd's.

"Maybe you didn't. But that's where he was last Saturday. He got there at ten and spent the night."

There was a moment's pause. "You do know that don't mean he couldn't have killed his ex-wife, right?" Rafe asked. "Cause she was dead long before ten o'clock."

"I know that. But he didn't kill her. Ronnie Burke did. Or Dear Elizabeth."

There was another beat. "Who?"

It was beginning to sound something like a refrain. "That's right. I guess I didn't tell you that, either."

I went over the information I'd already given Grimaldi.

"So you're gonna stay away from the real estate office until you're sure she's gone, right?" Rafe said when I was finished.

"I'm going to stay away from the real estate office until Tim crawls to me on his hands and knees and begs me to come back. And then I'll only do it if he grovels well enough."

I could hear the laughter in Rafe's voice. "That's my girl."

"I am going back to Nashville in the morning, though. I have an appointment at Fifth and Main at eleven, to get started working on the rentals. And when I'm done there, I'll probably just go home."

"I oughta be home by tomorrow night, too," Rafe said. "Still trying to track down a couple old friends of Jolynn's, but otherwise, there's not much more I can do here."

"I'll look forward to seeing you tomorrow night, then." I did my best to sound demure, but my inner self was jumping up and down at the thought.

"You too, darlin'." He sounded amused, like he knew exactly the pictures scrolling through my mind of what would be happening tomorrow night.

"Call me if anything changes."

He said he would. "See you tomorrow, darlin'."

"See you," I said, and hung up.

So that was that. I leaned back against the pillows and closed my eyes.

The case was solved, more or less, and only the cleanup was left. And Tamara Grimaldi would take care of that, so Rafe didn't have to. He could come back home, and go back to work drilling the recruits at the TBI. And I didn't have to do anything more, either, except stay away from the LB&A office until Grimaldi could carry off Liz.

Todd was safe. Ronnie Burke and Dear Elizabeth couldn't use their sex tape to embarrass him, or discredit him, or blackmail him, or whatever it was they'd planned to do with it. Jolynn would go in the ground quietly. Todd might turn to Marley for consolation, and maybe, finally, I could stop feeling guilty for not loving him.

Life was good.

I smothered a yawn, and then rolled off the bed before I could fall asleep where I lay. It doesn't do to go to sleep with makeup still on and contacts still in and dirty teeth. Tomorrow was another day, and if I didn't take care of face and mouth now, I'd regret it then.

Twenty-One

Mother looked more like herself the next morning. The photographs of Ronnie and Dear Elizabeth were conspicuously absent from the kitchen island, of course, and so were any bridal magazines, but she no longer looked like the rug had been pulled out from under her. Her hair was done, her makeup was done, she was nicely dressed in linen slacks and a silk blouse, and her expression no longer had that stricken look it had had yesterday. She even managed to ask, nicely, how my evening had been.

"It was good," I said. "Marley's doing very well. She looks like a different person. She's gained weight, and stopped smoking, and cleaned up the place. The house looks great. Marley looks great. Oliver seems happy."

"That's wonderful," Mother said warmly. I don't think she really meant it—I'm sure she probably couldn't care less one way or the other; not that she wasn't happy for Marley, of course—but we Southern Belles are adept at putting other people at ease and making them believe they're the most important thing in the world to us.

"I'm very happy for her. After everything that happened, she deserves it." The only thing missing from her life, that I could see, was a dad for Oliver, and with luck, even that would work out.

I wasn't about to tell my mother about that, though. Todd obviously wasn't ready to share it, and Marley had told me in confidence. So I just said, "I'm driving back home this morning. I have to go to work."

Mother's brows drew together. "Alone?"

"Rafe will be back by this evening. I spoke to him last night. And both he and Grimaldi have told me to stay away from the real estate office until they come up with enough evidence to arrest Dear Elizabeth. As long as I do that, I won't be in any danger."

I probably wouldn't be in any danger anyway. Although if Liz knew that the jig was up and the police were closing in on her and Ronnie, who knew what she might do? "And anyway, I'm sure they're keeping an eye on her. They won't just let her float around out there without any kind of surveillance. If she leaves the office and comes anywhere near me, someone will stop her."

Mother nodded, but still looked a little worried.

"So what are you planning to do today?" I asked. It was an effort to distract her, but instead I managed to do the opposite. A shadow crossed her face, and she frowned.

"I was supposed to meet Frances and the florist, to start picking out the arrangements. But with this hanging over us, there's no point in it."

"There's a point in not tipping off the criminals before the police can arrest them," I said. "And if you suddenly cancel for no reason, Frances might wonder why."

Mother looked torn. "If we order flower arrangements, Frances will have to put down a deposit. And she might not get it back if the wedding doesn't come off."

And as I'd pointed out yesterday, Frances was likely to need all her money to post bail for her son and future daughter-in-law shortly.

"Maybe you could just look at the flowers, but not order any? Say you have to think about it before you make a decision?"

"Ye-e-e-s..." Mother said. "What if Frances finds something she really likes, though, Savannah? I can make an excuse for the florist, but how do I talk Frances out of ordering something?"

I had no idea. Frances had struck me as a strong-willed sort of person. She might not listen to Mother. And anyway, I'd hate for my mother, who knew what was going on, to somehow tip Frances off and have Ronnie and Dear Elizabeth catch on that they were about to get arrested.

"Maybe I should give her a call on your behalf," I suggested, "and tell her you're feeling unwell and you'll have to postpone the meeting with the florist."

Mother looked hopeful.

"Would you like me to do that?"

She made a moue. "Would you mind, darling? I don't like to disappoint anyone."

That was a bit rich, but I bit my tongue. "Of course not. What's the number?"

She rattled it off, and I dialed and waited for Frances to answer. When I reached her voicemail, I left a message explaining that my mother was feeling under the weather and had to cancel their appointment to look at flowers. "I'm sure she'll give you a call when she feels better." I wanted to hang up right there, but politesse forced me to add, "It was nice to meet you yesterday," before I disconnected.

"That was nice," Mother said approvingly.

"Yes, well, I didn't mean it."

"That's all right," Mother said. "We all say things we don't mean."

"I'm trying to stop doing that. Life's much nicer when nobody lies."

"It wasn't a lie..." Mother demurred weakly.

"Sure it was. It wasn't nice to meet her at all. She was a horrible old witch, and very rude. And while I can refrain from telling her that, at least to her face, I don't want to have to lie about it and pretend I enjoyed her company, either. The world would be a much better place if people stopped saying things they don't mean."

Mother had no answer to that. I slid off the stool. "I'm going home. When Rafe and I decide what we're going to do about getting married, would you like an invitation?"

Mother's mouth dropped open, and she gaped at me, goldfish-like.

"We will be getting married," I said. "I want my baby to have a father, and I want to have a husband, and anyway, I love him. I'd like for my family to support us, but I know how you feel, so if you'd rather we just got married on the sly and didn't let you know until it's done, we can do that, too."

Mother's mouth closed, and then opened again. No words came out.

"Why don't you think about it?" I suggested. "I don't think we're ready to do anything in the next few days. Even a quickie ceremony will take a bit more than two days to pull off."

Mother blinked.

"I mean, I realize that you don't see a reason to celebrate, but we have friends who are happy for us, and they'll want to have a party. Dix and Catherine will probably want to attend, too. They like Rafe, for the most part. And of course there's David, who might need a little time to get used to the idea. Rafe's son, you know? I don't know whether Rafe has told him about the baby and about us getting married yet. I don't know how he'll feel about it when he finds out. So with all of that, we'll have to wait at least a few weeks, I think. I'll have to get a dress, too, and find a tux for Rafe. So why don't you just give it some thought, and then let me know."

Mother blinked. And then swallowed. And then nodded.

"Good," I said. "I'll get out of here and let you get on with your day." I almost said 'life,' but that would have been a little too pointed. "I'll talk to you later."

Mother nodded, mesmerized.

I sailed out of the kitchen and down the hall, scooped up my overnight bag from the floor in the foyer without breaking stride, and erupted through the double doors like the heroine in an epic drama. And then I swept down the stairs and folded myself into the Volvo, and peeled out of the driveway with a spurt of gravel, and headed in the direction of home.

JUST OVER AN HOUR LATER I pulled off the interstate into East Nashville. It had been an easy drive. Morning rush hour was over, and the weather was good, so traffic had been a breeze. I hadn't taken my foot off the gas pedal the whole way.

It was still late May, but summer in the south can be a real killer. Heat was rising from the pavement, and shimmering above the hood of the car as I made my way through the streets of Historic Edgefield. The 1916 fire had demolished more than 700 of the Victorian houses in what had once been a summer community for the fancy folks who spent the rest of the year on the other side of the Cumberland River, but there were still enough Victorians left—along with the more recent Craftsman bungalows and brick Tudors—to make for a very pleasant drive. And while the 1998 tornado had ripped a mile-wide path through this area, tearing out every tree above a certain height and age, the new growth had been filling in nicely over the past decade and a half.

It was too early to head over to Fifth and Main. Shannon wasn't expecting me for almost another hour, and I had absolutely no desire to visit my old apartment. I had no idea whether the police had released it as a crime scene yet, or whether it still sported yellow tape across the door, but either way, my bed was still inside, and I didn't want to look at it.

And I had promised both Grimaldi and Rafe I wouldn't go to the LB&A office. Besides, Tim didn't want to see me, anyway.

So I ended up going to Brew-ha-ha. I had been too busy putting my mother in her place earlier to eat anything for breakfast, and if I didn't start working until eleven, it wasn't like I could stop for lunch at twelve. So I ordered a glass of decaf sweet tea and a bagel sandwich for a late breakfast/early lunch treat, and settled in at a table by the window. And no sooner had I bit into my sandwich than the door to the outside opened, and Dear Elizabeth walked in.

The bagel threatened to lodge in my throat. For a second, I panicked. My first instinct was to look away, to pretend I hadn't seen her, but that would be silly, not to mention suspicious. And besides, she'd already noticed me. She'd stopped just inside the door to look around, and had noticed me sitting here. Acting like I didn't recognize her would be stupid. So I gave her a tight smile and continued chewing, hoping she'd chalk my reaction up to the mouthful of bagel rather than my being startled.

She looked like she hesitated for a moment, too—maybe she wasn't any more eager to deal with me than I was with her. If what I suspected about her was true, I'd give me a wide berth in her shoes.

But here I was, and here she was, and since we were both trying to pretend that nothing was wrong, she came across the floor toward me. "Savannah."

The smile looked fairly genuine. If I hadn't known better, I would have believed that she was just mildly embarrassed to see me under the circumstances, given that I'd been given the boot from LB&A.

I swallowed. "Liz. Hi."

As surreptitiously as I could, I examined her, taking care not to stare so hard that she noticed. But I wanted to make sure I hadn't made a mistake, that she really was the same woman who'd been in the photographs with Ronnie Burke.

And she sure looked like she was. In the pictures, her hair was long and flowing and she looked casual and relaxed. Now her hair was pulled smartly back into a bun and she was wearing a business suit and heels. But the face was the same, I was almost sure. And the name was the dead giveaway, as far as I was concerned.

"You're not going to the office, are you?"

There was a tiny wrinkle between her brows, the same kind that my mother gets when she's perturbed about something but doesn't want me to know.

I shook my head. "Oh, no. I have an apartment just down the street, at Fifth and Main. I'm going there."

"I heard about that," Liz said, pulling out the chair opposite and taking a seat. She didn't even ask first. "The murder, right?"

I nodded.

"Have the police closed the investigation so you can get into your apartment again?"

It sounded like just ordinary curiosity, something anyone might ask, but I caught a glimpse of avid interest in the depths of her eyes.

Of course, I pretended I didn't. "I don't know much about it," I said casually, "but I think they're getting close to making an arrest."

It was probably safe to say that much. Naturally I wouldn't mention that the arrestee was likely to be her.

"Really?" She lowered her voice. "Who? Have they told you?"

"Well..." I coughed politely, "my boyfriend works for the TBI, you know? So he tells me things sometimes, that aren't common knowledge."

She blinked, twice, and I wondered whether I was laying it on too thick. Then she twitched her chair a bit closer. "You can tell me. Who are they arresting?"

"Well..." I said, leaning across the table and lowering my voice another degree, while at the same taking another, up close and personal look at her. She was definitely Dear Elizabeth. "Rafe is in Atlanta looking into Jo... the victim's past. Including her ex-husband. He's the one they're suspecting. Remember when you told me my sister came to see me at the office on Saturday?"

She nodded.

"My sister wasn't in Nashville on Saturday. And she doesn't look anything like me. That was the dead woman. She used my computer to contact her ex-husband and ask him to meet her."

"And he did?" Elizabeth breathed.

I nodded. "One of the neighbors saw him. I think they're planning to make the indictment tomorrow."

The indictment of Ronnie Burke, at any rate. But as Rafe had told me more than once, the closer to the truth you can keep a lie, the more likely you'll sound like you're telling the truth. Especially when you're someone like me, who isn't the world's greatest liar. Rafe can tell any kind of whopper and make anyone believe it, but I'm not quite that accomplished. I stick close to the truth whenever I can.

"Wow," Elizabeth said. She hesitated a second, and then she got up. "I really just came in to grab a cup of coffee on the go."

"That's fine," I said graciously. "I don't want to keep you."

She smiled. "It was nice to see you."

"You, too. Are you settling it at LB&A OK?"

"Oh, you know..." She waved a hand. "I'll see you later, Savannah, OK?"

"Sure," I said, and watched as she walked to the counter and ordered her coffee to go. She was on the phone—probably to Ronnie—before she'd even started the car. She was driving a dark SUV, incidentally. The kind of car Shannon Duncan said she'd seen on Thursday night.

I waited until the SUV had cleared the parking lot before I pulled out my own phone and dialed Tamara Grimaldi. "Detective."

"Ms.... Savannah."

"It wasn't my fault."

There was a pause. "What wasn't?"

"I was just sitting here quietly having a glass of tea and a sandwich when Dear Elizabeth walked in. I'm nowhere near the office."

Not technically true. The office was a few blocks away. But I wasn't there. Hadn't been there, or on my way there.

"Did you speak to her?" Grimaldi demanded.

"She saw me. So yes. She came over to the table and sat down."

"What did you tell her?"

"Nothing," I said. "Just that you're planning to arrest Todd tomorrow."

There was another pause. "Really?"

"Well, it wasn't like I could tell her you were going to arrest *her*."

"No," Grimaldi said. "I'm glad you didn't tell her that."

"You *are* going to arrest her, though. Aren't you?"

"Once we have the evidence we need. She's under surveillance, and there's no reason to think anyone else is in danger."

In that case, why was everyone telling me to stay away from her?

"It's better not to take any chances," Grimaldi said. "I'd hate to be the one to tell your boyfriend that you got hurt on my watch."

I wouldn't want to have to tell Rafe that, either. "He's coming home tonight. Unless something happens so he needs to stay longer, I guess."

"As far as I know," Grimaldi said, "there's nothing more that needs doing in Atlanta."

Good. "So Todd's off the hook for now?"

"Not entirely. He had motive, means, and opportunity. But he's not at the top of the suspect list."

"Because of Ronnie Burke and Liz."

Grimaldi didn't deny or confirm that. "Please stay out of trouble, Ms.... Savannah. I have a busy day, and I don't have time to yank your butt out of the fire."

Which she'd have to do with Rafe out of the way, I guess.

"I'm not planning to get in any trouble," I said. "I'm going to Fifth and Main. I'm going to sit in an office and work on short term rentals for the rest of the day. If you're keeping an eye on Liz, and

Sheriff Satterfield is keeping an eye on Ronnie—and I assume he is, right?—I'm perfectly safe. Just make sure that whoever is following Liz around knows that if she goes anywhere near Fifth and Main, I need a warning."

"Spicer and Truman are switching off," Grimaldi said. "I'll make sure they both know where to find you, and to sound a warning if Ms. Pettigrew goes within a block of the crime scene."

"And the office. Don't forget the office."

"How could I?" Grimaldi said and hung up.

I returned to my decaffeinated tea and sandwich.

I WASN'T LATE GETTING TO FIFTH and Main, but when I walked in, Shannon was pacing the floor like an expectant father. She glanced at the clock on the wall when I came through the door, but since it was eleven right on the nose, it wasn't like she could say anything. Maybe she was the type who believed that unless you were five minutes early anywhere, you were late. Mother had instilled proper manners in me, too, including punctuality, but she had impressed upon me that it's never polite to arrive early and risk catching someone unprepared. So I'd sat in the car until it was two minutes to eleven, and only then had I made my way across the courtyard to the office.

However, I've also been brought up to apologize when I make someone feel uncomfortable, even when it's their own doing, so I had my mouth open when I caught myself. I hadn't done anything I needed to apologize for. "Hi," I said instead, brightly. "Have you been waiting long?"

"Just a few minutes." She sounded disgruntled. Another apology bubbled up—my mother indoctrinated me very well—but I squashed it.

"What do you want me to do?"

Shannon took a breath. When she let it out, she looked a little happier. Or perhaps just a little less impatient. "This is the Fifth and

Main HOA office. Prisca uses it sometimes, and so do I. Most of the time it's empty, since we both have other jobs."

I nodded. "Prisca works in advertising, right?"

She nodded.

"What about you?"

"Financial planning," Shannon said.

"Good for you." I don't have enough finances to plan anything with them—it's more a hand-to-mouth or paycheck-to-paycheck kind of existence—but with a baby on the way, Rafe and I should probably start thinking about college funds and the like.

Of course, we should probably get through the wedding and the birth first. Neither's a cheap proposition.

"There are three vacant units in the building at the moment," Shannon said, "in addition to yours." She rattled off the unit numbers. "They've been in use as corporate rentals, and are fully furnished, but not particularly friendly or welcoming. I thought you might be able to help with that. You have such great taste. And there's a little money in the coffers that isn't earmarked for anything else, that you could use to spruce them up a bit. New curtains and throw-pillows, that kind of thing."

"Sure," I said. I never turn down a chance to go shopping, especially with other people's money.

"Here's the HOA debit card." She rattled off the PIN code and made me repeat it back. "I think there's about a thousand dollars you can spend, give or take a ten or twenty."

"I'll keep it under nine-fifty," I promised, already looking forward to picking out pretty things. My own apartment had been furnished on a shoestring, after I walked out of the townhouse I'd been sharing with Bradley with nothing but my clothes and the Volvo. Shannon might think I had good taste, but it was simplicity born from necessity and a lack of funds.

"These are the keys." She dropped them on the desk. "You can start by having a look at the units and deciding what you can do to jazz them up a little more, and maybe make them more attractive to businesswomen and to tourists. That's mostly who rents short term B&Bs, right?"

From my experience, yes. That and prostitutes, although they may not care what their surroundings look like, as long as the bed is comfortable.

I didn't say that to Shannon, of course, but maybe she read the thought as it meandered through my mind. Or maybe the subject just wasn't very far from either of our minds.

"So what's new with the case?"

"The murder?" I hesitated. But I'd told Dear Elizabeth that an arrest was imminent; it wasn't like I had a reason to lie to Shannon, or tell her something different. She wasn't even involved. "I think the police are closing in on someone."

"Really?" She stiffened like a Pointer.

"That's what I heard. My boyfriend's been in Atlanta for the past two days tracking down clues."

"What kind of clues?"

"I haven't been there," I said, "so I don't really know the particulars, but I know he's been talking to people who knew the victim when she was married, and who knew her husband, and I guess he's spoken to friends of hers, and probably gone through her apartment looking for connections to anyone up here, you know. How she came to know the people who killed her, that kind of thing."

Shannon nodded. She looked a little pale, but that could have been just the florescent lighting in the office. It tends to wash people out, especially when they're pale to begin with, and Shannon was a blue-eyed blonde with fair skin.

"I'm fairly sure they'll be making arrests either today or tomorrow," I told her, trying to be comforting. The idea of a murderer—or two—wandering around loose, isn't a comfortable feeling. It wasn't comfortable for me, seeing as it was my apartment that had been the crime scene, and my lookalike that was dead. And I imagine it was uncomfortable for Shannon, who might be dealing with a lot of panic from the other residents. For all I knew, they held her responsible for everything that went on at Fifth and Main, and were blaming her for this.

She opened her mouth, but before anything could come out, we heard rapid footsteps in the hallway outside. My head turned in the direction of the door, and so did Shannon's.

As the knob turned, my heart skipped a beat, and I was absolutely certain it would be Dear Elizabeth coming through the door. That she'd given Spicer and Truman the slip, and was coming to kill me, because I'd said something over coffee at Brew-ha-ha that had tipped her off that the police were onto her. I knew I hadn't said anything like that, but nonetheless, my heart was knocking against my tonsils as I watched the door fly open.

Twenty-Two

Prisca Miller stood on the doorstep, hair flowing over her shoulders and temper snapping in her eyes. "What's *she* doing here?!"

The finger she pointed at me quivered with righteous indignation. Or with something else. Fury, or general unhingedness. She certainly was acting out of all proportion upset.

"I'm working," I said calmly.

"I hired her," Shannon said at the same time. "To handle the rentals. She's been very successful marketing her own apartment."

"Successful?!" Prisca was so upset she was practically spitting. "She rented her place to a prostitute who got herself strangled! In *our* building!"

"It isn't your building," I said. "You don't own it."

"I live here!"

For looking so together and poised, she sure wasn't holding it together very well right now.

"The corporate rentals aren't working out," Shannon said, in the voice of one trying to talk a jumper off a ledge. Or a man with a gun into lowering it. "But if we revamp them, make them look a little more updated and more appealing to tourists and people coming in for other reasons than to work, and we let Savannah market them in the places where she marketed her own unit, we could potentially rent them out a lot more. And get more money into the HOA accounts."

"I don't care about the money!" shrieked Prisca. "I care about not having prostitutes coming in and using our building for sex!"

"I'm sure the people who live here already have sex," I said, trying to maintain my own calm.

Rafe and I had certainly made good use of my bedroom—a bit icky to think of, now that someone had been murdered there—and Prisca didn't look like someone who had taken a vow of chastity. Shannon, for all that she appeared so buttoned down and proper, was probably having sex, too. We were, on the face of it, three healthy, unmarried women in our late twenties or early thirties, and it was unreasonable to think we weren't getting it on with somebody. I'd had two celibate years between divorcing Bradley and falling into bed with Rafe, but unless the other two were in that kind of situation, I was willing to bet they got regular sex. And the whole building consisted, to a large degree, of single tenants, or couples with no kids. The location and setting—studios plus one and two bedroom apartments and townhouses near downtown—appealed to professionals or retirees, so there was probably a whole lot of casual sex going on on any given Friday night.

Prisca turned furious eyes on me, and I took a step back. She seemed a bit unbalanced on the subject, frankly, and while I'm sure she had a good reason, she made me uncomfortable. She was so angry I was concerned for my safety. Any moment now, I was afraid she'd pick up a stapler and beat me to death with it.

"I wouldn't do that again," I tried to reason with her. "After what happened, I'd be very, very careful about anyone who wanted to rent a unit. I'd do background checks and make sure, as much as I could, that none of them were prostitutes. Or criminals of any other kind."

How I'd manage that, I had no idea, since it isn't like they advertise it when they are, but whatever it took to calm her down, right?

"You can't imagine I was any happier than you about this murder," I added, appealing to her sympathy. "She died in my bed!"

Prisca growled. Like a grizzly bear. Or a Doberman Pinscher.

So much for that. I was casting about for something else to say, something that might calm her down and keep me from being attacked with office supplies, when my phone rang.

Saved by the bell. Literally.

"Excuse me." I dove for my bag, next to the desk.

"They're getting ready to arrest someone," I heard Shannon explain to Prisca as I dug the phone out of the bag and looked at it. Rafe's number flashed on the screen. "It'll be over soon. People will forget that this happened here."

I pushed the button on the phone. "Rafe?"

"Darlin'..." The connection was scratchy and awful. His voice kept going, but I literally only caught a letter here and there. Not even words, just the sound of his voice going in and out.

"I can't really hear you," I told him. "Do you want to hang up and call again?"

"Can't. I'm..." *Scratch, scratch.* "...car..."

"Can you repeat that?" I glanced around, at the windowless office with its thick concrete walls. "I'm sort of underground, and I guess maybe the connection is bad."

Which didn't make a lot of sense, given that the office was probably set up for wireless internet. Then again, maybe that isn't how cell phones work. Technology isn't really my strong suit.

"I'm... *scratch, scratch*... home!" Rafe said. His voice was louder but no easier to understand, since it wasn't anything he was doing that was causing the problem.

"You're home?"

"No! I... *scratch, scratch*... home!"

Sure. "You're on your way home?" I guessed. "You're coming home? Halfway home? Almost home?"

"Yes!"

OK, then. I had no idea which of my guesses was the right one, whether he was on his way, or halfway here, or close, but he was coming home. *Good.*

"Where... *scratch, scratch...* you?"

"Where am I? I'm at the Fifth and Main office. I told you I'd be here this morning. Shannon hired me to work on the empty units, remember?"

"Effing shit," Rafe said furiously, and I heard the sound of a car horn in the background, along with another muttered curse and what I assumed was the squealing of brakes. That, of course, came down the line with no interference.

"What's wrong? Are you OK? Are you hurt?"

"Idiot drivers," Rafe snarled. "Listen, darlin', I need you..." He dissolved into static again.

"I need you, too," I told him.

"No! I mean... *scratch, scratch...*"

"I can't hear you. Maybe I should just hang up and you can..."

"No!"

"OK, OK." To me, it made more sense to try to establish the connection again, just in case we could get a better one next time, but maybe he was driving through an area with a lot of interference, or something.

"Tried... call... twice," Rafe said, "...couldn't... *scratch, scratch...* through. Don't wanna..."

Ah. He had tried to call me twice before, and hadn't been able to get through. He didn't want to risk not getting a connection again at all.

"Fine. Just talk slowly and clearly. I'll do my best to keep up."

He growled. For a second, I thought it was Prisca, but she and Shannon were now both standing there watching me try to make sense of my boyfriend.

Just so they could hear what I had to deal with, I turned the phone to speaker, and the scratchy static filled the office, along with occasional bursts of Rafe's voice. I had given up asking him to repeat anything, since I pretty much missed whatever he said the second time, too. Much easier just to let him talk, and then do my best to piece the scraps of words together into something coherent.

"...album..." Rafe said. "Jo... *scratch, scratch*... friends... *scratch, scratch*... time ago..."

"OK." He'd found an album? A photo album, presumably, although I supposed it might be an old-fashioned vinyl record, too. They used to call those albums, didn't they?

And it had something to do with Jolynn and maybe a friend. The person in the photograph, or maybe on the album, was a friend from a long time ago?

My thoughts turned to Victoria Wallace, the girl who had rented the apartment a few weeks before Jolynn. She'd said she was in Nashville to record a song. Did that have anything to do with anything? Grimaldi had tracked her down and made sure she'd been in town to record, just as she'd said she was. Surely Grimaldi would have told me if something about Victoria Wallace wasn't kosher. Wouldn't she?

"Recognized her..." Rafe's voice said.

"Recognized who?"

All I heard back was static, and then, "...HOA meeting."

"Someone at the HOA meeting?" That would take Victoria Wallace out of the running, anyway. She'd been back in Canada, or Michigan, or wherever she'd come from, long before this Monday.

"...friends!" Rafe said. "... picture... *scratch, scratch*... murder."

"What?"

Over by the desk, either Prisca or Shannon made some sort of movement. I heard it, but by the time I turned around, they were both standing like statues, staring at me. For being made so differently, they looked remarkably alike in that moment: both with pale faces and staring eyes. I swear I could smell fear in the air, like the odor of perspiration.

Not that anyone smelled of sweat. Prisca's perfume was musky and Shannon's powdery.

"... gotta..." Rafe said vehemently.

"What?"

"Fucking goddamn connection!" That, too, came through loud and clear. Before the line dissolved into static again, as soon as he said, "Where..."

"I'm in the office," I said, taking a wild stab at guessing what he wanted. "Downstairs at Fifth and Main. With Prisca and Shannon."

"Fucking sh—!"

OK, then.

"We're perfectly safe," I told him. "There's been no sign of Dear Elizabeth or Ronnie."

"Don't care about... scratch, scratch... or effing Ronnie!"

There was an awful lot of f-bombs in this conversation. That usually means Rafe is upset, because normally he remembers to censor that particular word when he talks to me.

"What do you want me to do?" I asked, in an effort to calm him down.

It didn't work. "Didn't you... *scratch, scratch...* I effing said?! She... *scratch, scratch...* you gotta... *scratch, scratch...* outta there!"

That was clear enough, anyway. And not just to me.

"Come on," Shannon said. She grabbed my arm and propelled me from the office. For being so short—several inches shorter than me— she had a strong grip. And she didn't even give me time to pick up my purse on the way. She simply hustled me out of the room and into the hallway, leaving Prisca to stare after us. "Let's go."

Sure. I scrambled to keep up, since my heels were an inch or so higher than Shannon's, and since she had my arm in a grip that approached anything Rafe had ever managed when trying to remove me from somewhere he thought I shouldn't be.

Speaking of Rafe... The phone was still in my hand, and I lifted it. "We're leaving now. Getting out of the office. I couldn't really catch everything you said, but I'm getting away from her." The phone was silent. Eerily so. "Rafe?" I said. "Rafe?"

But somewhere between the office and the hallway I must have lost the connection. Maybe it really was a matter of being on the bottom floor of this bunker. No radio waves or whatever cell phones use could penetrate through the three feet thick concrete walls.

Technology is great, except for when it doesn't work anymore.

Or maybe Rafe just had hung up so he could keep both hands on the wheel while he drove.

I dropped the phone in the pocket of my skirt and scrambled after Shannon down the hall. "Where are we going?"

"Somewhere safe," Shannon said, without even glancing over her shoulder.

"Out?"

She didn't respond, but she kept moving, purposefully. A door at the end of the hallway opened into a stairwell, and Shannon began to climb. Perforce I did too.

"Is Prisca from Atlanta?" I asked breathlessly after half a story.

Shannon glanced at me over her shoulder, but didn't respond.

That made the most sense, anyway. Shannon was obviously trying to get me away from Prisca.

Truth be told, I was really quite impressed with the way she had managed to piece together so many of Rafe's disjointed utterances into something that made sense. And she didn't even know him as well as I did!

I turned my attention to putting thing together, too, behind the curve.

Rafe had found a picture of Jolynn with someone he recognized from the HOA meeting. It made sense that that would be either Shannon herself or Prisca, since it wasn't likely to be Mr. Sullivan or his septuagenarian love interest. And it would explain why Prisca was so bent out of shape over the prostitution thing. Maybe she'd been an escort, too, and if so, Jolynn showing up here and getting herself murdered must have made Prisca feel very worried. She had a good job now, a nice home and a fancy car. She was head of the home owner's association. She was respectable. Like Todd, she might not appreciate her former connection to a prostitute—or to prostitution—being made public knowledge.

When she'd shown up in the office downstairs, she'd looked ready to kill me. Or at least ready to kick my posterior from the building.

Maybe I was an uncomfortable reminder of something she'd rather forget. Everyone agreed I did look rather a lot like Jolynn, or she like me.

What if Ronnie and Dear Elizabeth hadn't killed Jolynn? What if Prisca had?

It had never really made sense to me that they would; it was just that we had no other suspects. Todd hadn't killed her, and who else was there?

So I had made up a scenario that made sense to me: one in which Jolynn had figured out what they were trying to do, and wherein she had refused, because she still had fond feelings for Todd and didn't want to be a party to publicly humiliate and embarrass him... and so Ronnie or Elizabeth had strangled her before she could tell Todd what they were planning.

And on the face of it, that would work. But it was very much a case of making the theory fit the facts, rather than vice versa. It obviously wasn't what Rafe was worried about. He must have come up with a different connection to Jolynn, a connection that gave someone else a reason to kill her.

What if that someone was Prisca? What if they'd been friends and colleagues in Atlanta before Prisca moved here? And what if Prisca recognized Jolynn, or Jolynn recognized Prisca, and Prisca felt compelled to get rid of her before Jolynn could ruin Prisca's new life?

I could imagine it only too easily. Jolynn had figured out who Ronnie and Elizabeth's target was, and decided she didn't want to be a party to ruining Todd's life. She could have just walked away, but that might have made Ronnie and Elizabeth unhappy, and if Jolynn knew about the lawsuit and that conspiracy to commit murder charge Todd was getting ready to levy against Ronnie, she might have thought it safer not to upset her temporary employer. So she looked around for another way out, and lo and behold, here was Prisca, a former escort, too. What would be easier than to tell her old friend, "I'm not going to do it. But unless you do, I'll tell everyone what you used to do for a living? I'll ruin your brand new, happy life."

And Prisca, not wanting her brand new, happy life ruined, had strangled Jolynn. And had walked out of there with the camera they'd planned to use to trap Todd, since she knew it would have recorded the murder.

Hell—heck—Todd had even told me he'd seen a couple of women outside in front of the townhouses when he arrived on Saturday night. What do you want to bet one of them was Prisca, fresh from killing Jolynn and on her way to her own house?

"Did you happen to run into Prisca in the courtyard on Saturday night?" I asked Shannon. "Coming out of my building? Around seven?"

We had reached the third floor now, and were moving briskly along the corridor.

Shannon shot me a look over her shoulder. "How did you know?"

"Good guess. Someone told me he saw a couple of women in the courtyard at that time."

"Yes," Shannon said, stopping in front of a door. "I met her coming out of your building. We stopped and talked for a couple of minutes." She opened the door and gestured me in.

"What's this?" I stepped across the threshold into a furnished unit. "Your place?"

She shook her head. "One of the corporate rentals."

One of the ones I was supposed to be renting out. Check.

I looked around. "Not bad. It could use a little redecorating, though. Some feminine colors and tchotchkes."

Shannon didn't answer, just closed and locked the door behind us.

"So what are we doing here?" I added. Besides hiding from Prisca.

She turned to me. "What has your boyfriend found out?"

I stared at her. "Are you kidding? You heard as much of that conversation as I did. It was impossible to make out most of it."

She didn't respond, and I added, "In fact, it seemed like you did better than me. You were the one who got us out of the office before I realized there was anything to worry about."

It was almost supernatural, in fact, that she'd been able to extrapolate so much from the scattered information I'd only been putting together in my head on the walk up here.

Almost as if she'd had prior knowledge.

"What did you and Prisca talk about on Saturday night?" I asked.

Shannon sighed. "The weather."

"Excuse me?"

"And the difficulty in finding a good man to date."

I stared at her.

"I can't believe how dim you are," she told me.

I blinked. Really?

I didn't feel particularly dim. Only yesterday, I had figured out who was trying to frame Todd, and why. Surely that argued a certain degree of brains. Something a step up from 'I can't believe how dim you are,' at least.

Part of me wanted to ask what had given her that impression, but I figured that would only prove her point. So I closed my mouth and thought about it instead.

What was it I wasn't getting?

Rafe had seen a picture of Jolynn with a friend, someone he recognized from the HOA meeting.

Shannon had met Prisca coming out of my building just before seven on Saturday night.

Or perhaps Shannon, coming out of my building on Saturday night, had met Prisca.

Duh.

The pieces rearranged themselves in my head. What if it wasn't Prisca Rafe had recognized in the picture with Jolynn? What if it was Shannon? That would explain the frantic phone call. He had no reason to expect I'd be seeing Prisca today, but he knew I had an appointment with Shannon.

And it would also explain something I hadn't thought anything of at the time, but something I realized now: earlier, when Shannon had explained about the corporate apartments and the debit card, she'd complimented me on my taste. But she had never, as far as I knew, been in my apartment.

Sure, it could be a reflection on the way I dressed.

Or she could have been there with Jolynn.

She was watching my face, seeing the thoughts chasing one another. Probably seeing realization dawn. I don't have a poker face, or anything resembling one. I'm a horrible liar, and most of my thoughts are only too visible on my face.

"It was you," I said. "But..."

Her face twisted. "I don't look like an escort?"

To be honest, she didn't. Prisca was tall and curvy, with a stunning face and pouty, red lips. I could easily see her hanging on someone's arm at a fancy party—and going back to his hotel with him afterwards. And Jolynn had been pretty, with long wavy hair and—I assumed—a decent figure.

Shannon was... average. Not ugly, but not particularly pretty, either. Short and a little chubby, with fluffy, blond hair.

She fisted her hands on her hips. "You think Marilyn Monroe looked like Marilyn Monroe when she woke up in the morning?"

I hadn't ever really thought about it, but no. Probably not. I mean, I don't look like me when I get up in the morning. My mother certainly doesn't look like my mother until she's put on her face and done her hair.

It wasn't morning, though. In fact, we were getting close to noon. And Shannon was fully dressed, in a suit and sensible heels, with her hair fluffed and sprayed in place.

She looked professional. Capable. In charge. Like she knew exactly what she was doing.

It wasn't a reassuring thought.

"What happens now?" I wanted to know, while I looked around, surreptitiously, for something I could use as a weapon. I had my phone in my pocket, and in a pinch I suppose I could throw it at her, but I didn't have my purse. If I did, I could have hit her with it. It has a long strap, and like most women, I keep enough stuff in my purse to make it nice and heavy.

Or—if she'd allow me the opportunity—I could have pulled out one of my small self-defense lipstick canisters, one with a tiny knife and one with a triple dose of pepper spray, and let her have it.

But my purse was downstairs in the office with Prisca. Who had nothing to do with any of this, and who probably had no clue what was going on.

Shannon bit down on her bottom lip. "I don't know. I didn't think I'd have to kill anybody else."

"You don't have to kill me," I pointed out, helpfully. "You could just walk away."

"And have you call the cops before I get out of the building? No, thanks."

It didn't really matter whether I called the cops or not. Rafe was onto her by now, and that probably meant Grimaldi was, too. After he got off the phone with me, he would have called her. Unless he'd called her first. I'd be very surprised if she wasn't already on her way here.

Naturally, I didn't mention that to Shannon. "You can take my phone," I said, digging it out of my pocket and holding it out. "Just tie me up, or something. Give yourself time to get away."

She looked like she was actually thinking about it, and I pushed my advantage. "One murder is enough, don't you think? I mean, it's understandable that you'd want to get rid of Jolynn. If she told anyone what you used to be, she might have ruined your new life."

"Bitch," Shannon said, her face darkening. "And all because she got hired to do a job she didn't want to do once she figured out who the mark was."

"She cared for her ex-husband." As far as I was concerned, it was the one redeeming thing about the whole tragic fiasco.

Shannon snorted. "She didn't wanna get in trouble is more like it. Said if she went through with it, he'd have her up on charges so fast her head would spin. That he wasn't the type to let himself be blackmailed, especially not by his ex-wife."

And she might have been right about that. I hadn't given it a whole lot of thought, but now that I did, Ronnie might have been reaching a bit with this plot. It hinged on Todd being willing to forego the indictment if he got embarrassed enough. And like most of us properly brought-up Southern gentlemen and ladies, he's loath to make a public spectacle of himself—or be made a public spectacle of. But he's also a lawyer and a public prosecutor, and I found it hard to believe that he'd put his own emotional comfort above prosecuting a dirty businessman for fraud and murder.

There was a sound out in the hallway, a faint thud—like from a door closing; perhaps the door to the stairwell we'd used to come up here—and then what might have been footsteps. Shannon and I both looked at the door.

Now would have been a fine time to attack her, with her attention distracted, but I didn't have a weapon, and to be honest, I was afraid to do anything that might harm the baby.

I know what I was hoping for—Tamara Grimaldi to come bursting through the door, gun drawn—but instead, there was a timid knock. "Shannon? Are you in there?"

It was Prisca, of course. I guess she'd sat in the office for long enough to realize we weren't coming back, and she had come looking for us.

Shannon scowled at me. I got the message: don't answer.

I might have answered anyway—it wasn't like she was holding me at gunpoint, so what was she going to do if I spoke?—but before I had the chance to open my mouth, there was the sound of a key being inserted in the lock.

Shannon swore.

"This is ridiculous," I told her. "You're unarmed. So am I. I'm pregnant, so I'm not going to risk attacking you. You can just walk out of here. Get in your car and drive away. If you're lucky, you can make it to the interstate before the cops arrive. And the Kentucky state line is less than an hour away."

She didn't answer. She couldn't, really, because the door opened and Prisca stood on the threshold, looking like her beautiful, vacant self. "There you are." She held out my purse. "You left this downstairs."

"Oh." It would be strange if I didn't reach for it, so I did, with a sideways glance at Shannon. She didn't say a word.

"Thank you," I told Prisca.

She nodded, her brows wrinkling. "Are you OK? You look a little pale."

"I do?" I didn't feel pale. Although I was here, locked in a small apartment with a murderer, so perhaps it might be understandable if I were.

"Maybe some lipstick would help," Prisca said.

Oh.

Yes, lipstick would definitely help.

I dove into the bag while Prisca turned to Shannon. "Everything OK?"

"Everything's fine," Shannon said impatiently. "You can go back downstairs. We're just taking a look at the corporate rental units."

It sounded reasonable. I wondered whether Prisca would buy it.

She looked around. "It could use a little more pizzazz, I guess. Some green plants, some throws and pillows, maybe some new artwork..."

I dug a lipstick canister out of my bag. It was silver. The last time I'd had to use my knife and pepper spray—on Sheila's murderer, who was just about to kill Marley—I had accidentally pulled out the wrong canister, and then had to fumble for the right one. So when I went to replace the spray, I made sure to get canisters that didn't match. That way, I'd know exactly what I was pulling out of the purse without having to open it.

Silver meant spray. The knife canister was red.

I popped the top off and exposed the tiny nozzle.

"Some new curtains..." Prisca said, gesturing to the windows. Shannon looked that way, not at me, and I brought the spray up and aimed for her eyes.

The rest was pretty anticlimactic. Shannon collapsed in a screaming heap, rubbing her eyes and probably making the spray sting worse. The door to the hallway opened again, and Grimaldi came through, holstering her gun. "Guess I won't be needing that." She pulled the pair of handcuffs from the middle of her back instead. "You OK?"

She glanced at me.

I nodded. "Fine. I don't think she was going to do anything to me. When she realized Rafe recognized her, I think she just panicked."

"You can tell the judge that," Grimaldi said, cuffing Shannon and hauling her to her feet. "It might help."

Maybe. But either way she'd be spending a lot of time in prison for Jolynn's murder. And besides, I wasn't entirely sure I wanted to make things easier for her.

"Stop by my office this afternoon to make your statement," Grimaldi told me. She marched Shannon out without waiting.

"I will," I told her back. And turned to Prisca. "Thank you."

She watched until they were gone around the corner and then answered. "Like you said, she probably wasn't going to do anything to you."

Maybe not. But Prisca had still brought me my bag and my pepper spray at an opportune moment. And, it seemed, she'd brought Grimaldi, too.

"Did you call the detective?"

Prisca shook her head. "She showed up a minute after the two of you had left. Until then, I didn't realize anything was wrong."

As expected, Rafe must have called Grimaldi. Wonder how far from Nashville he was at the moment?

"We should go," Prisca said, gesturing to the door.

I guess we should, although I was getting the distinct opinion she was trying to get rid of me.

"With Shannon gone, I don't suppose you intend to use the corporate rentals for short term B&B purposes anymore," I said on my way past. I didn't even pose it as a question, that's how sure I was of the answer.

Prisca looked at me.

"I didn't think so," I said, and walked out.

Twenty-Three

"Prisca Miller did not come here from Atlanta," Tamara Grimaldi said over dinner the next evening.

The previous evening, after the incident with Shannon at Fifth and Main, she'd been busy handling Shannon's arrest and, I assume, putting together a case against Shannon, since Shannon hadn't really been a suspect at all until Rafe saw the picture of her and Jolynn in Atlanta. Everything moved kind of quickly from there.

And then, of course, there was Dear Elizabeth to deal with. She wasn't guilty of murder, but she was still swept up along with Ronnie Burke in the indictment against Stonegate Development on Friday morning. By Friday afternoon, both Ronnie and Liz were behind bars. Spicer and Truman were off surveillance duty, and all the appropriate charges had been filed against everyone concerned.

By Friday at six, my brother came knocking on our door, overnight bag in hand. He had dropped off Abigail and Hannah with Catherine and Jonathan, and was all set to go exercising with Rafe in the morning.

After we had installed him in one of the empty bedrooms on the second floor, my boyfriend dragged me into our bedroom and closed the door, and then turned to me, eyebrow arched.

"Sorry," I said sheepishly. "It was my idea. He wants to beef up before he takes his clothes off with Grimaldi."

The other eyebrow arched, too. Not something I see often.

"At least I assume that's what it is," I added. "When I suggested he could go exercise with her, because she's in good shape too, he said that yes, she is. So I assume he's self-conscious."

"It's gonna take more than a session or two in the gym to turn your brother into something other than a desk jockey," Rafe said.

"I know. I'm sure he knows, too." I put my hands against his chest and leaned in, feeling muscles quiver and tighten under my palms. "Just humor him. Spend an hour or two with him and make him realize Grimaldi probably doesn't care that he doesn't look like you."

"Me?" He looked comically surprised. "Darlin'..."

"I don't mean you specifically." Grimaldi had told me once he wasn't her type. "But she spends all her time around law enforcement types. Guys like you, who are in really good shape. She probably likes Dix because he isn't. He's normal."

"I'm not normal?"

"Of course you're normal. You're just in really, really good shape."

Really good shape. A shape that was distracting me to a rather large degree at the moment. When Dix rang the doorbell, Rafe had just walked in the door himself not five minutes earlier, and he had had me backed up against the wall in the hallway with his mouth on mine and his hands under my blouse. The interruption hadn't sat well with either of us.

"He'll probably spend a couple minutes unpacking," Rafe said, pulling me closer, so my front was flush against his. His breath was warm against my ear. "You could join me in the shower."

He slipped his palms down my back to push my hips against his.

I shivered.

I'd already had a shower that morning, but I supposed having another wouldn't hurt. And it had been a while since we'd done anything as athletic at sex in the shower. During the first trimester of carrying this baby, there'd been a lot of missionary positioning and very careful thrusting, none of it outside our nice, soft bed.

But since the first trimester was officially over today, I guess maybe Rafe wanted to celebrate with some more adventurous love-making. "I could do that..." I said.

"Or we could just stay right here and be really, really quiet." He bent his head to nuzzle the side of my neck, his lips warm, moving south. At the same time, his hand was moving north along my thigh, pulling the skirt with it.

"Not sure I can be that quiet," I admitted, a bit breathlessly.

He chuckled. Outside in the hall, a door opened. My brother's voice said, "Sis?"

I dropped my forehead to Rafe's shoulder with a groan. He dropped his hands. "We'll pick this up later. Go entertain your brother, darlin'. I'll be out in a minute."

I nodded, and pulled my clothes straight, all the while cursing my own big mouth, to have extended this invitation, and cursing my brother, for having accepted it.

So Rafe took his shower, and then we got dressed and went out to dinner. A double date, with Dix and Tamara Grimaldi. First time ever.

The detective came straight from work, still in her business suit and shirt, and still with her mind on her cases. Which was how she came to sit across the table from me to say that Prisca Miller didn't come to Nashville from Atlanta.

I shook my head. "I realized that, once I figured out that Shannon was the one who killed Jolynn. I mean, Prisca could still have been from Atlanta, I suppose... But she isn't?"

"Small town girl from Mississippi," Grimaldi said. "No connection to Atlanta or to Jocelyn Rivera whatsoever."

I grimaced. "It's my own fault. I only heard part of what Rafe said, and I assumed Prisca was guilty instead of Shannon because of the way she looked."

"Always a dangerous thing," my boyfriend remarked. And he should know. He'd certainly been on the receiving end of plenty of prejudice because of the way he looks.

I nodded. "I really should know better than to judge based on that. But I took against her from the start because she flirted with you. And then I always look at women like her and worry."

He tilted his head to look at me, quizzically. "Why?"

Why? "She's attractive and sexy and..." And not as fishbelly-white as I am. "I guess I just always think that she's the kind of woman you should be with."

"Because she's black?"

I blinked. OK, so maybe I haven't gotten as good at direct confrontation as I'd like to think I have. And maybe not as comfortable with plain speaking as I'd like to think, either. At least not when someone else is doing the speaking and confronting.

My mouth opened, and then closed again.

"I thought we'd gotten past that, darlin'," Rafe said, while Dix and Grimaldi watched me from across the table. My brother winced sympathetically as I squirmed.

"It isn't that," I tried, "so much..."

Rafe arched that single brow, and I sighed. "OK. Maybe it is that."

"I'm black, so I should be dating black girls? And you're white, so..."

"No!" God, no. Of course not. And if he mentioned Todd Satterfield, even obliquely, I would hit him. "Prisca's beautiful, and exciting, and exotic, and... and everything I'm not."

Especially now, when I was getting fatter by the day, and couldn't fit into any of my sexy clothes anymore. And is there anything less appealing than a woman who loses her breakfast in the toilet bowl every morning?

"And it isn't that you're black." Which he wasn't, anyway. His mother had been as blond and blue-eyed as mine. "It's that you're..." I looked him up and down. And since I couldn't find the words to describe what he was, I ended up with, "—you."

Which said it all, really.

"You deserve someone as..." I tried again, but couldn't come up with anything better than, "as special as you are, and instead you got me, and my mother, and a whole town who looks at you sideways and thinks you've ruined me, and then I see someone like Prisca trying to get your attention, and I think that maybe you'd be better off with someone like her."

"No," Rafe said.

"What do you mean, no? That's what I think!"

"No, I wouldn't be better off with her."

Oh.

"And I don't care what your mama thinks. Or what anyone else in Sweetwater thinks. Or what the whole damn world thinks. You ain't getting rid of me."

"I don't want to get rid of you," I said. "I want to marry you and keep you forever."

"That can be arranged," Rafe said.

And that was the point where Detective Grimaldi had had enough. "OK, you two," she said. "Either knock it off or get a room. You're turning my stomach."

"Sorry," I said. "It's just..."

"I know what it is. Do it on your own time. Let the rest of us eat our food in peace."

I rolled my eyes. *Fine.* "So Prisca's from Mississippi. Shannon's the one from Atlanta."

It was Rafe who nodded, his fingers warm and hard around mine. "And it damn near scared a decade off my life when I saw that picture."

"I'm surprised you recognized her at all," I admitted. He'd brought the photograph back to Nashville with him, so I'd gotten a look at it yesterday afternoon, and Shannon had been right: she did clean up well. Dressed in a skimpy cocktail dress and high heels, with her hair long and flowing over her shoulders, and with smoky eye shadow and bright red lipstick, she didn't look anything like the dowdy executive I'd met.

"It took a couple minutes," Rafe said. "I knew she looked familiar, but I couldn't place her. And then I realized you'd gone to meet her..."

"She understood what you were trying to say better than I did."

Obviously, since she knew things I didn't.

"When she grabbed my arm and hustled me out of the office, I thought she was getting me away from Prisca." I shook my head. "It wasn't just that Prisca looked more like an expensive call girl, by the way. It was the fact that she made such a big fuss about the prostitution thing. I thought she was trying to deflect attention from the murder to make herself look less guilty."

"A logical assumption," Grimaldi nodded. "But instead it was Ms. Duncan who had the sordid past, and the reason to commit murder."

Rafe let go of my hand to take a sip of his beer. "Did she confess?"

"Not much else she could do under the circumstances," Grimaldi said. "Yes, she made a full confession. Claimed she had no plans to hurt you," she nodded to me, "which supports your impression that you weren't in danger."

"She didn't behave threateningly. I think she just panicked when she heard Rafe's phone call."

Grimaldi nodded. "She claims she killed Ms. Rivera in a panic, too. That she didn't see another way out. Ms. Rivera threatened to destroy the life Ms. Duncan had built here, including her burgeoning relationship with a man who knew nothing about her past, and she was afraid of losing everything."

"So she strangled Jolynn."

Grimaldi nodded.

"And took the camera."

"She kept it," Grimaldi said. "And gave it to me."

Yowch. "Did it show the murder?"

Grimaldi nodded, her face set. After a moment, she took a sip of her wine. I deduced she hadn't particularly enjoyed watching that piece of the evidence.

"Todd brought the indictment against Ronnie Burke and Stonegate Development this morning," Dix said, after a quick glance at her. That's my brother: always ready to change the subject to spare a lady's feelings. Unless that lady is his sister and she's being interrogated by her boyfriend on an important subject, of course; then he's only too happy to watch and cheer. "Ronnie's in jail in Columbia, and his mother is trying to scrape up enough money to pay the million dollar bond. Needless to say, the wedding's off."

It was my turn to wince sympathetically. "How did Mother take it?"

"I didn't talk to her," Dix said, "but I spoke to Audrey, and she said Mother was at home in bed with the alcohol and the smelling salts."

I giggled. Dix didn't.

"Are you serious?" I asked.

"That's what Audrey said."

Good Lord.

"We took Elizabeth Pettigrew into custody this morning, as well," Grimaldi added. "She's being held in Nashville, since she isn't being charged with any crimes in connection with the Stonegate Development case. ADA Satterfield doesn't believe she was a party to the blockbusting and real estate fraud—she's just the designer, hired after the land had already changed hands and the deeds transferred— and he also isn't charging her with conspiracy in the case of Ms. Collier's overdose last year."

She glanced at Rafe, who nodded. "That was Ronnie and Billy."

"With a go-between," I reminded him.

"And she's already on the hook for the murders back in May. I'm OK with her not swinging for my mama."

Good, because with the deal she'd made, that was the best we were going to get. Mary Kelly would do time for killing several of my classmates, but she would not be doing time for hiring Billy Scruggs to kill LaDonna on Ronnie Burke's orders. And if Rafe was OK with that, I guess I didn't have much choice but being OK with it, too.

I turned back to Grimaldi, and to the subject of Dear Elizabeth. "If Todd isn't charging her with anything, what is she doing in jail?"

"She's being charged with facilitating prostitution, running a brothel, and violating the Mann Act," Grimaldi said.

"Man Act?"

"M-A-N-N." She spelled it. "It's a federal law from 1910, named after Congressman James Robert Mann of Illinois, and it's better known as the White-Slave Traffic Act. The Mann Act makes it a felony to engage in interstate transport of any woman or girl for the purpose of prostitution or debauchery."

Debauchery. Wow.

"So when Ronnie and Liz arranged for Jolynn to come to Nashville from Atlanta to sleep with Todd, they committed a felony?"

Grimaldi nodded. "ADA Satterfield added it to the charges for Mr. Burke. We're prosecuting Ms. Pettigrew ourselves. They'll both be going away for a long time. Also, we're considering whether to charge them both with felony murder in the death of Ms. Rivera."

"How can you do that? They didn't kill her. Shannon confessed."

"Felony murder is when someone is killed during the commission of a crime," Rafe explained. "Back when I was young and stupid, if I'd decided to hold up a liquor store, and I took your brother with me, and he got shot dead by the guy behind the register, I could be charged with the murder."

"How? You didn't kill anyone!"

"No," Grimaldi said, "but that's how it works. Ms. Pettigrew and Mr. Burke knew they were committing a crime when they hired Ms.

Rivera. The fact that she was murdered during the commission of this crime, makes them guilty of felony murder."

"Wow."

Grimaldi nodded. "Crime never pays."

No. But the way this was piling on, I was almost feeling sorry for Dear Elizabeth. She could have had no idea what she was letting herself in for when she allowed Ronnie to talk her into helping him get out of the coming indictment.

Then again, I had no way of knowing who talked whom into what. It could just as well have been her idea from the start.

"I guess Ronnie knew about Jolynn from living in Sweetwater," I said. "Everyone knows everything about everyone else there."

"I imagine your mother probably told Ronnie's mother about her," Grimaldi said. "Commiserating over the wedding plans. Ronnie's new fiancée, so much more suitable that his first wife, and your new boyfriend, so much less suitable than your first husband."

She glanced at Rafe. "No offense."

He grinned. "None taken. I'm sure she put it in just those words, too. And went on and on about how much better it woulda been if Savannah'd just married Satterfield instead. Who had an unsuitable first wife of his own. No better than she oughta be."

I nodded. "That sounds like my mother. She would have told Frances Burke every last detail about Todd and Jolynn's life. And mine and Rafe's. Including where I work and what I do for a living. I suppose Liz hired on with LB&A to keep an eye on me?"

Grimaldi nodded. "That's her story. She was also Shauna Bangs, going through the process of renting the apartment once, to get the lay of the land before she had to do it again. A dry run, if you will. A rehearsal."

Good to know. So I hadn't actually, truly, rented my apartment to any prostitutes. Jolynn, yes, but she hadn't come to Nashville to turn tricks. Perhaps that shouldn't have made me feel better, but it did. "Any chance I can get you to share that information with Prisca Miller?"

Grimaldi's lips twitched. "I'll be happy to do that."

The food arrived just then, and we got busy eating. It was a few minutes before the conversation picked up again.

"So what are you going to do now?" my brother wanted to know. "I don't think Tamara telling Prisca Miller that you didn't actually rent your apartment to any hookers is likely to make her change her mind about having you work there."

No, indeed. I would not be handling short term rentals for Fifth and Main. And it was just as well, because I wasn't sure I wanted to work there. Not just because Prisca didn't like me and because she'd be hard to get along with, but because Jolynn's murder had soured me on the place. It was the last in a long string of bad things that happened in my apartment, and I was ready to move on.

"I'm not sure," I admitted. "Tim told me I wasn't welcome back at LB&A unless I rustled up some new business, and I haven't. The whole real estate thing has turned out to be a lot more difficult than I expected. I've had my license for almost a year, and I haven't sold many houses at all. For the most part, I've spent the past year sitting open houses for other people and tracking down murderers. And no one pays me for that."

"And won't start now," Rafe said. "Don't even think about it. Tracking down murderers ain't good for you. Or for my blood pressure."

"I guess it's no good asking you to quit the TBI and open a PI agency, then."

He stared at me.

"I was thinking you could be Sam Spade and I could be Effie Perine," I added.

"Roleplay on your own time," Grimaldi instructed. "And please, Ms.... Savannah, don't go into crime fighting. I'm not sure Nashville could survive it."

That was surely giving me a little too much credit, but OK. "I guess there's only one thing for me to do, then," I said.

Dix took the bait. "What's that?"

"Follow in Barbara Botticelli's footsteps and start writing steamy romance novels." I smiled sweetly. "I was thinking I could be Barbara's younger sister, Bianca Botticelli. Or maybe Daniela Donatello. Or Romilda Rafael."

That last one had a certain poetic justice, as far as I was concerned.

My own Rafael stared at me. "Over my dead body!"

I did my best to look innocent. "What's the matter? Don't you want to be immortalized in print?"

He looked nauseous. "Ain't no way I'm letting a bunch of women read about what I do in bed."

Dix chuckled. Even Grimaldi looked like she had to work hard to keep from laughing.

"A bunch of women have already read about what you do in bed," I informed him. "Elspeth sold a lot of those Barbara Botticelli books."

He shook his head. "The stuff she wrote about never happened. Not with me. The one time we got together, I was eighteen, drunk outta my mind, and beat half to a pulp. It was over in less than five minutes. And I don't imagine it was any better for her than it was for me."

"But look at the success she had turning those five minutes into book after book. Just imagine what I could do with all the time we've spent together!"

"No. So help me God, if you write a single word about—"

I giggled, and he squinted at me. "You're joking. Ain't you?"

"Not necessarily. I did think about it."

"No." He shook his head. "If you wanna write, write about something else. Real estate, or dead bodies, or knitting. Not sex. Specially not sex with me. Nobody wants to read about that."

"You'd be surprised," I thought, but I didn't say it. "I have to do something," I said instead. "And if I can't sell real estate..."

"You don't have to do anything, darlin'. I can afford to feed you." He very nicely refrained from telling me that he was pretty much doing that, and everything else, already. "In six months, the baby's coming. I'll have to provide for the two of you then. Might as well start now."

He had a point. However...

I reached out and took his hand, lacing my fingers through his. "I appreciate it. But my whole life, I was brought up to find a man and let him take care of me. That's why I married Bradley. And when he cheated, I was alone, so I had to learn to take care of myself. And maybe I haven't done the best job in the world, but I don't want to go back to being taken care of. I don't want to be Rafe's wife and the baby's mother and nothing else. Not that there's anything wrong with being your wife and the baby's mother, but—"

"I get it." He ran the pad of his thumb along my knuckles. "Maybe I should have a chat with Tim. See if I can't talk him into taking you back."

"If anyone can do it, you can." In fact, I'd pay money to watch. Rafe would have Tim wrapped around his finger, and offering me my job back, so quickly I'd probably get whiplash.

"As for the rest of it," Rafe said, and paused.

"Yes?"

"Wife?"

Uh-oh. "You did propose," I pointed out. "Remember? You told my mother and the sheriff that we were getting married."

"I remember."

"So...?"

"When d'you wanna get married?"

"Soon," I said. "While I still look OK in a wedding dress."

"Where d'you wanna get married?"

"I don't care, as long as you're there, too."

"And a couple of witnesses," Dix added. "Don't forget that."

Truth be told, I'd almost forgotten that he was there. And Tamara Grimaldi, too. They'd both been very quiet while Rafe and I had our conversation.

My future husband contemplated them for a moment before he got to his feet and pulled me out of my seat. "You don't mind if we cut out a little early?" he asked. "We got some talking to do."

Dix shook his head. "Not at all," Grimaldi told him. "I'll make sure Mr. Martin gets back to your house in one piece."

"Just give me a key so I can get in," Dix added. "And don't wait up."

No worries. We'd be hitting the sheets as soon as we walked through the door at home.

I dug my key out of my purse and gave it to him. "Enjoy your dinner." *And take your time getting back to the house afterwards.*

"C'mon, darlin'." Rafe put a hand on my back to guide me toward the door. A woman who was sitting at a table to our left looked up and kept looking as we moved past.

"You know," I told him as we skirted the other tables and headed for the front of the restaurant, "Most women would be happy to read about what you do in bed. I think you're selling yourself a bit short."

A corner of his mouth curled up. "Ain't nothing short about what I do in bed, darlin'."

"Exactly! And that's why I think most women—"

"Forget it." He pushed open the door and followed me out into the steamy humidity of the late May evening. "The only story I'm interested in, is ours. Yours, mine, and the baby's. And I don't wanna share it with nobody else."

Fair enough.

"You know," I told him, as we made our way across the parking lot toward the Volvo, "I'm crazy about you."

He grinned. "That mean you're gonna let me take you home and do wicked things to you all night long?"

"The wickeder, the better," I said.

"Hold that thought," Rafe told me, and unlocked the door to the Volvo.

ABOUT THE AUTHOR

New York Times and USA Today bestselling author Jenna Bennett (Jennie Bentley) writes the Do It Yourself home renovation mysteries for Berkley Prime Crime, and the Savannah Martin mysteries for her own gratification. She also writes a variety of romance for a change of pace.

FOR MORE INFORMATION, PLEASE VISIT HER WEBSITE: WWW.JENNABENNETT.COM